MOONPATH

MOONPATH

Lorna Hart

L̲ineage Independent Publishing
Marriottsville, MD

ISBN (paperback):!9781958418062
First printed in the United Kingdom

Publisher: Lineage Independent Publishing,
Marriottsville, MD, USA
Maryland Sales and Use Tax Entity: Lineage Independent
Publishing, Marriottsville, MD 21104
www.lineage-indypub.com
lineagepublishing@gmail.com

To my family (you know who you are) and the friends who have read this story in the early stages and encouraged me to continue.

Contents

Foreword

I am honored to be part of Lorna Hart's debut novel. When I was first introduced to Lorna (virtually, that is; we have never met in person), I was instantly impressed by her determination to tell a compelling story that is loosely based on her own life events. When I received the first sample of her work, it convinced me that she should be part of the Lineage Independent Publishing team.

New to publishing, Lorna quickly realized that there is more to writing a book than just 'writing a book.' Grammar and punctuation are only a small portion of that work. More important is the ability to evoke emotional responses from readers – myself included – and Lorna has done that right from the first paragraph. I was hooked.

As the story unfolded, I could see the Lebanese coast. I could feel the environments in which the main characters lived. I could even smell the marketplace in Tripoli and see the sidewalk cafes of Paris. More importantly, I could sense the emotions of her characters, from protagonists to villains. Lorna's imagery and her ability to paint a scene with words brought the story to life. Her narrative was so vivid that it brought back memories of my own travels to the Middle East and within Europe.

During the course of our collaboration, I also discovered that Lorna is quite an artist. She designed and painted the artwork for the cover, as well as the wonderful sketch we agreed to use as a chapter separator when publishing conventions would have left us with a blank page. It certainly made my job as an editor and publisher less difficult.

I hope that "Moonpath" is not Lorna's only work. Though it has taken her ten years to put it together, she's now jumped the high hurdle of first publication. I look forward to working with her on her next works.

Michael Paul Hurd
Author/Editor/Publisher
Lineage Independent Publishing

Prologue

Under the light of a full moon, the city of Beirut lay sleeping. A taxi drove through the fringes of the city and turned north along the coast road, following the contours of the rocky shoreline. The rocky hillsides bit like jagged teeth into the land which rose sharply upwards to the foothills of the mountains, black against the starry sky. The night was calm and quiet. The only sounds to be heard, apart from the engine of the elderly taxi, were the hiss and suck of the sea on the pebbled shore and the soulful Arabic love songs playing quietly on the car radio.

As the car motored on, the moon seemed to be moving in the same direction, almost as if it were curious to know who traveled so late in the night. The moonlight was cool but so bright it almost seemed to radiate warmth.

Two men sat in the front seats of the car, chain-smoking and occasionally exchanging a word or two. In the usual fashion of Lebanese taxis, the interior of the cab was ornately decorated with fringes and the occasional dusty ostrich feather, its ancient springs seeming to sway in time to the music. In the rear sat a little girl, her cheek pressed against the cracked leather upholstery that smelled faintly of sweat, perfume, and a thousand other faint reminders of previous travellers. The girl leaned back against a small woman dressed in shabby black clothes whose head nodded sleepily.

The man in the passenger seat turned and looked back at the old woman and the child. His cold eyes lingered over the child speculatively, in a way which troubled her. She dropped her gaze and snuggled closer to the woman and eventually the man turned to look at the road ahead.

The child lifted her eyes and gazed at the moon as it appeared to race along parallel to them, dropping a glittering path over the restless sea. She had lived in the city all her short life and had seen glimpses of the sea shimmering over the rooftops, but she had never been to the seashore. She was astonished to see how huge the sea was. As they had left the city and driven into the countryside, it had surprised her to see the land on either side of the road almost devoid of buildings.

They travelled through a harsh, rocky landscape softened in places by areas of lush vegetation, palm trees and spiky patches of plants. Occasionally the lights of small villages flickered through the vegetation. Beside the road lay small fields sown with crops in orderly rows. The little girl was tired and confused but soon, soothed by the moonlight, the music and the warm comfort of the woman's body, she fell deeply asleep.

Chapter One - Beirut

The week had started like every other. The old woman, Sofia, had gone to her work, cleaning the apartments of the wealthy people in the large block where they lived. Sofia's tiny apartment was in the rear basement, just two hot, stuffy rooms with tiny, grubby windows. A miniscule primitive bathroom was in the hall and an equally basic kitchen stood in the corner of the main room. Sofia and the child slept together in the bedroom in a lumpy double bed and Hassim, Sofia's troublesome son, slept in the living room whenever he was short of money and had nowhere better to go.

Sofia wore an eternally anxious expression on her round face. She had a small, upturned nose and wiry, black hair with a grey streak at the front. Her clothes were inevitably dark coloured and shabby, and she always covered her hair with a scarf or shawl. She had been poor all her life, although, when very young, she had been married to a good man. He worked at whatever jobs he could find to support his wife and child, but they had always struggled. Sadly, her husband died young, forcing Sofia to work as a cleaner to support herself and her wastrel son, Hassim.

The manager of the apartment building, Mr. Khalid, liked Sofia and appreciated that she was a hard worker who could be trusted not to pilfer from the people whose homes she cleaned. However, he did not trust Hassim at all and often hinted quite forcefully to Sofia that she should not allow him to stay with her. Sofia was afraid to deny her son a place to stay when he needed it, as he had a fearsome temper. When he had no money, he would either bully her to give him cash or help himself to money from her purse.

When she was able, Sofia would take Millie, the little child she cared for, with her when she cleaned the apartments. When the owners were home, this was impossible. On those days, Millie had to stay by herself in the little apartment while Sofia worked.

They had not always lived in this poky little flat. Not so long ago, they had lived in a lovely apartment with Rachel, Millie's mother. Millie could still remember her mother's lovely long, golden-brown hair. She could still smell her perfume and hear her laughter, like a lovely echo, but the details of her mother's face were beginning to fade from her memory. All she was sure of was that those times had been happy, much happier than now. They had been a small, cosy family, just Millie, her English mother Rachel, and Sofia, who had been Millie's nanny from when she was a toddler. Sofia had looked after their home and took care of Millie while her mother worked. Millie grieved for the loss of her mother and the time when she felt safe and loved.

Hassim had rarely been able to pester his mother in those good days. A concierge, who would only allow people in with the permission of the tenants, guarded the entrance hall of the block of flats, day and night. Sofia had loved working for Rachel. For the first time in her life, she had a good wage, a lovely room to sleep in, a sweet child to take care of and a kind and understanding employer. She had felt protected from her greedy son. Hassim had hung about outside the apartment entrance to try to catch Sofia as she went out to buy groceries and to bully her for cash, but he could not get inside.

One evening, when Millie was nearly four years old, her mother had gone to work but had never returned. Sofia awakened the following morning to find Rachel was not asleep in her room as usual, and her bed not slept in. When Rachel had not arrived home the following morning, Sofia, worried out of her mind, had called the police. They had been unable to find out what had happened to Rachel. She had gone to work that evening, and afterwards had been seen leaving the casino on her own. She had, quite mysteriously, completely vanished. Her car was never found.

Some days later, Sofia had packed a few suitcases with their clothes and took Millie in a taxi to where they lived now. Millie was still utterly bewildered by the disappearance of her mother and did as Sofia bid her without question. The rent of Rachel's apartment was due, and Sofia did not have enough money to pay it. Instead, the landlord offered Sofia the job, including the small flat, of cleaning the apartments in another block he managed.

Sofia had to go to work straight away cleaning the palatial apartments in the building above them. At four years of age Millie could only accept their new life, but she would constantly daydream about her old life. She told herself that, one day soon, her mother would return, and everything would be as happy as it once was.

One day Hassim, again in need of money, came to the basement when Sofia was out working. He searched amongst his mother's things but could find no money. He sat for a while, looking at Millie speculatively.

"Put your shoes on, Millie, and come with me. We are going to make a little money."

He took Millie into the city center and forced her with threats and slaps to beg from the people sitting in the pavement cafes. He pointed towards the groups of tourists he wanted her to beg from. They would look at the tiny child with big hazel eyes and a cloud of soft brown curls, and their hearts would be touched. Millie felt a natural embarrassment and humiliation at having to beg. She would approach each person obliquely and lay her tiny hand, palm up, gently on their knee. She could not look them in the eye and would simply gaze into the distance. If the people did not give her money, she would simply remove her hand and quietly move on to another person. It was rare that the sight of the pretty child in a grubby dress did not move someone, and invariably they would press a few coins into her hand.

When Millie had a handful of coins, she took it to Hassim, waiting around the corner. If he did not think she had tried hard enough, he would pinch her arm painfully and send her out to try again. Millie did not cry and never told Sofia that Hassim made her beg. He had threatened that he would take her away if she did and that she would never see Sofia again. Whenever he was short of money and Sofia was away, he would come to the little apartment and take Millie out to beg. Millie was as frightened of Hassim as Sofia was but soon learned not to show it. If he saw she was afraid, he would be even more cruel and vicious.

Some months went by and then one night, Hassim returned after an absence of a few days. When Millie slept in the back room, he told his mother he had found her a new job with a nicer apartment.

"But I like this job here," said Sofia nervously, biting her lip. She did not trust her son at all.

"But this job has a better place to live with lots of rooms. It is out of the city in the countryside. You will earn much the same money, but you will have more room," wheedled Hassim.

"I suppose you will be getting something out of this?" Sofia knew her son did nothing for anyone if it did not benefit himself even more.

Hassim frowned. He stood up and leaned over his mother menacingly. She flinched away from his foul breath. "I suppose I could always take the kid out begging from the tourists," he said smirking slyly, knowing his mother would hate that. She did not know that he had already forced Millie to beg. Sofia sighed; she would have to take the new job to try to protect Millie. She reckoned that Hassim would not visit them often if they lived outside the city, as he liked to be amongst the action. Sofia did not know exactly how he earned his money, but she was certain it was not through hard work.

The next day Sofia told the manager of the apartments that she was leaving for a new job that her son had found her and, although he was annoyed, he understood. A gentle lady like Sofia could not easily stand up to a man like Hassim. In the end he shrugged; there were plenty of people looking for work and, he reasoned, that scumbag Hassim would no longer have an excuse for hanging around the apartments.

Millie was surprised when Sofia started packing their things again. "Where are we going to now, Sofia?" Her nanny replied that they were going to a nicer home. In her heart she hoped that what she said was true.

Two days later, in the evening, Hassim came around and helped them carry their bags up to the street at the side of the apartment block where an old Mercedes taxi stood waiting at the curb.

"OK," Hassim said, "hurry up and get in the car," and he threw all their bags into the trunk. He pushed Sofia and Millie roughly into the back seat, slammed the door and got into the front seat next to the driver.

"You know the way, don't you, Ahmed?" he said to the driver, a swarthy man with a hooked nose and long greasy hair.

"Yes, I know the way to the village, but I don't know which house."

"That's OK," said Hassim, "I know which one it is."

They both lit cigarettes and Hassim turned on the radio, twiddling with the tuner until he found some music he liked. Millie looked out at the city streets passing by. She wondered where they were going and worried that when her mother returned, she would not know where they had gone.

Millie wished she were still back home with her mother. She remembered feeling safe and happy and completely loved by her mother and Sofia, who had a little bedroom of her own behind the kitchen. Sofia did all the cleaning and cooking, but always had time and patience to amuse Millie. She would give the child a little rag to dust the furniture or let Millie help her prepare the meals. Sofia spoke no English and just a little French, as do most Lebanese people, but always spoke to Millie in her native Arabic. In this way, Millie learned to speak Arabic, but Rachel always spoke English to her child.

Because she worked at night, Rachel used to sleep late into the morning. When she woke, she would play with Millie. Then, after dinner, she would dress in something beautiful and go to work. Millie had no idea what her mother's 'work' was, she just wished she could go with her, but her mother said it was impossible, that children were not allowed there. Rachel was a dancer in a very lavish revue in a grand and elegant casino outside the city. Rachel could have lived in the village near the casino where many of the other people in the show rented apartments, but she loved living in her beautiful apartment in the city and considered it worth the half an hour's drive in her little car to and from work every day.

When Rachel disappeared, two of the dancers who worked with Rachel at the casino came to the apartment to see if she was sick and why she had not come to work as usual. Sofia told them Rachel had not arrived home two nights ago and she had no idea where she was. Millie cried constantly for her mother in those days. Sofia held her tight and whispered that her mother would come soon, but the police had not been able to trace Rachel's movements after she left work. No trace was found of her or her car, and after a few weeks without results, the police activity diminished and finally ceased altogether.

Now here they were, a few months later, driving away from the city lights to yet another new place. Millie sighed sadly, closed her eyes, and eventually she went to sleep.

Chapter Two – The Big House

Suddenly, the car veered sharply off the coast road, startling Sofia and Millie awake. They were driving up a stony unpaved road that zig-zagged up the hill away from the sea. The road was steep and full of potholes, causing the taxi to lurch from side to side. Ahmed, the driver, grumbled about the damage to his car. Hassim laughed scornfully, "The suspension on this old crate was long gone anyway."

They climbed higher until the hiss of the sea on the shore grew fainter. They approached a small hamlet where no lights showed, and all was quiet, but bathed in the silver blue light of the moon. Beside them was a high stone wall surrounding a large house separated by some distance from any other dwelling. Hassim shouted to Ahmed, "This is it! Stop here," and the car came to a halt.

Hassim jumped out and shouted to his mother and Millie to get out. They quickly gathered up all their bags and followed him to an arched wooden gate of wide planks, with huge black hinges, set in the wall.

"Wait there, Ahmed," called Hassim to his friend, "I'm coming back to the city with you."

He pulled a bunch of keys from his pocket and unlocked the gate, its rusty hinges groaning from lack of use. Hassim, taking out a torch, led them across a dark garden to a short flight of stone stairs leading down to a doorway, their feet rustling through fallen leaves. The door was hidden in the shadow cast by the stairs going up to a verandah. It was hard to see where they were going with only the light of the moon and the faint light from Hassim's torch. He unlocked the door at the bottom of the steps and as he pushed open the door a stuffy, damp smell wafted out. They shuffled into the room peering around in the dim ray of moonlight shining through two very dirty windows.

Hassim shined his torch round until he found a candle stuck in the top of an old bottle and struck a match to light it. Sofia and Millie could see little in the shadows cast by the candle. An old iron bedstead stood in one corner with a grubby mattress. Sofia pulled a knitted blanket out of one of her bags and persuaded the exhausted child to lie down on the bed to sleep.

Hassim gave his mother a set of keys to the house and gate, then handed her a small wad of money. He told her that there were a few shops in the nearest village a short walk up the hill. As he turned to go, he warned his mother, "Don't get friendly with people round here and don't tell them your business."

"Why?" said Sofia, "I have nothing to hide!"

"That doesn't matter," he replied insolently, "but the woman who owns this house prefers the caretaker not to get too friendly with the locals, that's all."

"Who is the owner? Is she living here?" said Sofia.

"No," said Hassim, "She lives abroad, in Paris or somewhere, and never comes home, but she likes the house to be taken care of, just in case. You don't need worry about her; you just take care of the place and don't ever bring anyone local here. Don't let the kid talk to anyone. I will come every week or so to bring your wages and make sure everything is okay."

He told his mother to lock the gate after he had gone, and after a minute she heard the taxi turn around and go back down the hill. Sofia sighed and felt her way carefully back down into the basement. She locked the door and lay down on the bed next to Millie to sleep.

The next morning, Millie woke first and saw that Sofia still slept soundly. She got off the bed, careful not to disturb the old woman. The sun shone through the grimy windows and motes of dust floated around her as she walked round their new home. The stone floors were gritty with dirt, and the few threadbare and faded rugs were thick with dust. The basement was spacious with low arched ceilings. Several "rooms" led off a large central space, each with a stone archway and a vaulted stone roof.

One of the 'rooms' facing the windows had seats built into the walls, topped with oblong cushions in faded red and blue stripes. These were edged in tatty, faded fringes and tassels. Two of the curved arches had faded red curtains at the front, held back with frayed cords. In these curtained off areas were rusty iron bedsteads with stained, elderly mattresses. In the central area stood an ancient velvet-covered sofa with ornate scrolled arms and legs on which could be seen traces of gold leaf, long since worn away. One of its original legs was missing and a block of wood had been nailed in its place.

Millie was very intrigued by the arched ceilings and the old furniture, which had obviously once been beautiful but was now shabby and left abandoned and unwanted in this basement. She ran her fingers over the fabric of the old sofa: it was soft and velvety. The cushions were of a stiff, once glossy fabric edged with moth-eaten fringes and ragged tassels.

Only two large arched windows, high up near the ceiling, brought light into the basement, both obscured by years of dirt and cobwebs. Under one window stood a stone sink and wooden draining board. Beside it was an old stove with a shelf above. Millie found a door leading into a dark and clammy bathroom where there was a chipped rolltop bath streaked with green under the dripping taps of a chipped enamel water heater. On the other wall was a toilet and sink with an old spotted mirror on the wall. She turned on the tap of the sink and leaned over to drink some water, then rinsed her face and hands. There was no towel, so she shook her hands to dry them.

Millie went over to the basement door and, finding it unlocked, she went up the steps into the garden. It had high stone walls around it, much too high for Millie to see over. The house was situated at the back of the garden, facing towards the sea. There was a wide marble staircase, curving from the garden up to a large verandah, edged by a marble balustrade. At the back, high arches framed the French windows. The arches supported the floor above and there was another verandah up there too, but it did not have a staircase leading up to it.

Millie wandered across the garden. A wide stone path wound around a patchy bit of grass, thick with fallen leaves and dried petals. Overgrown bushes lined the walls, their branches reaching out and catching at Millie's clothes as she passed. Some were rose bushes and one or two had a few blossoms. Millie held a rose and dipped her nose appreciatively into the cool pink petals, breathing in the delicious scent. Two palm trees grew among the other bushes, their fronded heads reaching high above the walls.

She walked on round the garden and looked at the wide stairway curling upwards. She hesitated, then walked up the marble stairs, weather-stained and with dead leaves forming brown drifts in the corners. When Millie reached the verandah, she turned and found that she could see over the high wall to the sea. She sat on the top step and, with her elbows on her knees, rested her cheeks on her hands. The marble step was cold under her bottom.

The house stood high above the coast, but Millie could still faintly hear the sea hissing back and forth across the narrow pebble beach far below. The land below the house sloped steeply and was mostly rocky, with patches of grass or prickly bushes. To the right was a stand of gnarled and twisted trees with sparse, grey-green leaves. The trees appeared to be struggling to grow in crevices between the rocks and small patches of spiky weeds grew in their shade.

On the left-hand side of the house the road, which they had traveled up the night before, zigzagged down the hillside, lying quiet and undisturbed in the morning sun. Behind the house, the road ran up into a small village of plain, square houses, some with walled gardens. Beyond the village lay the mountains rising to the east, dark green forest hugging the lower slopes. Alongside the sea lay the coast road, running north to south. In the distance the cars on the road looked like a child's toys.

Millie got up and wandered about the verandah, kicking at the leaves, which lay in deep, rustling drifts against the house. She cupped her hands to peer into the windows, but curtains had been closed inside and all she could see in the dirty glass was her own faint reflection.

"Millie, where are you?" Sofia stood at the top of the steps to the basement.

"I'm here," called Millie, "I am coming." She ran down the wide marble stairs, warming as the sun grew stronger.

"Come and help me. I brought our breakfast with me, but we will go to the village later to buy some more food."

Before they went to the village, Sofia looked around to see what they needed. There was electricity in the basement but there were no light bulbs in the sockets. Sofia would buy some so they would have better light than just candles. She found an electricity meter up high in the corner and a switch to turn it on.

They unpacked two of their bags to take to the shops and left through the big wooden gate, locking it carefully behind them. They walked up the hill to the village and found a shop selling hardware and cleaning things. Close-by was another selling canned and dried foods, and a variety of vegetables. On a corner stood a small butcher's shop with a carcass of beef hanging in the back of the shop. The butcher was a short and swarthy man hacking at joints of meat on his counter. A small boy with a bored expression sat on a stool next to the animal carcass, listlessly waving a cloth to disturb the flies which buzzed irritably around, only to settle again on another part of the flesh.

Sofia bought a little meat and then went to the shop to buy rice, vegetables, and other provisions. They went into the hardware shop and bought light bulbs, a new broom and soap. The villagers were curious to see strangers in the village. Sofia smiled in a friendly fashion but said nothing. Several people looked closely at Millie as her unusual colouring captured their attention. Sofia noticed this and bit her lip. She decided not to bring Millie with her to the village again without a scarf over her hair. She remembered that Hassim had said to not let local people know their business.

They struggled home with their heavy bags of shopping and, after locking the big gate behind them, they worked to put their new home in order. They hauled all the bedding out into the sun to air. Sofia swept the floor and mopped it clean. She stood on a chair to clean the windows and sunlight lit up the room. She gave Millie a hand brush and set her to sweeping up the leaves on the stairs. These they gathered up and Sofia took them outside to throw them on the empty ground in front of the garden wall.

After making a midday meal, Sofia sent Millie out into the garden to play while she got the water heater working so she could wash their clothes. If there was any hot water left, they could bathe off the grime their bodies had accumulated from the cleaning.

Millie climbed the wide stairs to the verandah, now hot to the touch, and turned to look at the sea. The sky was bright blue but there was a wintry chill in the breeze blowing from the sea. From the verandah, Millie could just reach the top of the high wall surrounding the garden. She leaned forward so that she could see the land below the wall. It was rocky and uneven but there were patches of tall weeds growing in the shade of the wall. Millie heard someone whistling and a boy appeared driving a small flock of goats with a stick. He sat down in the shade of the wall as the goats browsed on the herbs, and soon seemed to be taking a nap.

Climbing down from the verandah, Millie explored the garden. Under one of the overgrown bushes, she found a water tap which was dripping on to a patch of grass growing green and lush. Suddenly Millie spotted a small green snake curled up in the moist grass in the shade of a bush. It looked at her intensely with glittering eyes and moved its head restlessly from side to side. Millie ran screaming for Sofia; she had never seen a snake before and instinctively she feared it. Sofia came running and Millie cautiously showed her where the snake was lying. Sofia was not afraid of snakes herself, although she knew the little snake was poisonous. She went and found a long, forked stick and unlocked the big gate to the street. She picked up the snake with the stick, carried it outside the gate and dropped it on the ground in front of the house.

"Be watchful in the garden," she said to Millie, "A snake bite can make you very ill. They mostly like to stay where it is damp and cool, so always look before you touch the bushes." Millie nodded her head vigorously; she would not forget this advice. She had been terrified of the tiny snake's glittering eyes.

Sofia and Millie enjoyed living in their new home once it was clean and Sofia made it as comfortable as she could. It was more spacious than their last tiny apartment. They both enjoyed the fresh air, and the peace and quiet of the countryside, so much nicer than the noisy city streets crowded with people and thick with traffic fumes. Sofia had less work to do, and she was less tired at the end of the day.

After Sofia had cleaned the basement to her satisfaction, she decided they would work on the garden together. She found some old garden tools in a little building hidden behind overgrown bushes. Sofia checked for snakes carefully and then she cut back the bushes.

When they had a big pile of branches and leaves, they carried them outside and made a bonfire on the wasteland to burn it all up. Sofia also added some bits and pieces of broken furniture from the basement. Soon the garden, the wide marble stairs and verandah were looking neat and spruce. Responding to the care they had received, all the bushes soon put out fresh growth and new flower buds. In this busy fashion, their first few weeks at the house passed peacefully.

One day they heard a car wending its way up the hill. It stopped by the gate. The big gate opened, and Hassim appeared. Sofia and Millie stopped gardening, and apprehensively watched him saunter over to them. They had been so busy and contented that they had almost forgotten about him. He had a chilling effect on their good mood, like a dark cloud passing over the sun.

He ambled round, inspecting everything, and then went down to the basement to see what they had done there. He came back up the stairs and said, "You've done a good job, Mother. The owner will be pleased, and I can report good progress to her agent. Now, I want you to arrange things for some other people to live here."

"Who would that be?" answered Sofia anxiously, "I thought we would live here by ourselves."

"A man I know needs somewhere for his woman and son to stay for a while," said Hassim.

Sofia was upset by this news. She had begun to feel that she and Millie were safe here in the country and now she was expected to make room for strangers. She knew that Hassim was unlikely to share any of the money he might receive from this man. In fact, she doubted that she was receiving more than a fraction of what Hassim was being paid for her taking care of the property.

As she had a thousand times before, Sofia wondered what she had done to deserve such a nasty man for a son. She did not bother to argue with him. She knew from experience that Hassim might be even more harsh and spiteful if she questioned his actions.

"Here is some more money, Mother, and it must last you longer this time. Make the rooms suitable for the woman and the kid by this time next week." Hassim left and they heard the car drive away down the hill.

Sofia sighed and continued with her gardening. Millie looked at her anxiously. "Why is Hassim bringing more people here, Sofia?"

"I don't know, Millie, but I am sure he will be making money out of it." Sofia attacked the rose she was pruning with a vengeance to vent her annoyance.

The basement was finally ready for the extra people. They would have to share the kitchen and bathroom but there was enough room for separate sleeping and sitting rooms with a little rearrangement of the furniture. Only the curtains hanging in the archways gave any privacy at nighttime. Sofia and Millie had not bothered to draw the curtains before, but Sofia decided that she would do so when the new arrivals came.

A week later, a car stopped outside the big gate. Through it came Hassim, accompanied by a fat man with a bad-tempered expression and a painfully thin woman with a weary face who was holding the hand of a big, clumsy-looking boy with an unseeing stare. Hassim led the way into the basement and signaled his mother to show them to their space. The woman sank onto the bed and pulled the boy protectively close to her. The two men went back to the car and brought in some bags which they dumped on the floor. Then, without a word, both men went out and drove away.

Sofia and Millie stood looking at the two newcomers. The woman was so thin that her clothes hung loose on her. Her dark hair was threaded with silver and was tied back in an untidy knot. The boy sagged against his mother, his eyes devoid of any connection to the world around him. A little thread of drool hung from his lip.

"I am sorry," said the woman wearily, attempting a smile. "I am sure that you do not want us here. I am Nabila, and this is my son, Ali. He was damaged at birth and can't do what other children his age can do, but he is usually no trouble."

Sofia was touched by the obvious sadness of this woman and by the plight of the son. She sat beside her and put a sympathetic arm around Nabila's shoulders. "Don't upset yourself, we must make the best of things in this world, don't you think? Won't your husband be staying here with you?"

Embarrassed, Nabila lowered her head, "No. For many years he sold my body to other men. I have been ill and now my looks have gone. I no longer interest men, so he wants me and the boy gone. He wants to live free, probably with a younger woman who he will no doubt force to go with men to bring him money. He hates to work for a living."

Her heart swelling with sympathy, Sofia said, "Never mind, you will be safer here, I cannot imagine it would pay them to bring men such a long way from the city."

"I am not sad to be away from him. It is a blessing I am truly grateful for, but I am afraid he will not pay Hassim the money for our keep."

Sofia snorted, "I don't think you need to worry about that. Hassim can look after himself!"

Nabila made herself and her son comfortable in their rooms. Millie peeped shyly around their curtain and

Nabila smiled at her. Millie smiled back, perhaps it would not be so bad to have Nabila and her son to live with them, although she could see that the boy was strange. He did not smile and his head leaned to one side, his lips hung open and he drooled a little all the time

Over the next few days, the two women got into a routine. Nabila did half the housework in the basement and most of the cooking, as she was a very good cook. She was not, however, very robust and could not manage the heavier work of the garden. When the garden was under control, Sofia took the set of keys for the main house and went in once or twice a week to sweep and dust the whole house, even though she knew that it was unlikely that anyone was coming to live there. She felt a responsibility to the absent owner to keep it clean and habitable.

On warm sunny days, she would open the French windows to air the rooms, keeping the drapes pulled across so the sun did not fade the upholstery and carpets. When she did this, Millie would creep up the verandah stairs and peep in at the beautiful things in the rooms. It reminded her of her mother and the lovely apartment they had lived in, and she always felt a pain in her heart. Why had her mother gone away? Where had she gone and did she wonder if her little girl was missing her? These sad thoughts would overcome Millie and the tears would fall for a while, but with the adaptability of a child, she would dry her tears and turn her eyes away towards the sea. She always found the sound of the waves on the shore soothing and comforting.

One day Sofia returned from the shopping with a big smile on her face, carrying a sack.

"I have a surprise for you, Millie, because you have been such good girl, and have worked hard to help me in the garden."

She placed the sack on the ground, and it moved! Millie ran to open it and inside was a scrawny white kitten with big green eyes and an ugly ginger blotch under its nose, like a large, uneven moustache. The kitten blinked at the sunlight and took a few steps towards Millie and gave a tiny "Miaow". Millie was enchanted and knelt to stroke the tiny animal.

"Is it mine?" she asked Sofia as she gathered it gently into her arms.

"Yes, child, all yours. Perhaps he will be useful to catch mice when he has grown a bit."

The kitten snuggled against Millie, purring loudly. He put his little face up and rubbed it against Millie's cheek. Millie had never had a pet before and she was ecstatic. Sofia said that the man in the hardware shop kept a cat to catch the mice in his storeroom which had given birth to a litter of kittens. He had given the others away, but no one wanted this ugly little one.

"Thank you, thank you, Sofia, I think he is lovely," and she sat on her bed to pet and cuddle him.

"What will his name be?" said Nabila smiling. "He looks as if he has been dipping his nose in the soup pot, with that ginger blob under his nose."

This made Millie giggle. She thought for a while and then she said, "I will call him Peter. My mummy used to read me a book about a rabbit called Peter."

A month went by peacefully until Hassim visited again. He gave his mother and Nabila some money, told them to make it last, and then he noticed the cat sitting on Millie's lap.

"What's that thing doing here. You're wasting your money feeding it," he said angrily, and he made a move to grab the kitten.

"No, wait," said Sofia quickly, grabbing his arm. She saw Millie's eyes go wide with fear as she clutched the kitten to her chest. "The cat will be useful to keep down the mice in the house. You don't want the owner complaining that mice have nibbled the furnishings, do you?"

"Oh, well," said Hassim frowning. "I suppose you can keep it as long as it does catch mice. Otherwise, it goes, you understand?" Millie and Sofia nodded their agreement, hoping that Peter would learn to catch mice as soon as possible.

The months passed and Millie was happy. Sometimes she got bored as she had no way to exercise her brain. She wished she could go outside the garden walls to explore and be free like the boy who looked after the goats, but Sofia would not allow her outside alone. Hassim came only rarely and would leave them enough money to last until his next visit. The two women knew they had a period of peace until he came again and so they could relax and feel easy.

Nabila's husband never came, and Nabila was extremely relieved about this. As her spirits improved, her health improved also. They breathed clean air in the country and ate good food, and Nabila grew stronger and smiled more.

Sofia was getting older and she suffered with pain in her joints. She had worked extremely hard her whole life and it had taken a toll on her health. Nabila took over the cleaning of the main house and the washing of their clothes, as scrubbing their garments in hot water made Sofia's fingers stiff and painful. Nabila often insisted that Sofia took a chair into the garden to sit in the sun to rest. When the sun became too hot, she would move to sit in the shade under the marble staircase.

The garden thrived under their care. The roses and the other bushes flowered profusely. All day long the garden hummed with bees and other insects. Birds visited the garden and Millie would feed them crumbs of bread. The warmth of the sun heated the paving stones until Millie and Ali could not walk on them without shoes. In a corner of the garden the two women had planted some tomato pips and trained the resulting vines up against the garden wall. Millie loved to eat the ripe tomatoes straight from the vine.

Millie could not play with Ali, as he was always lost in his own little world. He was only interested in staying close to Nabila. He sulked and made moaning noises when his mother made him sit in a chair by himself while she worked. All he wanted was to cling to his mother's skirt and suck his thumb noisily. Sometimes he would look at the cat with a tiny bit of interest, but he was very clumsy and more likely to fall over the cat than to pet it. He took no notice of Millie at all unless his mother gave her attention when he would grunt angrily and try to pull Nabila away.

Millie was happy she had Peter to play with and to love. The kitten was Millie's comfort and her companion. His playful antics would make her laugh. He could not get out of the garden but, as he got older, he would promenade along the top of the wall, surveying the countryside and making little growling noises if he spotted a goat or a rabbit, or a bird flying across the sky. Millie became anxious when he walked along the wall and would try to tempt him back into the garden with a little piece of food.

Several times a year at the weekend, a large group

of families would come out of the city in a convoy of cars. They would have a picnic in the little wood down the hillside, cooking food on portable barbecues. They would play drums, sing and dance till the sun went down. Millie would listen to the laughter and music as she watched from the verandah and feel rather lonely. She felt a yearning for something but did not know what it was. She wished she could go and join in, they seemed to be having such a good time.

With the two women to share the work, they did not need Millie's help, but they gave her little chores to do every day. It was the way things were for women of their culture. Ali never had to do any chores, as he was not capable of doing anything properly. If Millie was doing her chores, Peter would go and curl up next to Ali. The boy never showed any affection towards Peter but seemed in his own peculiar way to enjoy the company of the little cat.

Very occasionally, Ali would become upset for no discernible reason and he would roar with anger, pull at his clothes, and try to bang his head against the wall. When he had one of these episodes, Nabila had no choice but to stay with Ali and hold him tight to prevent him hurting himself he eventually calmed down.

Except for when Hassim came, time passed quite peacefully for the two women and the children, until Millie was about eight years old. Sofia was not sure what the little girl's birth date was, so they could not celebrate her birthday. As Millie had grown out of her clothes, Nabila cut down some of her old dresses to fit her, and Sofia bought her a warm jacket and trousers in the village. She bought them too big so they would last longer, and Millie had to roll up the sleeves and the trouser bottoms. Ali was now taller than his mother, but although he grew very strong, he still had the mind of a small child. He could not speak and still merely grunted to his mother, who always seemed to know what he wanted.

Millie was growing to resemble her mother very much, although she was unaware of it. She was a pretty child with a small, heart-shaped face and hazel eyes, fringed with brown lashes tipped with gold. A few freckles dotted her nose, and when she smiled, she had dimples in each cheek. Sofia brushed her hair each morning and braided it into a long plait falling down her back. When Sofia brushed her hair out like a soft fan on Millie's back, the old woman would get tears in her eyes remembering that Rachel's hair had been the same curly light brown streaked with blonde.

One day Hassim arrived and for once he bought with him Nabila's husband, Mohammed. Nabila was terribly upset to see him and went into her bedroom with the curtains drawn much of the time he was there. Mohammed completely ignored her and Ali. Nabila had peeped out from time to time and was relieved to see that he was not interested in her and he had not noticed the improvement of her health and looks. She was very curious to know why he was there but did not dare ask.

The two men sat around in the apartment, instead of leaving quickly as usual, and Hassim ordered Sofia to cook them a meal. They ate and talked, and all the while they talked, they were looking at Millie in a way which made the little girl feel extremely uncomfortable. After they had eaten, the two men went up into the garden and up the marble stairs to the verandah to smoke. Nabila came out of her bedroom and crept up into the garden after them. She hid in the shade of the staircase to listen to their conversation as she had noticed them glancing at Millie, and the way they had looked at the child made her blood run cold.

She heard the two men taking about Millie, their

cigarettes glowing in the gloom.

"Yes, she is coming along very nicely, isn't she?" said Hassim.

"A lovely girl," agreed Mohammed. "I expect she will bring you a lot of money."

"All in good time, all in good time," said Hassim, "She is a bit too young for the client I have in mind. He likes them young, but he likes them to have breasts, however small, and she has none yet."

"That is true," agreed Mohammed, "She has no breasts at all."

Nabila had heard enough. She tiptoed quickly back down to the basement and looked at Millie. The child was still small, and she hoped it would be some time before she developed to the point that she was in danger. Millie was looking anxious, so Nabila smiled reassuringly. Millie smiled back, feeling better.

When Millie was asleep, Nabila whispered to Sofia what she had heard.

"He is my son, Nabila, but he is a very evil man. I am ashamed that he would plan to sell a child to a stranger in such a terrible way," and Sofia started to cry.

"We must try to think of a way to prevent this," said Nabila. "Hopefully, we have a bit of time as she has not started to develop yet."

"This is true," said Sofia drying her tears.

"Shhh," said Nabila, "They are coming back down."

Hassim came down into the basement and gave his mother her money. It was more than usual so she knew he would not be back for a few weeks. The two men left; when the two women heard the gate clang shut behind them and the car drive away down the hill, Sofia and Nabila gave a sigh of relief.

Sofia called Nabila into her bedroom. She reached under her bed and brought out a small suitcase. It had belonged to Rachel, Millie's mother. In it were stored important looking documents, some letters and a passport with Millie's photo from when she was a toddler.

Sofia whispered to Nabila the story of how Rachel had disappeared and how they had been forced to leave her apartment. She told Nabila that she could not read and so did not know what the papers in the case were about. She had taken them to keep them safe for Rachel in case she returned, and because she thought they might be important to Millie in the future. Perhaps one day they would help her to find her mother or her mother's family.

The two women looked at the papers together. Neither could read, so the papers were of little use to them. There were also some photographs in the case. One was of Rachel holding Millie as a baby, another of Rachel on her own in a beautiful evening gown, and one of her with a handsome, smiling man on a sailing boat, her hair blowing out behind her in the wind.

"She is very beautiful," said Nabila. "Don't you have any idea where she is?"

"I never heard a single thing about her from that day, but I think she must be dead because she loved Millie so much and she was a wonderful mother." Sofia wiped a tear from her eye. "Yes, I am sure she must be dead. She would never have left her little girl alone."

They placed all the papers back in the case and hid it under Sofia's bed again. The old woman said to Nabila, "Hassim does not know anything about this case and the papers. I think he might even throw them away if he did because he obviously has plans for Millie. Please never tell him about them. Because I am getting old, if anything happens to me, tell Millie about them, and make her understand that they are important."

"Please don't worry, Sofia." Nabila put her arm round the older woman. "I will keep her things safe and, if I can, I will protect her from Hassim."

After several months, Hassim began visiting more often than he had before. Each time he appraised Millie to see if she were beginning to develop. The two women became more anxious each time he came in case he became impatient and decided to take Millie away before she reached puberty. They never went shopping together so that Millie was never left alone in case he came when they were away.

Millie was aware of their anxiety, but they had always been nervous of Hassim and so she did not understand why they were more on edge than usual whenever he came. The added tension was not good for the old woman and Sofia sometimes found it hard to get her breath. She would sit and clutch at her chest gasping with the effort to breathe.

"Are you in pain, Sofia?" asked Nabila gently.

"I keep getting a sharp pain in my heart. Perhaps it is because I do not know how to protect Millie from Hassim." Nabila hugged Sofia, but she did not know what to do either.

One terrible morning, Nabila woke to find that Sofia had died during the night. She woke Millie and told her the sad news. Millie cried and cried, her tears falling on Peter until his fur became quite wet. He wriggled out of her arms and went out in the garden to groom his fur. Ali was upset by all the tension, too, and started to roar and bang his head on the wall. Nabila didn't know which child to go to first.

Nabila sent Millie out into the garden with her cat then pulled the little case out from under Sofia's bed and hid it among her clothes. That afternoon, Hassim arrived but showed little emotion when told his mother had died. He grudgingly went to the village to sort out the business of Sofia's burial. Millie was still distraught and lay on her bed cuddling Peter when he would submit to it. She was old enough to realise that Sofia had been her protector, and the old woman had taken the place of her missing mother in her mind. She wondered what would happen to her now.

Chapter Three - Shock

Hassim sent his taxi driver friend away when he was told his mother was dead. He told Ahmed to return in two days when the burial was over.

He asked Nabila if she would take over the job of taking care of the property. She agreed to stay on because she had nowhere else to go and because she hoped to think of a way to protect Millie from Hassim's evil plans. She and Sofia had been spending as little as they could and had buried a little store of money in a tin box under one of the rose shrubs by the garden wall. Nabila had a vague plan that, when she had sufficient money, she would take her son and Millie on the bus to Tripoli in the north. This city was in the opposite direction to Beirut where Hassim spent all his time. Nabila had some cousins living there, although she had not seen them for years. She hoped her relatives might take pity on them, and let them stay until she could find another job and a new place to live.

Hassim gave her some money and, when his friend came in his taxi, he went back to the city. He told Nabila to take good care of Millie and not to take her to the village when she went out. A few days later, Nabila had to go to buy food. She took Ali with her as she could not leave him alone. While she was gone, Hassim arrived and came in the big gate. Millie was sitting up on the verandah with Peter, looking out at the sea. She had been thinking about Sofia, her heart aching. She missed the old woman terribly.

Hassim called out to her, "Come down here, Millie, I want to take you to the city to buy some new clothes."

Millie did not want to be alone with Hassim. "No, thank you," she replied politely, "I don't need any new clothes."

Hassim's face flushed red with anger. Somewhere deep inside him was a guilty feeling for what he had planned for Millie, but he angrily repressed this feeling and shouted at the child.

"You come down here right now and do as I say."

Millie, carrying Peter in her arms, came down the stairs very slowly, hoping all the time that Nabila would come back. When Millie reached the bottom of the stairs, Hassim grabbed her arm and Peter fell to the floor. When Millie tried to reach for the cat, Hassim grabbed Peter by the back legs and swung him hard against the wall. The cat fell dead on the ground, and with a scream, Millie pulled her arm free from Hassim's grip and ran over to Peter. She picked him up gently. His head fell back, and his eyes had glazed over. Millie knew he was dead.

Hassim's face was scarlet with anger.

"That damn cursed animal," he shouted as he caught hold of Millie's arm again, forcing her to drop Peter's body on the ground. He dragged the sobbing child out of the gate and locked it behind them. He pushed her into the back of the taxi, got in the back with her and told the driver to drive and fast.

Nabila was just walking back down the road with Ali and the shopping. She saw Hassim push Millie into the car and she started to run, but she was too late. The taxi sped down the hillside, skidding on the stony road. Nabila went sadly back inside the gate, knowing that she had been too late to save Millie. When she went into the garden and saw Peter's body lying on the ground, her heart sank. She did not know whether Hassim would ever bring Millie back to the house, but resolved that, if he did, as soon as he went away again, she would pack their things and take the children away immediately.

All the way to the city Millie sobbed with fear and grief for her cat. She knew that something terrible was going to happen. Hassim usually had a lazy insolent grin on his face. Now he frowned and looked angry. He slapped her and told her to stop bawling. She managed to stop crying but she was shivering with fear, wondering where they were going and knowing there was no one to rescue her.

When the car reached the city, Hassim directed the driver a large white house on the edge of the city. Apart from a large front door guarded by a wrought iron gate, all the windows were high up and the house had a shut away, forbidding appearance. He directed the driver round to a narrow street at the rear of the house and told him to stop. Hassim pulled Millie out and, keeping tight hold of her arm, he knocked at a black door. The door opened and an old woman motioned them in. She was dressed from head to foot in black, showing only a pinched, mean face, her small black eyes shadowed by bushy brows meeting in the middle. The door shut behind them. Millie saw they were in a dark, musty smelling hallway. The old woman took hold of her arm as tightly as Hassim had done and told Hassim to go away and to return the next day.

Hassim left, and the old woman took Millie up some uncarpeted stairs to another long, dark hall. She opened a door and pushed Millie in. They were in a large, elegant bathroom with cool green tiles. The old woman told Millie to take off her clothes.

"I don't want to," said Millie tearfully. She was shivering uncontrollably. "I just want to go home."

"Well, you can't, not yet, so do as you are told. Take off your clothes," the old woman said, her voice harsh and cold. She pinched Millie hard on her arm and Millie began to cry but complied.

Millie felt very afraid, and her heart was beating so fast she felt her chest would burst. She did not know why Hassim had brought her to this place, but she knew it would be for something bad. With Hassim, things were always bad if Sofia or Nabila were not there to protect her.

The old woman ran water into the huge roll top bath. She undid Millie's long plait and made her get in the bath. She scrubbed Millie from top to toe and washed her hair. When she judged Millie was spotlessly clean, she helped her out of the bath and handed her a soft white towel. Millie usually enjoyed a bath and liked being clean. If she were not so filled with dread, she would have enjoyed the luxury of this huge and imposing bathroom.

The old woman helped her dry herself and rubbed Millie's hair briskly. Then she dressed Millie in a long, white dress embroidered with tiny white flowers. The dress was made of thin, flimsy material and Millie felt very vulnerable as she could see her arms and legs right through the cloth. She wondered if it were a nightdress. It was the middle of the day, surely, she didn't have to go to bed yet.

The old woman took her down the corridor again and led her into a small plain bedroom, with a single bed in the corner. A chair stood under the window which was covered on the outside by decorative metal bars. The bed was covered in a shabby bedspread.

"Wait here, said the old woman, "I will come back and brush your hair when it is dry,"

As the old woman left. Millie heard the key turn in the lock outside. She could not imagine what she was doing here or why she had been locked in. Maybe Hassim had arranged for her to become a servant in this house. This was a very worrying idea as Millie only knew what Sofia had taught her, and she had not asked Millie to do more than simple little jobs like sweeping or washing dishes.

Millie looked out of the window. All she could see was the bare brick walls of the building opposite. As there was nothing to see outside, Millie sat on the bed. She felt rather chilly but dared not get under the bedclothes. A long time passed. Millie was very thirsty and hungry too. She lay down and pulled the bed cover over herself to try and get warm as she had started to shiver again.

She thought about Peter and the terrible way he had died. and she cried salty tears. Everyone and everything she loved had been taken away from her. First her mother, then Sofia and now Peter and Nabila. She thought of Peter's sweet ugly face and the way he squinted his eyes at her to show his affection. She remembered his soft body lying close to her in the night, soft purrs rumbling though his body. Eventually she cried herself to sleep.

The sound of the key in the door woke her. The old woman came into the dark room, putting the light on as she entered. Millie sat up and tried to straighten the bedclothes.

"Never mind about that," said the old woman impatiently, and producing a hairbrush, she proceeded to brush Millie's hair. She brushed it briskly and none too gently.

"Ouch!" Millie squealed.

The old woman grunted and carried on until Millie's hair hung soft and shining down her back.

"Where is Hassim? When is he coming back for me?" Millie was starting to feel very frightened indeed. The old woman, cold and indifferent to her feelings, did not answer her and merely sniffed. Millie longed to be back in familiar surroundings. She felt instinctively that she was not safe in this house.

"Be quiet, girl, if you behave yourself and do as you are bid, all will be well," the old woman said as she straightened the flimsy dress.

"What do I have to do?" said Millie.

"All you have to is to please the master, then you can leave. Now stop talking and remember to be polite and respectful to the master."

With that the old woman took hold of Millie's wrist in her bony fingers and led her down the corridor and up some stairs. At the top of the stairs, she opened a plain wooden door and they walked into a wide passageway. This was a complete contrast to the part of the house she had seen before. It had a high ceiling and a floor carpeted in a deep shade of red. On top of the carpet were many silky Persian rugs patterned in shades of dark red, blue and green. The walls were papered with red and gold paper. There was faint sound of Arabic music behind one of the ornate, wooden doors on either side of the passage.

The old woman stopped outside the door where the music was coming from and knocked.

"Enter," said a quiet voice.

The old woman opened the door and pulled Millie into the room. "The girl is here, Master."

A man rose slowly from a gilded chair, upholstered in red velvet. The walls were covered in wooden panels, carved in an ornate style of strange beasts, birds and exotic flowers. The windows were covered by plush red drapes and the room was dimly lit. In the corner was a great metal birdcage with a green parrot pacing up and down on its perch. In another corner was a huge carved bed with a purple and gold coverlet. The room was oppressively hot and there was a sweetish, cloying smell in the air.

The man signaled the old woman to leave the room and she went out, bowing obsequiously as she went. He walked towards Millie, who was shivering with fear despite the heat in the room. The man was tall and languid, with a thin face and a long, beaky nose. His eyes were large and glittered moistly but had an unfocused look as if he were half-asleep. The whites of his eyes were bloodshot and yellow. His hair was long, tied back and hung in greasy strands down his back. He wore a long, blue robe decorated with gold embroidery and his feet were bare, long horny toenails bent over the ends of his toes.

The man walked round behind Millie, lifting her hair as he walked.

"Please can I just go home now. Nabila will be worrying about me," she whispered, twisting her hands together nervously.

The man pulled Millie's hair with a sharp jerk, "You will go home when I say you go home. Get on the bed!"

"I don't want to," said Millie backing towards the door. The feeling of fear was increasing, and her heart was beating wildly.

Suddenly the man grabbed her and threw her on the bed. She screamed and scrambled off the bed and ran to the door. She frantically tried to open it, but it was locked. The man walked towards her; his face suffused with anger now. He grabbed her again and pushed her onto the bed. He stared coldly down into Millie's eyes. Millie stared back into those cruel eyes, frozen with terror. Holding her tightly by her wrists, the man callously stole her innocence forever.

When he was done, the man got off her and let go of her hands. Sobbing with fear and utter confusion, Millie crawled off the bed; her instinctive urge was to escape this terrible man. He chased her round the room, cursing as she dodged round the furniture. Millie saw a walking stick leaning against a table and grabbed it. As the man got near her again, and flailing the stick in a blind panic, she swung it between his legs and then hit him hard on the arm.

The man doubled over, clutching at his crotch, howling in pain. He grabbed Millie with his uninjured arm and threw her against the wall. Falling to the floor and gasping for breath, Millie lay feeling sure the man was going to kill her now. Using his uninjured arm, he wrenched the stick from Millie's hand and beat her with it. He then pulled a tasseled bell rope that hung down next to the bed and unlocked the door. Afterwards, he went over to the bed and lay down, curled into ball of pain.

There was a tap on the door and the old woman came in.

"Take this brat away and then come back, I want to talk to you," ordered the man.

The old woman grasped Millie by the arm, sharp nails digging into her flesh, and dragged her back down to the small bedroom where she had been before. Millie's clothes were on the bed. The old woman told her to put on her own clothes, then went out and locked the door behind her. Millie dressed herself, with some difficulty as she was bruised and stiff, and sat on the bed. She could not stop shaking with shock and fear. She did not understand what had just happened to her.

Chapter Four - Consequences

After a while, Millie heard the lock turn. The door opened and the old woman came in.

"Do you need the bathroom?" she asked Millie, seeming indifferent to the ordeal that she knew the child had been through. Millie nodded, her head down, and the old woman took her to the bathroom and waited outside, then took her back to the little bedroom again and locked her in.

Millie lay on the bed and tears trickled from her eyes on to the pillow. Apart from Nabila, there was no one to care what happened to her. Eventually, despite the pain, she cried herself to sleep.

She woke in the morning to feel the sun on her face. She rubbed her eyes and gasped in pain. Her face was sore where the man had hit her, and she could hardly see out of one of her eyes. The old woman came and took her to the bathroom. Millie looked in the mirror and gasped. Her face was swollen and she had many bruises on her face and body. She was terribly thirsty and drank some cold water from the tap.

Then the old woman took her down to the street door where Hassim was waiting, his face like thunder. Hassim's taxi-driver friend was waiting outside and they drove back out of the city to the big house. Hassim unlocked the big gate and pushed Millie inside.

"You stupid little fool. Why didn't you behave yourself? The master was angry and would not pay me all he promised me. You cost me a lot of money." Hassim then started to hit Millie, his fists landing cruelly on the bruises she already had. She screamed but he continued to beat her until she fell to the ground and then he started kicking her.

Hearing the noise, Nabila ran up the basement stairs, followed closely by her son, Ali, her face white with horror.

"Leave her alone! What have you done to her?" she screamed, and she grabbed at his arm to pull him away. Hassim turned round and punched Nabila hard in the stomach and she doubled over in pain. He started to kick at her instead of Millie.

Suddenly Hassim fell to the ground and Nabila saw that Ali stood over him with a big stone in his hand. Ali could not stand to see anyone hurt his mother, but he had no concept of having done wrong. He simply wanted to stop Hassim hurting her. When Nabila had got her breath back, she looked at Hassim. He was lying on the ground and not moving, blood pooling on the paving stone under his head. His eyes were closed.

Nabila went over to Millie and helped her up. The poor child's face was swollen and red, and she had bruises all over her body. Nabila kissed Millie gently on the cheek and led her quickly down into the basement, calling Ali to come too. When they were all down there, she locked the door and they all sat.

Nabila held the two children close, waiting for Hassim to wake up and bang on the door. The minutes passed and all was quiet, so Nabila hoped he had gone away. Ali was distressed and clung tightly to his mother's dress. Nabila hugged him and coaxed him onto his bed and stroked his head until he fell asleep.

Nabila gasped as she saw the extent of the evidence of violence all over Millie.

"The man hurt me. He beat me with a stick," whimpered Millie between sobs. "Why did he do that?"

Nabila sighed and shook her head, "I don't know, Millie. There are bad people and good people in this world. That man and Hassim are both bad people. I will not let them hurt you again. We will go away tomorrow, somewhere far away, where Hassim will never find us."

"Nabila," said Millie. "What happened to Peter?"

"I buried him under the rose bushes, where he liked to lay to keep cool."

Millie buried her face in Nabila's lap and cried for herself and for Peter. She had known he was dead as he had not moved when he fell on the ground, but it hurt so much to have lost the little cat she loved so much. It would have comforted her now to have him to cuddle. Nabila kissed the little girl's cheek and wrapped a blanket around her as she was still quivering with shock and pain. Then she fetched the little case of documents and pictures from under her bed, thinking the pictures would distract her.

"Sofia gave me this case for you before she died, Millie. It was your mother's and there are papers and photographs of her inside. Would you like to look at them with me?"

Millie nodded, and together they looked at the things in the case. Nabila showed Millie the passport, "I think this is a passport for you and papers of your mother's.

A passport helps you to travel from one country to another and proves who you are. There is a picture of you as a small child in the passport."

Together they looked at the photographs. When she saw the picture of her mother holding Millie when she was small, she burst into tears. If only her mother were here now, to hold her and comfort her. Millie had never seen the things in the case before.

"These things may be important to you one day, Millie, and you must never speak of them to Hassim. We must look after them very carefully. Sofia said that they might one day help you find your mother, or your mother's family."

Millie had never thought of her mother as having a family. There had always been just the two of them and Sofia as far back as she could remember.

"Thank you, Nabila, for keeping them safe for me."

Nabila kissed her and tucked her in, "Go to sleep now, my darling, tomorrow we have a very long journey."

When Millie had gone to sleep, Nabila stood on a chair to look out of the window. The moon was bright and shone down into the garden creating deep shadows. Nabila could not see any sign of Hassim. Maybe he had gone! She quietly unlocked the door and climbed the stairs cautiously. She saw a pool of blood on the ground, but Hassim was nowhere in sight and the big gate had been left wide open. She peeped out and saw that the taxi was gone so Nabila guessed Hassim had gone back to the city with the driver. She was dreadfully afraid he would come back the next day. She knew that at first light they must leave and, when he came back, they would be long gone. She locked the gate.

Nabila had to shield her son from the consequences of his action in trying to protect her. She could not bear him to be separated from her: she was all he had in the world. She doubted that Hassim would tell the police Ali had attacked him. He was more likely to come back with some of his cronies and punish Ali himself.

She also had to protect Millie. She pondered how to cover their tracks, so they had a chance to get away. She decided they would walk across country through the woods and then down the coast road to the next village, so people would not immediately know which direction they had come from. There they could catch a bus to the next big town, Batroun, and from there they could travel on to Tripoli. If Hassim did bring the police (which Nabila doubted very much) and they tracked them as far as Batroun, she hoped they would waste time looking for them there. Hassim did not know about her cousins, and she didn't think her former husband would remember either. She hoped no one would have reason to think they had gone to Tripoli.

She spent some time packing some clothes and made packages of food to take with them. She went into the garden and dug up the money that she and Sofia had hidden. When all was ready, she lay down to sleep for a while. She got up just before the sun rose and woke the children. They dressed and Nabila draped a shawl closely about Millie's face to cover her bruises. She gave her trousers to wear, and a long-sleeved jacket. The day was cool and cloudy and so her clothes would not draw attention to her. They gathered all their things together and went out into the road. Nabila locked the big gate behind her and threw the key over the wall.

Chapter Five - Escape

Nabila gave each child a bag to carry and took the rest herself. Millie had a deep woven cloth bag with a long strap so that she could hang it over her shoulder and across her chest. At the bottom of the bag, Nabila had packed Millie's little case of papers and photos, with a few of her clothes on top. As he was stronger, she gave Ali a much larger bag to carry although he scowled and moaned about having to carry it.

Taking hold of the rest of her bags, Nabila hurried the children down the road. They turned onto the rough ground at the front of the house and headed towards the woodland some distance away to the right. As soon as they were safely amongst the trees, she knew they would not be visible from the village, and she hoped no one would notice which direction they had taken.

The rocky ground was uneven, and the prickly bushes caught on their clothes as they hurried along. Millie found walking fast difficult because of her bruises but, as soon as they entered the trees, Nabila slowed down. They walked downhill through the cool, quiet woodland, the pine needles scrunching beneath their shoes, and eventually emerged from the trees a short distance from the coast road. They scrambled up a rocky scree on to the dusty road. This was the first time Millie had been so close to the sea. On the narrow, pebbly beach lay a mounded tidemark of seaweed dotted with plastic cartons, broken plastic shoes and other trash washed in by the tide. Clouds of flies buzzed over the smelly piles of rubbish.

Ahead of them they could see a village which straddled the road. People milled about, going about their business and no one took any notice of them. Nabila knew that the center was the usual place to catch a bus in the coastal villages, so she looked around to see if anyone else seemed to be waiting. She saw two women with large bags waiting outside the village stores who might be waiting for a bus. She walked over with the children to a place behind them, as she was anxious not to attract any attention. She checked that Millie's shawl was pulled forward to hide her bruises.

After a while, an elderly bus drove into the square, belching out clouds of oily smoke. The women got on and Nabila asked the driver if the bus went as far as Batroun. He said it did. Whispering to Millie to keep her head down, Nabila helped the children onto the bus.

She paid their fares and herded the children to the unoccupied seats at the rear.

The bus drove out of the village. With much grinding of gears, it headed north up the coast road. Nabila relaxed for the first time since the previous evening, and the two children sat quietly. Ali was content if he was close to his mother, and because he didn't have to carry a heavy bag anymore. Millie was silent because the traumatic events of the last two days had left her in pain and utterly bewildered.

The bus was hot and very little breeze entered the windows. Everyone was sweating with the heat and the bus was filled with the odour of unwashed bodies. The sun was high in the sky when they reached Batroun and alighted from the bus, grateful to be in the fresh air again.

It was a busy and bustling town, and nobody took any notice of a woman with two children. They came upon a marketplace with stalls selling fruit and vegetables. They could smell a delicious aroma of cooked food coming from some of the shops. Nabila decided to save the food she had brought with them for later, so she purchased some stuffed pitta breads for them to eat.

The shawarmas were filled with a mixture of thinly sliced spit-roasted lamb and salad with mint leaves, and they were delicious. She had also bought some bottles of juice and oranges. They found a quiet, shady spot under one of the orange trees that lined the square and ate their food. Nabila coaxed Millie to eat but it was hard for Millie to chew as her jaw was so sore and she could not finish hers. Nabila gave it to Ali who wolfed it down.

Nabila asked a passing woman if she knew where the bus to Tripoli went from. The woman pointed to a large building in the square and told her that the bus stopped there. When they had finished their food, they walked over to a place a little nearer the bus stop. When the bus drew up, Nabila walked the children quickly over to the group of people waiting to board. She reminded Millie to keep close hold of her shawl and to keep her head down.

They climbed aboard and Nabila paid their fares to Tripoli. Her money was disappearing fast, and she prayed her cousins would take them in. She had no idea what she would do if they had moved or would not allow them to stay until she could get another job. The bus was quite full, but there were still spaces at the back. They squeezed into the rear seat with their bags on their laps. Nabila put Millie near the window to keep her away from the curious eyes of a large man sitting beside them.

The bus set off, still going north and parallel to the sea. The mountains were further away from the coast here and they passed orchards, green fields of crops and small farms. Millie gazed out at the sea and the rhythmic movement of the waves calmed and soothed her a little.

As the sun dipped down towards the sea in a blaze of pink and purple and gold tinted clouds, the bus arrived in Tripoli. Nabila had not been there since she was a young girl, but she remembered that the bus to her cousins' village, some miles distance from the city, started from the port area. However, the city had changed a great deal in the years since she had last been there, and inadvertently they got off the bus too early and were still quite a long walk from the port.

They stood in the street, with their bags gathered round them and Nabila went into a shop to ask the way to the port, telling the two children to wait for her. She came out and they set off in the direction the shopkeeper had suggested, eventually reaching an area near the port with shops and stalls selling vegetables, meat and seafood. The market was filled with people milling about, enjoying the cool of the evening. Nabila was getting anxious: they had to find the bus stop soon as it was getting quite dark. She had no money to spare to pay for a place to sleep the night.

Feeling desperately tired, Millie was dragging her feet. Gradually she fell behind the other two and Nabila, searching anxiously for the bus stop, did not immediately notice. People were milling around, and Millie suddenly noticed that she could not see Nabila or Ali. She ran around, dodging among the people, calling to Nabila. Nabila soon realised that Millie had disappeared, and she called her name anxiously. She scanned the crowd but could see no sign of the little girl. She and Ali walked round the market slowly, Nabila calling to Millie as they walked, but there was no sign of her.

Millie, meanwhile, was running round the market too, frantically looking for Nabila and Ali but could not find them amongst the crowds. Eventually she saw a road leading down to the sea. She remembered that Nabila saying that the bus went from the port, so she thought that maybe she and Ali had gone this way. At the bottom of the road, she saw that some boats were tied up to the harbour's edge, bobbing gently in the waves. The moon had risen and lit up the boats and the quayside almost as brightly as day but casting dark shadows. Some boats were quiet and dark, but one or two showed lights and Millie could hear voices talking and laughing.

A group of men lounging about smoking noticed Millie and called out to her. One of them came towards her as if to grab her. She whimpered in fear and took off running, not noticing where she was going. The men did not follow her, and she stopped running. Millie found some wooden boxes stacked up against the wall of a building and she hid behind them. She was exhausted and hoped that if she waited there, she would hear Nabila calling for her. She put her bag down beside her and laid her head on it and she soon fell asleep.

Nabila, dragging a grumpy Ali by the hand, was still walking around the streets close to the market looking for Millie. She looked for a long time then decided she had to find somewhere for the two of them to sleep until the morning. It was now too dark to see anything, people were leaving the streets, and Millie was still nowhere to be found. Nabila found a derelict building at the edge of town where she and Ali lay down to sleep. Nabila fretted about losing Millie and hoped she would be able find her in the morning.

Down by the quay, voices woke Millie. A couple were walking along the quay, laughing and bantering in a good-natured way. The man was tall with sparse, faded blonde hair, wearing a long-sleeved tee shirt and long, baggy shorts. He had a craggy, lived-in face, untidy eyebrows, and keen, blue eyes. He was carrying a bag of food in his arms. His companion was much shorter. She was wearing a cream sweater knotted about her neck and blue cropped trousers. She also had a bag in her arms. She had short blonde hair, twinkling brown eyes and a pleasant, smiling face. They were both tanned brown from the sun and sea air.

They passed Millie without seeing her, talking and laughing as they strolled. Millie sat up, suddenly alert.

The people spoke the same way as her mother had done, they used some of the same words! Millie had not heard anyone speaking in the same way since her mother had disappeared. She quickly left her hiding place behind the crate, took up her bag and followed the couple down the quay.

The couple climbed aboard a yacht. Although it was smaller and of a more old-fashioned type than some of the other boats moored beside it, it still looked big to Millie. The couple went down into the cabin and put on the lights. This made the night seem much darker to Millie and she felt safe enough to creep up on to the boat to listen to the couple talking.

She crept towards an open porthole on the side of the cabin and peeped in. She could hear the couple chatting while they unpacked their shopping. The man poured two glasses of red wine and the woman started to cook a meal in the tiny galley on one side of the cabin. The smell of the food made Millie's stomach rumble. She had not eaten for hours.

Millie listened carefully to the couple talking and laughing while they ate their meal. She liked the confident and happy way they talked; it reminded her so much of her mother. She did not understand everything they said, but much of it sounded familiar and she did not want them to stop talking. After they had eaten, the man washed the dishes and the woman lay on the seat under the window to read a book. Soon they were both reading quietly, and Millie had no more conversation to listen to. Despite the pain from her bruises, she was dreadfully sleepy and could hardly keep her eyes open.

She crawled to the front of the boat as quietly as she could. If she could hide and go to sleep for a while, she could listen to them again when she woke. Finding a sort of cupboard with a slatted door, she opened it and saw it was a small space with coiled ropes and some metal cans stored inside. There was a little space on top of the ropes, so Millie crawled into the locker with her bag and pulled the door to. She curled up and soon went to sleep.

Chapter Six - Voyage

At first light, Nabila woke up, stiff and aching from the hard floor of the ruined house where they had sheltered. She woke Ali and they went out to look for Millie. After hours of fruitless searching, Nabila reluctantly decided that she had lost the little girl. She had no alternative but to travel on to her cousin's house. She had Ali to protect, and Hassim might be looking for them. Reluctantly and sadly, she took Ali's hand and went to find the bus that went to her cousins' home.

On the boat Millie had slept soundly all night. She did not hear the couple get up the next morning and make breakfast. She did not hear them prepare to get under way. She gradually woke to the noise of an engine, and she could feel the motion of the boat moving over the sea.

She was afraid that the couple would be angry if they knew she had hidden on their boat, so she stayed quietly where she was. When they got farther from the land, the water got choppier. As the sun got stronger, the heat and the chemical smell in the locker became unbearable. Millie began to feel very sick and started to cry. Suddenly the locker door flew open. The man was there, bent over to look inside. He started back in shock.

"Hey, Marie, come here quick. There's a kid hiding in the locker!"

"You're kidding" came the incredulous reply and then the woman appeared and peered in at Millie.

The man reached in and pulled her out quite roughly. Millie squealed as he had touched one of her bruises, then she promptly threw up on the deck.

The woman pulled his hand away impatiently, "Stop it. You hurt her!" Marie pushed up the sleeve of Millie's baggy old jacket. She gasped at seeing the livid bruises on the child's arm, then she saw that Millie's face was swollen and bruised, and that she had a black eye.

"Jim, this kid has been beaten black and blue. Maybe she hid on the boat to escape from someone." Marie, gently took off Millie's shawl and saw that, under the bruises and swelling, was a pretty child.

"Look at her eyes and hair, Jim, she doesn't look Lebanese. I wonder what she was doing in Tripoli all by herself."

"I can't imagine," said Jim, "But we will have to go about and take her back."

"Wait a minute, love," said Marie, "You want to take her back to where someone has beaten her half to death?"

"We don't have a choice," said Jim, "If we don't, we could be guilty of kidnapping."

Marie said to Millie, "What's your name, love? Can you tell us your name?"

Millie racked her brain to remember the English words. "Me... Millie," she said haltingly.

Marie and Jim looked at each other. The child spoke a little English but not as if she spoke it every day.

"Where are your parents?" said Marie, and Millie shook her head as she did not understand.

"Do you have a mother and father?" said Marie.

"Mummy gone," said Millie and her eyes filled with tears.

"Who hit you?" said Jim, and Millie turned her big hazel eyes to look at him. The woman was gentle and kind, but the man seemed to be a bit less sympathetic.

"Man hurt and, and..." Millie paused, "Hassim hit me."

Marie and Jim looked at each other. "You want to return this child back to that kind of treatment?" said Marie angrily. "I will not take her back to that."

"Well," said Jim thoughtfully, rubbing his stubbly chin, "we'll go on for today and anchor up this evening and talk about it again. Why don't you take her below and give her something to eat and drink and see if she can tell you more."

Marie took Millie by the hand and led her below into the cabin. She noticed that Millie was hugging her bag close to her chest.

Marie gave her some fruit juice to drink, and the thirsty child drank it straight down, so Marie poured her another. She cooked some eggs and toast and put it before Millie, then noticed that her hands were very grubby.

"I'll just wash your hands, sweetie, and then you can eat your food."

Marie watched as Millie ate. She ate quite delicately, despite obviously being extremely hungry. Marie looked sympathetically at the sad eyes in the somber little face. Something dreadful had robbed this child of her happiness. What kind of people would beat a sweet child like this?

When Millie had finished eating, she thought for a while then said hesitantly, "Tank oo."

"Well, it's my pleasure, sweetie, you are very welcome. Would you like to have a shower?"

Millie looked puzzled, so Marie took her and showed her the shower.

"Shall I help you?" she said to Millie, "Just to show you how it works."

Millie looked nervously towards the door of the cabin. She remembered the old woman taking her to have a bath before the man had hurt her.

"Jim won't come down here, sweetie, he's busy, and we can shut the door, here look, we are all safe here on our own." Marie had quickly guessed that a man or men had frightened Millie very badly and she imagined what might have happened with a feeling of disgust towards such people.

She coaxed Millie out of her clothes and was shocked when she saw the extent of the cuts and bruises all over the child's body. Marie wondered she had any internal injuries, but she seemed to be physically okay apart from the bruises. She helped Millie have a shower and tried to shampoo her hair. This was difficult as she had sore places on her head and cuts on her ears and neck.

Marie gave Millie a pair of soft shorts and a tee shirt to put on. "Just until we have washed your clothes," she told the child.

Millie was tired in mind and body and submitted to all that Marie asked of her without resistance. She could not face thinking about anything and had shut down her mind. She had eaten, felt clean and fresh again, and her eyelids started to droop. Marie saw that she was sleepy and quickly went to their small second cabin. They used this tiny room for storage of their clothes and clean linens. Marie moved everything aside and made a space on the berth for Millie to sleep.

She went back to the main cabin to find Millie deeply asleep, her head on the table. She called quietly up the companionway to Jim, "Come down here, love. I need your help for a minute."

Jim came down the stair, "Did you find out anything?" he asked.

"Only that she is absolutely covered in bruises, and I suspect she has been sexually abused."

"Poor little mite," said Jim feeling very shocked. "What kind of monster would do that?"

"Could you carry her through to the little cabin for me?" said Marie.

Jim lifted Millie carefully and took her through to the cabin. She stirred slightly and moaned but didn't wake. He laid her on the berth and covered her with a soft cotton blanket.

Jim and Marie sat on the deck, drinking coffee. "I shall wash her clothes later, although they are a bit scruffy. Are there any more clothes in her bag?"

Jim opened Millie's bag. He pulled out a few, rather tatty clothes and then he pulled out the little case of documents.

"What's that, Jim?"

Jim opened the little case. They looked through the contents with amazement. There was a passport in the name of Amelia Caroline Randall, and carried a picture of a tiny child. Also in the case were pictures of a woman holding a baby, then a much younger but still recognisable Millie as a toddler, and one photograph of the woman with a very handsome man on a boat. Another large glossy photo showed the woman in a glamorous evening gown. There was a birth certificate for a Rachel Randall and one for Amelia Randall, which showed that Millie was very nearly nine years old, and that her birth had been registered in France.

"I can't understand this," said Marie, scratching her head. "She is obviously an English child, but she speaks so little English. It's weird."

"It is very peculiar. Anyway love, I agree with you. Something terrible has happened to this child, and it would be wrong to take her back. In any case, if these papers are genuine, she is obviously an English child. Whoever has had charge of her has done a damn poor job of taking care of her"

"Oh, I am glad you feel like that, Jim. I couldn't bear to see anything else so awful happen to that poor little soul. What do you think we should do?"

"I don't think the authorities would blame us for taking her with us if we can show that she has been badly treated and that she is possibly an English child," said Jim. "Perhaps we should go on towards Greece as we had planned and put into Piraeus. We can then contact the British Embassy in Athens and get them to see if they can find this child's next of kin."

"Okay, I agree, that's what we'll do," said Marie and she packed the papers back into the little case and put it back into Millie's bag. She kept the clothes out but decided not to bother washing them, they were just too old and worn. She wasn't that much bigger than Millie and she had plenty of things that Millie could wear. She did not throw Millie's clothes away as it seemed disrespectful to just dispose of her belongings however shabby they were. She put them in a bag and popped them into the cabin where Millie slept.

They upped anchor and set sail towards Greece. It would take longer sailing, but they only used the boat's engine to go in and out of port as a rule, or if there was no wind or if it were necessary to run ahead of bad weather.

Millie slept deeply for a while then started to dream. She dreamed she was riding on a boat out on the sea. The sun was warm, and she felt dreamy and happy. Then the sky turned dark red, and she saw that the boat was full of green snakes with bloodshot eyes. They all started to slither towards her, and she saw with horror that they all were growing thin bony arms. They reached her feet and started to climb up her legs, always staring at her with cold, glittering eyes. Panic rose in her like a red tide, and she woke up, stifling the scream that rose in her throat.

As she came fully awake, she remembered that she was on the boat with the two English people, and she relaxed. She willed herself to forget the dream and lay on the berth thinking for a while. She loved the feeling of the boat rocking up and down on the waves. She felt safe with Marie, but she was less able to trust Jim. She had always received love and affection from women but had experienced only frightening and painful encounters with men. Sofia and Nabila had tried to protect her. Perhaps Marie would protect her too, but she was small, and probably not very strong. Jim was extremely large and had wanted to take her back. Millie decided to keep a wary eye on Jim.

After a while, she got up and peeped out of the cabin door. Marie and Jim were both up on deck. She sat down in the room where she had eaten her meal and noticed that things were gone from out of her bag. She quickly looked inside; the clothes were gone but her little case was still there! She looked inside it, relieved to see that all the things about her mother were still safely there.

She waited in the cabin until Marie came down and she showed Millie where she had put her clothes and was relieved to see that the girl showed no particular interest in them. Marie showed Millie round the boat. She explained where everything was and demonstrated carefully until she was confident Millie understood that she must put on a lifejacket when she went up on deck while they were at sea.

Over the next few days Millie tried to keep out of Jim's way and was content to spend her time with Marie. Marie spoke slowly and clearly to her, and she started to remember more English words. Over the days it took to get to Piraeus, she found the confidence to start to speak her own language again, albeit a simple babyish version.

Millie told Marie about her mother, and how she had just gone away. Her nanny Sofia had looked after her as best as she could. She told her about Nabila and Ali, but she kept silent about Ali hitting Hassim with the stone. She wondered if Ali had killed Hassim, but if he was dead then she was glad. He had killed Peter, and he had taken her to the house where that horrible man had hurt her. Tears came into her eyes at the horrible memories and slid down her cheeks unchecked.

Marie saw that Millie was crying and hugged her. "Don't cry, sweetie. All the bad things are over now. Jim and I are going to help you find your family. You'd like that, wouldn't you?"

Millie didn't quite understand this, and she looked at Marie quizzically. Her only family was her mother, and she had gone away.

"You find my mummy?" she asked Marie hopefully.

Marie shook her head, "I can't *promise* to find her, sweetie." Secretly Marie thought that something bad must have happened to Rachel, or she would not have left her child alone and defenseless. "But your mummy must have a family, and we should be able to find them. We are going to a place called an embassy. There will be people there who can find your mummy's family."

When they got near the coastline of Greece, they anchored for a day near a little secluded beach. Marie coaxed Millie off the boat into the shallow water and tried to teach her to swim. The warm, salty water felt good, and Millie gradually relaxed and enjoyed being in the sea. Marie showed her how to hold her breath and open her eyes under water to see little fishes swimming under her legs. Millie was enchanted. The swellings on her face had gone down and the bruises were fading, although one of her eyes was still ringed with a shadowy yellow bruise.

They had a picnic of cold tinned ham, tomatoes and bread on the beach and lay basking in the sunshine. The sun dipped down below the horizon and, for a while, the sea and the sky were flushed with pink, orange and purple.

Before it got too dark, they gathered their things and climbed back on the boat, Millie was so relaxed and sleepy she allowed Jim to carry her back on board. They all sat up on deck to watch the stars come out.

The moon slowly rose into the sky, its light painting silvery streaks on the waves. Millie sat on the deck, wide awake now in the cool of the evening. with her arms wrapped round her knees gazing at the moon. She remembered the day she and Sofia had been driven out of the city, and how she had watched the moon following them along the coast road, and on into the countryside. Thinking of Sofia brought tears to her eyes.

The next day they were going to arrive at the place where Marie had said a man would be starting to look for her family. Another journey into the unknown would be ahead of Millie. She hoped Marie was right that, if her mother had any family, they would be glad to see her. Maybe she might even find her mother again.

Chapter Seven – Friends

The next morning, they sailed into Piraeus and tied up at the yacht marina. Jim went off alone to talk to the harbourmaster. He hoped they would allow him to telephone the embassy from there.

The port officials were helpful when he explained the situation, and soon he was speaking to someone at the embassy. He had brought Millie's passport and the two birth certificates with him and gave the embassy official all the information he had. He stressed the terrible beating Millie had received in case the official thought they should have returned her to the port where they had found her.

The man listened to his story and said, "I think you did the right thing to bring her here. The names in the passport and on the certificates should be easy to trace. Please will you give me an hour to see what I can find out and I will call you back. You will stay where you are, won't you?"

Jim agreed to be there in an hour and popped back to the boat to tell Marie. An hour later he went back to the harbormasters' office and took some beers with him. These were gratefully received by the port officials, and they passed the time in pleasant discussion about sailing and fishing, and the one that got away, as all fishermen do. The telephone rang and the harbourmaster answered it, then passed the receiver to Jim.

"My name is Charles Bertram," said a cultured voice, "And I do not have good news about the child's mother. I am afraid that, some twelve months after she disappeared, the mother's body was found up in the forest outside Beirut. It seems that she had been murdered, no one knows by whom. The police were alerted to the existence of the child but much too late.

By then the child's nanny had taken her away to another address. This was eventually traced, but when the landlord was questioned, he said that she had moved on with her son and the child, and that he had no idea where they had gone. Of course, the Lebanese police claim to have continued to make inquiries but, between you and me, I do not have confidence that they tried particularly hard.

We have managed to contact the child's family back in Britain. The grandmother, who is frail and elderly, lives with her daughter, the murdered woman's older sister. We are sending someone down from the embassy today to collect the child, and she will be escorted back to Britain. The grandmother is very grateful to you for the care you have taken of her granddaughter, and she wishes to have an address where she can write and express her thanks more fully."

Jim gave him their home address in England and told Mr. Bertram that they were sailing back to Britain but would not be back for at least two weeks.

"We are willing to take her back to Britain with us. We are on our way back to our home off the Hamble."

Mr. Bertram answered that he thought that unfortunately two weeks was much too long and that, in any event, arrangements were already in progress to fly Millie to her grandmother even as they were speaking.

"My colleague, Miss Janet Lang, will oversee collecting the child and taking her to the airport. She will escort the child all the way back to her relations. Can you bring her to the harbourmaster's office at 3.30 this afternoon? By the way, please do not try and explain to the child what happened to her mother. I think that it is preferable if her family decide when and how to tell her. Thank you once again for your efforts to help this child. It sounds as if she has suffered a very traumatic experience. It was fortunate for her that she ended up with you and your wife, and not some other person who might possibly have exploited her further."

Jim put down the telephone, his head aching from talking to a man with such a pompous turn of phrase. He went back to the boat and sat in the salon. He asked Marie to make some lunch, and he turned to Millie.

"Millie, I have spoken to a man at the embassy. He has already found your grandmother and you also have an aunt.'

Marie saw that Millie was confused.

"Do you know what an aunt is?" Millie shook her head. "Your grandmother is the mother of your aunt and your mummy. Well, since they found out that your mummy had a little girl, they have been looking for you. Your grandmother is a very old lady and could not come and look for you herself. She asked the police to find you, but they couldn't because you had moved."

Millie nodded, she had been afraid that her mummy would not find her when she and Sofia moved. "Have they found my mummy?" she asked.

Jim wanted to tell her the truth but could not. "I'm not sure, but perhaps your granny will be able to help."

Jim told them about the embassy lady coming that afternoon to take Millie on a plane to England.

"Oh, not so soon," said Marie sadly, she had become very attached to Millie and did not want to lose her so quickly.

"I did offer for us to take her back with us on the boat, but they had already made arrangements and the embassy chap said the grandmother wanted her back right away."

Millie looked from Marie to Jim, "I am going today?" She looked shocked and put her arms round Marie. "I don't want to leave you."

"Don't fret, sweetie. It will be lovely to meet your granny after all this time. We will come and visit you too, we promise, don't we Jim?"

Jim nodded. He knew Marie would be devastated when Millie had gone. They had never been able to have children of their own. Although they were usually content to be just the two of them, he could see Marie had quickly formed a deep attachment to Millie.

The time came and they packed Millie's stuff in her bag. Marie asked her if she wanted to keep her old clothes, but Millie shook her head. After all the time they had been sitting in the plastic bag they smelled bad, and anyway, they just reminded Millie of bad events. She liked the neat, comfortable clothes that Marie had given her, even if they were a bit too big.

A young woman was waiting at the harbourmaster's office. She was plump and had short brown hair in a bob. She was wearing a smart navy suit.

"So, this is Millie. Your grandmother is looking forward to seeing you and we are going to drive straight to the airport, get on a plane and we will be back in England by suppertime."

Marie stepped forward, "Millie needs you to speak a bit slower. She hasn't spoken any English for years and is still getting used to it."

Miss Lang's face fell. "Oh, I am so sorry, Millie. I will speak slower" and she smiled brightly at Marie and Jim.

"Say good-bye now, dear. We have plane to catch, and we need to hurry."

Millie hugged Marie tightly and touched Jim on the arm. "Thank you for helping me. I won't forget you."

Marie hugged her again and helped her put her things, including her little case of papers, in Miss Lang's car. As the car drove away, they could see Millie's sad little face looking out of the back window as she waved goodbye.

When she was out of sight, Marie burst into tears and Jim put his arm round her. They walked slowly back to the boat.

"We can write to her, Jim, can't we? And maybe we can visit her too?"

"Of course, we can, darling," he said, and there were tears in his eyes too.

Miss Lang was a fast driver and she drove with great concentration. They reached the airport just in time to get their flight. Millie's passport was no longer valid, but Miss Lang produced an official document from the embassy, and they were waved through.

Miss Lang talked to her during the journey, but she often forgot to speak slowly, and Millie couldn't understand much of what she said. Eventually Miss Lang gave up trying to chat and started to read a magazine for the rest of the plane trip.

They landed at Heathrow in the dark and Miss Lang hired a car. Millie's clothes were not warm enough for the chilly evening and she started to shiver so Miss Lang put the heater on high and soon she was warm. It was too dark to see much out of the window, and Millie eventually closed her eyes and slept.

Chapter Eight - Family

When she awoke, Miss Lang was shaking her arm. "We are at your grandmother's house. Come along, let's get you indoors before you freeze."

Millie took hold of her bag, holding it like a shield in front of her, and she climbed out of the car. The moon was full and showed the front of a pretty, stone house with red Virginia creeper growing all over the walls. Miss Lang pressed a bell at the side of the door. Millie heard the bell echoing inside the house. At last, the door opened, and a woman stood in the doorway, silhouetted against the light. At first Millie thought it was her mother and her heart leapt with hope. She started to move towards the woman, but then stopped. She saw it could not be her mother as the woman's face was cold and indifferent.

"So, this is the miracle grandchild." The woman said sardonically.

Miss Lang frowned disapprovingly; she had not expected such a poor welcome for this poor child. "Yes, this is Millie, and she has had some very unpleasant experiences," she said pointedly. "I am sure she will be very glad to be with her family after all she has been through."

"Oh, come in," the woman said impatiently, and she showed them the way down a hallway, lined with pictures in gold frames, and into a warm sitting room where a cheerful fire was burning in the fireplace. A thin, ethereal old lady was sitting beside the fire, two walking sticks beside her. Her eyes turned immediately to her granddaughter and tears appeared in her eyes.

"She looks just like Rachel at the same age," and she smiled, holding her hands out to Millie. Miss Lang pushed Millie towards her grandmother.

"Amelia, welcome home," she said, and she kissed Millie's cheek with dry, papery lips.

The old lady waved at Miss Lang to sit down and pointed to the chair next to her for Millie.

"I won't stop, if you don't mind," said Miss Lang. "I have a few days leave and I can get home tonight if I leave now."

"Well, thank you very much for all your help," said the old lady.

The aunt showed Miss Lang out, who turned and smiled at Millie as she left. "Be a good girl now."

Millie heard the car door slam and the sound of Miss Lang's car hurtling back down the drive. Her aunt came back into the room and sat down opposite her mother on the other side of the fire. The two women stared at this child, a complete stranger but still a member of their family.

Her grandmother took Millie's hand in hers. "We are very glad to have you here safe at last. You can call me Granny, and this is your Aunt Vicky. Are you hungry?"

Her grandmother spoke to Millie slowly and clearly, so she understood what she said, and she nodded.

"Would you be a dear and show Amelia to her room, and where to wash her hands," she spoke to Aunt Vicky, "and if you could also ask Irene to find a sandwich and a piece of cake for her, that would be lovely."

Aunt Vicky kept her face impassive until she and Millie had left the room, and then she looked at Millie coldly.

"This way," was all she said, and she led the way upstairs. She showed Millie into a pretty, feminine bedroom, decorated in blue and white.

"This was your mother Rachel's bedroom," said Aunt Vicky, "or to be more accurate 'the holy shrine'."

Millie put her bag down on the bed and then her aunt took her down the passage and showed her the bathroom.

"Wash your hands, and then come downstairs. Do you understand?"

Millie nodded and shut the bathroom door. She used the toilet and washed her hands. She looked at her reflection in the mirror. Her bruises were almost gone. She saw a hairbrush on a shelf, undid her ponytail and brushed the tangles out of her hair. She tied her hair into a ponytail, as Marie had showed her.

As she gazed in the mirror, she thought about the welcome she had received in this house. Her grandmother had seemed quite glad to see her, but her Aunt Vicky obviously was not. Millie wondered why. She went back downstairs. All the doors were closed and at first she was not sure which room was the sitting room, but she heard the two women talking behind one of the doors. She hesitated for a moment outside the door then she turned the handle and went in.

"Come and sit by me, Amelia." Her grandmother smiled and patted the chair beside her.

Millie sat down. "I am not Amelia, I'm Millie," she said.

"No, my dear," said her grandmother firmly, patting her hand, "that is not your real name. Your real name is Amelia Caroline Randall. That is what your mother named you. Millie was your pet name I expect, but your mother named you Amelia and that is what we shall call you. Is that all right?"

Millie nodded, but although her mother might have named her Amelia, she had always called her Millie. She felt very strange being called Amelia, as if she were being asked to change into another person. She decided to accept being called Amelia if it pleased these people, but she would always to think of herself as Millie.

Aunt Vicky had set up a table between them with little triangular sandwiches, some dainty slices of cake and a glass of milk. She handed Millie a small plate and pointed to the food. Millie took a sandwich and nibbled on it. It did not taste of much, but she was very hungry, and her grandmother encouraged her to take more. The two women watched Millie eat and then her grandmother suggested she go to bed.

"Good night, Amelia," said her grandmother, "come and give me a kiss," and she offered Millie her cheek. "Do you remember the way to your bedroom?"

Millie obediently kissed her grandmother goodnight and went upstairs to her bedroom. Marie had given her a pair of her own pyjamas to take with her, so Millie put them on. She climbed into the bed that had once been her mother's and looked around at the room. The bed was made of brass, with flower-painted china knobs at each corner. It was covered in a plump, white quilt with blue embroidery. Blue and white rugs sat either side of the bed on the cream carpet. A white-painted wardrobe stood by the door, and a desk of the same white wood was placed against the wall near the window.

The curtains were cream with a pattern of little blue flowers. Two pictures hung on the walls, one of flowers in a blue and white jug, and the other of fruit on blue and white plates. It was a charming room, but was the room of a young woman, not a child.

Millie liked the thought that this had been her mother's room. A battered old teddy sat on a shelf, so Millie got out of bed and took the teddy back to bed to cuddle. She closed her eyes. The bed was soft and cosy, the sheets cool and smooth against her skin. She had not been so comfortable since she had been a tiny little girl, sleeping in her own bed in her mother's apartment, and she quickly fell asleep.

Millie dreamt she was back in the garden at the big house where she had lived with Sofia and Nabila, but the house was different in the dream: the moon was shining down, making the garden a mixture of dark blue shadows. She was walking up the verandah stairs, which seemed to go on forever. She went into the house through the big French windows. Some candles were burning, their flames were guttering in the breeze from the windows.

Still in her dream, Millie turned to look out at the sea and put her hand on the curtains. Suddenly snakes, which had been hiding in the folds of the curtains started wriggling and wrapping themselves around her arms, their glittering eyes boring into her as they writhed around, trying to get at her face. She loathed the feeling of their bodies touching her skin...

She tossed and turned in the bedclothes that had become entangled around her body in her struggle to get free of the nightmare snakes. Her mind was suffused with panic, and she screamed.

Her bedroom door flew open, the light flicked on, and Aunt Vicky rushed in.

"What the devil is the matter?" Vicky said brusquely, her face twisted in an irritable frown as she stood over Millie, who was still struggling to overcome her terror, tears coursing down her cheeks.

"You have just had a bad dream. There's no need for all that screaming. You'll disturb Mother. Now pull yourself together and go back to sleep."

Millie's aunt left the room, turning out the ceiling light as she went.

Millie lay for a while, clutching the teddy to her chest. She hated dreaming about the snakes. They filled her with such unbearable horror. She had never actually touched a snake but in her dreams, she felt them cold and clammy on her skin. It reminded her of the man who had attacked her, and she shuddered with revulsion. She tried to think of nicer things so she could forget the dream. She imagined of being back with

Marie and Jim, the waves rocking the boat as she lay in the little cabin, with the moon shining down on her through the porthole like a blessing. Then she thought of her mother who had slept in this very bed and eventually drifted back to sleep.

Millie woke the next morning and for a moment she forgot where she was. The room was still dark, so she got out of bed, pulled back the curtains, and looked down into the garden. She saw a pretty, walled garden with many shrubs growing by the walls. It reminded her a little of the walled garden of the big house. The morning was damp and the trees beyond the garden wall were shrouded in mist. There was a smooth, lush green lawn, interrupted here and there by flower beds. A paved patio lay close to the house and a stepping-stone path meandered across the lawn to a wooden gate in the back wall of the garden. A little white dog ambled around the garden, sniffing at the bushes, and occasionally lifting his leg.

There was a knock on the door, and her aunt came in.

"Oh, you are awake. Good. Do you remember where the bathroom is?" Millie nodded. Her aunt's voice was brisk and not at all friendly. She made no mention of Millie's dream or of her screaming in the night and she did not ask her if she had slept well.

"The doctor is coming this morning to check you are okay so please have a bath. Can you do that by yourself?"

Millie nodded. She would prefer to bath by herself than under this woman's cold eyes. She felt a desperate longing for Marie and her eyes filled with tears.

"There is a fresh toothbrush in the bathroom, and everything in there is for you to use. I have my own bathroom, and my mother's bedroom and bathroom are downstairs. She is not well, and I don't want you to upset her. Will you please remember that?"

Millie nodded again, and her aunt swept out of the room. Millie went to the bathroom, cleaned her teeth, and had a bath. Then she went back to her bedroom and got dressed. She put on a clean pair of trousers and a cotton sweater that Marie had given her. The trousers were too big, and Marie had shown her how to roll up them up into cuffs and to pull the drawstring at the waist tight. She put on her plastic sandals, her only shoes, and went downstairs.

As Millie stood in the hall unsure where to go, a plump lady wearing a grey wraparound dress backed out of a room at the far end of the hall and turned round. She was holding a covered dish in each hand, and she smiled warmly at Millie. The woman had grey hair tied in a bun, with wisps escaping, and two round, rosy cheeks, topped with twinkling brown eyes.

"Ah, hello, young lady, you must be Amelia. Be a love and hold open this door for me?" And she indicated the door at the bottom of the stairs with her head.

Millie opened the door to see an elegant dining room, with a large table in the middle, covered with a crisp, white cloth. The woman put the dishes down on a side table and adjusted the matching lids.

"Scrambled eggs in that one and bacon in the other," she said to Millie. "Your granny will be along in a minute. Would you like a drink of orange juice?"

Millie smiled and said, "Yes, please," as Marie had taught her.

"My name is Irene and I have looked after your granny for donkey's years."

Millie looked puzzled, what did 'donkey's years' mean?

Irene noticed her expression and laughed. "Sorry, my love. I forgot for a minute that you have been living among the heathens. What I meant was that I have been with your granny for a long, long time. In fact, I was working here when your mum still lived at home. We'll have a lovely talk about your mum very soon. Would you like that?"

Millie only caught every other word of this exchange, but gathered that Irene knew her mother, and would talk to Millie about her. She liked that idea very much, so she smiled at her. Irene patted her cheek and bustled out of the room just as Aunt Vicky came in, pushing her grandmother in a wheelchair.

"Mother is feeling a bit wobbly this morning. Too much excitement, I expect," said Aunt Vicky with a pointed look at Millie.

"Good morning, Amelia," said her grandmother in a tremulous voice, "did you sleep well?"

Millie nodded and smiled at her grandmother, who smiled back and pointed to her cheek. Millie kissed her obediently, then sat down where Aunt Vicky indicated she should.

Aunt Vicky put some food on plates for Millie and her mother and brought the food to the table. They ate in silence and when they had finished, Aunt Vicky told Millie to go into the sitting room, then pushed her mother down the corridor back to her bedroom. Millie heard her grandmother say, "Be gentle, Vicky, she is only a child and must be utterly confused by all that has happened to her."

The door closed and Millie went to the sitting room and sat down. After a few minutes, her aunt came into the room and closed the door. She sat down opposite to Millie. She cocked her head on one side and narrowed her eyes.

"We have a great deal to talk about. When the doctor has been, we will go and buy you some new clothes," and she looked at Millie's clothes with distaste. "Then we must arrange for you to go to school."

"What is 'school'?" said Millie.

Her aunt looked at her with astonishment, "Have you never been to school?"

Millie shook her head,

"Can't you read or write?"

Millie shook her head.

Aunt Vicky was silent for some minutes. "That changes things a lot. I will talk to Mother about this. The other thing we have to talk about is an incredibly sad thing, I am afraid," but Aunt Vicky did not look very sad. She had a funny, twisted little smirk on her face.

"I am afraid I have some bad news. After she disappeared, your mother must have met a bad person because they killed her and left her body in some woodland where it was not found for a long time. Her handbag and passport were found nearby and that is how they knew who the body was. When they knew she was dead, the police tried to find you but could not trace you. It is a pity that your nursemaid took you away because, of course, you would have come to live here sooner and would have gone to school at the proper time."

Millie had known, somewhere in her mind, that her mother must be dead, but it was a terrible shock to hear that someone had killed her and left her lying in a wood like a bag of rubbish. Her mother had met a bad man, someone like Hassim or that other man. Hatred for such men filled Millie's heart. She was so angry that she could not cry.

Aunt Vicky watched in fascination the emotions passing over her niece's face as she absorbed this dreadful news. She had expected Millie to burst into tears, but instead she was obviously just furiously angry, and the child's fists were clenched as if she wanted to punch someone. She did not offer to hug or comfort Millie. Perhaps if Millie had been born in England and brought up properly as an English child, Vicky thought she might feel more sympathy for the child. As it was, Millie seemed to her to be merely an intruder, a foreigner seeking sanctuary in her home, and she was unable to see the child as part of her family, her flesh and blood.

Vicky was a very bitter woman. As a young woman she had married an ambitious man who had insisted that he did not want children. She had loved him so completely that she had agreed to this decision. She was more afraid of losing him than of not having children. After several years of marriage, she had been forced by his lack of interest in her to wonder if he had strayed. She had hired a detective and had discovered that her husband had a young mistress. When she had challenged him, he left her and demanded a divorce. When the divorce was final, he had married his mistress who immediately started to produce a litter of brats, one after another.

Although Vicky had been given a decent settlement by her husband in return for agreeing to a quick divorce, she had come back home to live in her mother's house. As her mother's health had deteriorated over the years, Vicky gradually settled for a life as her mother's carer. She had very little social life, although this was her own fault. She had lost all trust in men, and over the years, she allowed herself to fall into a habit of not liking people at all, with the sole exception of her mother. Although she loved her mother, in fact, Vicky was the dependent one. Her mother was the only person in the world she felt any love for. Therefore, unconsciously, and rather childishly, she saw Millie as a rival for her mother's affections.

Vicky had always been jealous of her mother's attention. When Rachel was born – when Vicky was three – she had been furious. Her mother had hoped that over time the two sisters would bond but Vicky had never learned to share with her sister and their relationship had always been one of being competitors rather than siblings.

Vicky had secretly been glad when Rachel had left home to be a dancer when she was only eighteen, against the express wishes of her parents. The family had had major arguments about Rachel's wish to go on the stage and relations with her father had broken down completely. Rachel had just packed her bags and left home to dance in shows abroad, and for some years they would receive occasional postcards, but never a return address. Eventually the postcards had ceased, and they heard nothing.

During those years, their father had died but the family had not been able to tell Rachel as they could not contact her. They had not known that Rachel had a child until her body was found and the police in Lebanon had informed the British Embassy that her friends insisted that she had a little girl. When the embassy checked they discovered that Rachel did indeed have a baby which had been born in France but registered as British. The police had not been able to find the child, and over the years, Rachel's mother had accepted that they might never find Rachel's child.

Then out of the blue, they had been informed that Amelia, now about nine years old, had been found by an English couple. It appeared that the child had been living with the Lebanese woman who had been her nanny. To make things worse, it seemed that the child had been beaten and abused very badly.

This was all too much to take in for the two women, who led such sheltered and unexciting lives. They had no resources to understand how to treat such a child. Millie's grandmother thought that just to give Millie a safe home and normal life would be enough. Vicky's emotions were much more complex. She resented the sudden appearance of a grandchild who had a perfect right to share her mother's love.

Millie looked at her aunt. She could see she resembled her mother but at the same time, did not look like her at all. Her mother was warm and loving, her eyes had always twinkled with love and laughter. If she had known what terrible things had happened to

Millie, she would have taken her in her arms and kissed the hurt away. Aunt Vicky just sat stiffly, having just told a child that her mother was dead, even worse murdered, and showed no sign of sympathy or tenderness.

Misery and anger flooded Millie's heart and she ran from the room, up the stairs and into her bedroom, slamming the door behind her. She flung herself on the bed and sobbed her heart out. The faint hope she had kept alive in her heart that she would find her mother and that life would be happy again had died. Her heart ached for her lovely, soft-hearted mother. *"Why did she have to die? It was not fair!"*

A terrible vision of her lovely mother lying dead in woodland, all alone and abandoned, just as Millie herself now felt. She felt no love for these two women, although maybe she could become fond of her kindly grandmother in time. They were her relatives, her family, but they could not comprehend what her life had been like, and Millie did not feel at ease in the genteel restraint of their home. She cried until she could cry no more. Her mother was gone, her grandmother was frail and ill, and her aunt seemed to actively dislike her. This puzzled Millie and made her feel angry too. She could not think of a reason why her aunt shouldn't love someone of her own family.

Then she heard a man's voice coming up the stairs. Irene opened her bedroom door and ushered in a short plump man with a pink, shiny face, and a kind expression.

"This is Dr. Morrison, Amelia. He wants to check you over to see you are all right. Will that be all right with you, dear?"

Millie sat up on the bed, full of apprehension. She wanted to refuse and for this man to go away, but she didn't dare to. She huddled back up against her pillows, clutching the teddy bear. The doctor smiled at her and patted her hand. He had a very gentle smile and Irene said soothingly, "It won't take long, Amelia. I will stay with you, if you like, and hold your hand. Come on, sweetheart, it won't take long."

Millie eventually let herself be persuaded to let the doctor touch her. The doctor examined her carefully. He listened to her heart and chest and checked her all over. Millie clutched Irene's hand, closed her eyes tightly and gritted her teeth. It reminded her of the horrible man who had caused her such pain and fear.

The doctor was gentle, and his hands were careful, but Millie kept seeing the horrible man's cold eyes and she shuddered as she remembered the pain he had caused her.

At last, it was all over. When she opened her eyes again, the doctor looked at her sympathetically and said, "All finished now, sweetheart. You were a very good girl."

Irene showed the doctor out and Millie was left alone again. Being examined had upset her very much, but instead of crying, for some reason she was just consumed with anger. Her bedroom door opened, and her aunt came in and stood at the end of Millie's bed. Her aunt's cold gaze wavered a little under the child's furious glare.

"Go and wash your face now. We are going to buy you some new clothes. It distresses Mother to see you dressed like that."

Not daring to refuse, Millie went to wash her face and she put on the cardigan that Marie had given her. Aunt Vicky was waiting by the front door with her coat on. They drove to a town and parked in a car park. They went into a large department store, and to the section for children's clothes. Vicky selected an assortment of items and held them up against Millie to judge the fit. She bought underwear, skirts and jumpers, some trousers, warm cardigans, and a coat. She added a scarf, a woolly hat and gloves. After that they went to the shoe department and had the saleswoman try on a selection of shoes and a pair of slippers.

Vicky never asked Millie if she liked anything and never gave her a chance to choose. Millie was initially not interested in the clothes, but some of them were made of fabrics that were soft and nice to feel. They had a faint but pleasant smell of newness, something that Millie had not experienced before. They carried their purchases back to the car and put them in the boot, then Aunt Vicky took her to a shop selling art supplies and toys.

"Mother wants you to have some things to keep you occupied until we can sort out the school problem. I will choose some things for you," and she proceeded to select drawing equipment and two jigsaws.

When they got home, Irene carried all Millie's new things up into her bedroom and helped her put them all away. She laid the drawing things and the jigsaw puzzles on the desk.

"It would be nice if you put on some of your new clothes and come down to show your Granny. Then you could say thank you to her," said Irene, patting Millie on the cheek. "Do you need me to help you?"

Millie nodded her head. *"Irene was so kind and understanding,"* she thought. She wished her aunt was as kind. Irene helped Millie put on a set of the new clothes and she went downstairs to thank her grandmother. She looked in the sitting-room, but no one was there.

"Granny is in her bedroom, Amelia," called Irene from the kitchen, "she's not feeling too good today."

Millie knocked on her grandmother's bedroom door and heard her call, "Come in."

Millie went over to the bed. Her grandmother was lying down, the little white dog Millie had seen in the garden curled up behind her knees. She was very pale and did not look well. She had violet smudges under her eyes, but she smiled sweetly at Millie.

"Amelia, this is Jack, my little Westie. You might like to play with him and take him for walks when you have settled down. You look so nice. Tell me, do you like your new clothes? Did Vicky get you some things to play with?

"Yes, Granny. Thank you."

"Did Vicky let you choose them?"

Aunt Vicky came in the room just then and said, "Of course I didn't, Mother, she has lived in the slums of Beirut for years. How on earth would Amelia have any idea what is suitable?"

"Even a child of the slums may have a preference of the colours they like, Vicky," admonished her mother gently. "Another time perhaps you could let her choose the colours, even if you decide what style is suitable. I am aware you are not happy about all this but perhaps, just to please me, you might try to be a little kinder. By the way, the doctor says he thinks Amelia has not suffered any physical harm, although he has sent off samples of her blood to be tested for infections."

"Amelia," said her aunt, "Go and take the dog into the garden, then see if Irene needs any help with the dinner."

Millie picked up the dog and went out into the garden with him. She wandered around and found a bench to sit on under a tree covered in pink blossom. The dog trotted around sniffing and ferreting in the bushes. Millie liked this garden. It was very different to the garden of the big house where she had lived with Sofia and Nabila. This garden was damp, and the air smelled like mushrooms. It had been raining and water dripped off the trees. Mosses like little green velvet pillows grew on the red bricks of the patio.

A stone wall surrounded this garden too but, unlike the one in Lebanon, it was low enough to see over. On the other side of the wall Millie could see fields and woods. In one of the fields, she could see fat, woolly sheep grazing with little lambs tottering at their sides. It was a very moist, lush landscape and it gave Millie a peaceful feeling.

The countryside back in Lebanon had been so harsh and arid. The plants and trees had struggled to find places to grow. The garden of the big house had been quite lush in winter, but in summer it had been hard work, watering the plants every day to keep them green. Even with all the care that Sofia and Millie lavished on the garden, by the end of summer everything had turned crisp and brown under the onslaught of the sun.

The countryside here in England looked soft and green, and somehow gentle. Little yellow daffodils like tiny trumpets grew in drifts all over the garden, and in the flowerbeds, all manner of plants were unfurling green shoots and sending out buds. Several trees round the garden were covered in pink blossoms. As the breeze blew, petals showered down and lay in pink drifts on the grass. Millie thought it was beautiful.

Her mother would have played in here when she was a little girl, and Millie suddenly felt as if her mother was here in the garden with her. She looked down to see that the little dog, Jack, was sitting at her feet, looking up at her with his wise little eyes. She leaned down to stroke his ears and he jumped up, putting his muddy paws on her knees. It was comforting to Millie to stroke the friendly little dog. He wagged his stump of a tail and licked her hand. They went into the kitchen together to find Irene rolling out pastry.

"Oh dear, is that mud all over your new trousers? Naughty Jack!" Irene washed her hands and sponged the mud off with a damp cloth. Jack climbed into a basket beside the Aga and curled into a ball.

"That's better, we don't want you getting into trouble, do we?" Irene winked at Millie and smiled. Millie smiled back.

Irene popped an apron on Millie and set her to work cutting out pastry rings for jam tarts, and then she helped peel the vegetables for dinner. All the time they worked together, Irene kept up a constant chatter about her mother Rachel and Aunt Vicky when they were children. Some of the chatter Millie could understand and some she didn't.

Irene said that her mother had always loved dancing and was always to be found with the radio on, dancing around to the music. She told Millie that Rachel's father, her own grandfather, had favoured Rachel and had been angry and utterly disappointed when she insisted on becoming a dancer.

Rachel had initially not been happy at being sent away to boarding school, explained Irene, but she had quickly grown to like it, especially as she was allowed to take dancing classes there. When Rachel had left school, she had refused to go on to college. She was determined to get a job as a dancer against her parents' wishes.

"Very attached to her mother is your Aunt Vicky," said Irene. "I think you arriving has put her nose out of joint a little bit." Millie did not understand this remark at all, and when Aunt Vicky came into the kitchen to see if dinner was ready, Millie could not help peering at her nose to see if there was anything wrong with it.

Her grandmother was too ill that evening to come to the dining room for her dinner and had a tray in her room. Millie and Aunt Vicky ate alone and mostly in silence. Occasionally Aunt Vicky would correct the way Millie ate, or held her fork, or say that she must not drink so noisily. Millie tried hard to do as she asked, but her aunt seemed determined to find fault with everything she did, tutting under her breath at every small error.

After dinner Millie wanted to see her grandmother but Aunt Vicky peeped in at her and said she was fast asleep. She told Millie to go to her room and play so Millie went up to her room and sat at the desk. She opened the drawers as she had not looked in them before. She found some drawings of ballerinas, some used pencils and crayons and a few rather battered photographs of Rachel as a plump baby, sitting on her mother's lap, and one of Rachel with a huge white cat curled up on her lap. How strange, thought Millie, that her mother had loved a white cat too. She sat thinking sadly of her kitten and how he had loved to be cuddled, purring with pleasure as she stroked him.

Over the next few weeks Millie realised that her grandmother was too frail to spend much time with her, and that her Aunt Vicky was never going make the effort to learn to love her. It would have been so good to have felt wanted, and for her mother's family to be glad to have her to live with them.

Millie had felt more loved with Sofia and Nabila, and with Marie and Jim, than she was living here. Aunt Vicky gave off powerful waves of animosity towards Millie. She felt instinctively that this was terribly unfair, and she felt resentment towards her aunt in return. She kept her hostility hidden as she was afraid of being sent away. She was accustomed to keeping her emotions hidden and had learned from Sofia and Nabila to keep a blank expression on her face even when she was afraid. That was how they had all coped with Hassim and the threatening atmosphere he created.

At dinner that evening, without her grandmother again, Aunt Vicky told Millie that Marie and Jim had telephoned to ask how she was.

"I should like to talk to them," she said to her aunt. Aunt Vicky pursed her lips and frowned. It seemed to Millie as if her aunt did not want her to have any pleasure or happiness at all. A few days later, Aunt Vicky was out and when the telephone rang, Irene answered it.

"Oh yes, she's right here, I'll put her on," and with a smile she passed the receiver to Millie. Millie put it to her ear and was thrilled to hear Marie's voice.

"Millie sweetie, how are you? Are you happy? Are you having a wonderful time with your grandmother and your aunt?"

Tears came into Millie's eyes at the sound of Marie's dear voice. Irene had gone tactfully into the kitchen.

"I miss you so much." Millie sniffed away her tears. "My grandmother is not well, and I do not see her much. Aunt Vicky does not like me, I don't know why. It is a nice house and I like the garden. I am sleeping in my mummy's bedroom. There is a little dog here and I have some new clothes. And a doctor looked at me."

All this came out in a tearful rush. Millie could not resist the kindness in her friend's voice.

"Poor little girl," said Marie sympathetically. "I tell you what, Jim and I will come and see you on Saturday and take you out for a while. Put that nice lady back on the phone and I speak to her about it."

Millie called Irene, and passed her the telephone, "Marie wants to speak to you."

Irene spoke to Marie and nodded her head several times. She said to Marie, "I expect I shall forget to mention it until Saturday morning. I think that would be best, then it will be too late to telephone you to cancel, won't it?" Irene winked at Millie and passed the telephone back to her. Millie smiled gratefully at Irene, she obviously understood about Aunt Vicky.

Millie and Marie chatted happily for a long while. Marie told her that she and Jim were not going sailing abroad again for a while. They both had to work and save up enough money to go off again in a year or two. Jim was working as a teacher and Marie was working in an office, which she said was terribly boring. They chatted happily then Millie remembered that Marie had not known that her mother was dead.

"Marie, my mummy is dead. Someone killed her and left her lying all on her own in a forest. I so hoped that one day I would see her again, and now I never will."

"I'm so sorry, sweetie. That is terribly sad. But you have your grandmother to love you, don't you?" Marie didn't tell her that the embassy man had told them not to tell her about her mother.

"My granny is very kind, but she is not well, and I am not allowed to see her much."

Marie was starting to see a clear picture of how things were for Millie, and she felt deeply disappointed for the child. After all the horrible events she had lived through, she deserved to be in a warmer and more loving family situation than seemed to be case.

"Well, we have Saturday to look forward to, don't we?" said Marie. "It might be best not to mention that I telephoned, sweetie. Do you understand?"

"Yes," said Millie. "I want to see you again, and Jim."

They said their good-byes, and Millie put the phone down.

Millie went into the kitchen and gave Irene a hug. "Thank you so much. I am so happy to speak to Marie again."

Irene hugged her back, "That's all right, dearie. Our little secret though?"

Millie nodded. They sat down together at the kitchen table and had tea and biscuits.

Chapter Nine – Retribution

Hassim opened his eyes. He was lying in the garden of the big house looking up at the stars. His head hurt, so he put up his hand and felt blood running down his face. Then he realised that stupid kid, Ali, had hit him with something. It must have knocked him unconscious for a while.

Hassim got up and immediately felt unsteady. He grasped the wall for support, feeling very dizzy. He thought of going down to the basement and giving Ali a good hiding but decided he didn't feel strong enough. Ali was a big, strong kid and might just get the better of him. He decided to go back to the city with his friend and come back when he had recovered. He looked outside the gate, worried that Ahmed had gone, but he was there, fast asleep and snoring behind the wheel of his car. Hassim woke him up and they drove back to the city.

When he got back to his squalid room, Hassim looked in the mirror. He had blood all down his face and on his clothes. He washed it off and examined the wound on his temple. It was not large, but there was some bruising. Washing the cut made it bleed again, so he lay down on his bed with a grimy towel pressed to the wound. He lay stewing with fury and planned what he would do when he returned to the big house.

He swore to make Ali regret hitting him and, if Nabila objected, he would punish her too. He would go back as soon as his head stopped bleeding and take Millie away. He knew a man who ran a brothel specializing in young girls. He reckoned he could sell her for quite a bit of money. He didn't want to be her pimp himself because he suspected she would never submit without a fight, and he didn't have a suitable place to keep her locked up. She might be too hard to handle, and Hassim was basically too lazy to try.

The next day he returned, driven by his friend Ahmed. He unlocked the big gate quietly and tiptoed down the basement stairs. He threw open the door, hoping to give them all a nasty surprise, but he was the shocked one. They had gone.

Hassim was incandescently furious. He went out in a rage and told Ahmed what had happened. They discussed where the runaways might have gone. They decided that Mohammed might know where his ex-wife would go, and whether she had relatives where she could find refuge.

They drove back to the city and went looking for Mohammed in all his usual haunts, eventually finding him in a café, drinking coffee with his latest girl. Hassim explained what had happened and how Ali had smashed a stone down on his head. Mohammed was amused to hear this and laughed.

Hassim jumped up, clenching his fists furiously. "Your idiot son is a raving lunatic. He could have killed me!"

Mohammed laughed, "Don't be stupid, that's just a love tap. You got off lightly. Seriously, though, I seem to remember that Nabila has some relatives somewhere up north, but I can't remember where."

"You are useless. Well, if you remember any more, you'd better let me know," Hassim hissed.

Mohammed agreed and turned back to his girl. Hassim couldn't let it rest and decided to go back to all the villages around the big house to ask if anyone had seen Nabila and the two children getting into a taxi or onto a bus. They drove up as far as Batroun and asked around in the marketplace. They found no one who remembered seeing a woman, a big boy and a little girl getting on a bus.

Hassim was incensed that Nabila and the children had got the better of him. Not only had they fooled him, but now Nabila was not taking care of the big house and he would lose his income from that, too. He swore an oath that if he got hold of any of the three of them again, he would make them all sorry they were born.

Some weeks later, Hassim encountered Mohammed in the street. He said that he had spoken to the owner of the shop Nabila had been working in when he first met her. This man had remembered that she had relatives somewhere near Tripoli, but he didn't know exactly which village.

Hassim paid Ahmed to drive him to Tripoli and they asked around in the markets. Eventually they found a old man at a stall selling drinks who, after scratching his stubbly chin for a while, remembered a woman buying some drinks for a big, stupid-looking boy and a smaller child swathed in such a big scarf that you could not see its face. Hassim looked at Ahmed, a twisted smile on his face. That had to be them.

"Did you see where they went?" Hassim demanded.

"No, I didn't but, in the evening, I saw the woman and the idiot boy going round and round the marketplace as if they were looking for something and the other child was not with them."

Hassim was very surprised to hear this. Nabila would not have deliberately left the child alone so she must have accidentally lost Millie. That was not good; the girl could be anywhere now. Somebody else might be making money from her instead of him. The thought of this made him seethe. All those years of waiting for her to get old enough to bring him a profit and she had escaped him. He thought of Rachel, Millie's mother. The stuck-up English woman had thought she was too good for him too, and she had learned her lesson. It would serve her right that her daughter might be earning her bread on her back right now with some fisherman from Tripoli on top of her. Hassim smirked at the thought.

He decided to cut his losses and go back to the city. He would return to Tripoli occasionally and he swore, if fate ever put either Millie, Nabila or Ali in his path again, they would regret it to their dying day.

Chapter Ten - Transition

Millie was up early on Saturday morning, bathed, dressed and tidy well before breakfast. She went to say good morning to her grandmother, who was feeling a little better and was sitting up in bed reading the paper. While Millie sat with her grandmother, they heard the telephone. Aunt Vicky picked up the receiver and listened, a frown appearing on her face. She pursed her lips irritably and said, "Well, I suppose as you are already nearly here, you had better come along."

Aunt Vicky put down the phone with a crash, "The cheek of these people, just announcing that they are here and can they take Amelia out for the day. These people have no manners."

Millie's grandmother called out from her room, "What is it, dear, is something wrong?"

"It is that couple who found the child. They just called up out of the blue saying they want to take Amelia out for the day. No warning, they just turn up," said Vicky crossly.

"Well, Vicky, they did rescue Amelia and bring her back to safety. I think it is kind of them to come all this way. We do owe them some gratitude for taking care of Amelia, don't we?"

Vicky looked sternly at Amelia, and the look said that she was sorry that Marie and Jim had rescued Millie.

"Well, since they have presented us with a *fait accompli*, you had better go and get ready to go out," said Aunt Vicky.

Millie went, keeping her expression bland but as she ran up the stairs she was smiling. A little while later the doorbell went, and Marie and Jim stood on the doorstep. As Aunt Vicky rather rudely did not ask them in, Millie grabbed her coat and ran to say goodbye to her grandmother.

Marie and Jim had a little open-topped sports car. There were two tiny seats in the back, just big enough for Millie. They drove off and went to the coast. They took Millie to a funfair, and they went on all the rides that Millie had the courage to try. They ate hotdogs and ice cream, and toffee apples. Jim won her a big, floppy teddy bear at the shooting gallery. Millie had never had so much fun in one day in her whole life. They walked across the wide green area of grass leading down to the beach. They crunched along looking for interesting pebbles.

Marie said, "I used to paint pictures on pebbles when I was a kid. I painted mermaids and boats on them."

"What's a mermaid?" said Millie. Jim and Marie looked at each other. This poor child had missed so much. They tried to describe what a mermaid was and burst out laughing at Millie's puzzled face. They all ended up laughing and ran down to the sea's edge to dodge the waves. As evening approached, they took Millie back home carrying her new teddy and a bag with a few interesting pebbles to paint pictures on.

As they drove down the drive to her grandmother's house, Millie leaned over the seat and kissed Marie on the cheek. "Thank you so much for today. I had a lovely time, and I will always remember it."

Marie slipped a little card into Millie's hand. "This is our address and all the telephone numbers where you can reach us. Keep it safe. If ever you need us, you know you only have to call or write. Whatever happens we will always be your friends, won't we, Jim?"

Jim nodded, "Remember, Millie, you only have to call."

Millie felt so grateful to Marie and Jim. "Thank you. I will remember."

They said goodbye at the door and drove away. Millie rang the doorbell. Irene answered and said, "Well, I can see somebody has had a good time."

Millie grinned at her, "I did."

"Well, go and tell Granny all about it, she's on her own at the moment."

Millie ran in to her Granny's bedroom and told her all about her day.

"I hope you will paint a picture on a pebble for me," said Granny.

"Oh, I will," said Millie and she ran off up to her room.

A few days later a small parcel arrived for Millie. It was from Marie and Jim. The parcel contained a book all about mermaids and a set of paints. Millie studied the pictures of mermaids with great interest.

Because Millie had never been to school, it was not easy to solve the problem of her education. After several telephone calls, Aunt Vicky located a retired schoolteacher, living nearby, who was prepared to come to the house and teach Millie. The aim was to get her up to a standard good enough so that she could attend mainstream school.

The teacher, Mrs. Bellman, was a widow and was very pleased to have a temporary job to supplement her pension. She turned up on the next Monday morning with a pile of books and other teaching aids. Irene showed her into the little study near the front door and sent in Millie, who was feeling a little nervous.

Mrs. Bellman introduced herself with a smile. "Well, Amelia, I understand you have never been to school."

Millie nodded, although she was not altogether certain what "school" was, but she knew she had never been there.

"We are going to work hard to teach you to read and write so that you can go to school and be with other children. Have you any books of your own?"

Millie showed her the book about mermaids.

"Wouldn't you like to be able to read the words in this book by yourself?" said Mrs.Bellman.

"Yes, I would," said Millie eagerly.

"That's good," said Mrs.Bellman. "So, let's begin."

Every weekday was school day for Millie, and the weeks flew by. Soon she was reading quite well and writing simple words. Mrs. Bellman was a good teacher and enjoyed using her skills again. It was much easier teaching one child instead of thirty and, with such intensive attention and, being an intelligent child, Millie learned fast. Mrs. Bellman had brought a pile of children's books with her, and she read the stories to Millie as a reward for her trying hard during her lessons.

Millie enjoyed her lessons and could soon read simple children's books. The joy of reading was so thrilling to her, she read voraciously and soon moved on to increasingly harder children's books which Mrs. Bellman would borrow from the library for her. She read all evening up in her room after saying goodnight to her grandmother. She would read so late that Aunt Vicky, when she went to bed herself, would come into Millie's room and order her to stop reading and go to sleep.

Mrs. Bellman was extremely pleased with Millie's progress and told her grandmother and Aunt Vicky that she would soon make up lost time in reading and writing. However, she thought that Millie would not be on a par with children her own age in other subjects. Primary school children take part in lots of activities connected with such subjects as as art and history, and of course Millie had missed out on all these things. Nevertheless, Millie's grandmother was pleased with her progress.

Now that they had reading and writing well under way, Mrs. Bellman proposed concentrating on basic arithmetic. Millie was not so keen on this subject and found it much harder to learn than reading and writing. Mrs. Bellman wisely kept the lessons reasonably brief and gave Millie art and craft lessons to try and give her a more rounded experience of learning.

One day, after two hours of concentrated effort on arithmetic, they spent an hour making some paper flowers out of tissue paper and green wire. By the time Mrs. Bellman was ready to go home, they had made a small bunch of flowers.

"Perhaps your grandmother would like to see your flowers, Amelia. It is time for me to go home now, so while I put on my coat on, why don't you pop in and show them to her"

Millie thought that was a lovely idea and she tapped on granny's door and went in. She immediately saw that something was wrong. Her grandmother was lying crookedly on her pillow. Her eyes were shut, and her mouth hung open. She was not moving at all. The little Westie, Jack, was whining and pawing at the bedclothes.

"Irene, Irene, come quickly, something's wrong with granny!"

Irene and Mrs. Bellman came rushing into the room. They saw at once that Millie's grandmother was not breathing. Mrs. Bellman took Millie and Jack out of the room, and Irene stayed behind but whispered to Mrs. Bellman to call an ambulance and the doctor. Mrs .Bellman sent Millie to take Jack into the garden while they waited for the doctor to arrive.

Millie wandered round the garden. She had seen Sofia when she died so she knew that her grandmother was also dead. It had been obvious when Sofia died, that what made Sofia alive had gone, leaving her shell behind. Millie had been fond of her grandmother although her health had made her fragile and often unable to cope with Millie's childish energy. When she had been well enough for a visit she had smiled very lovingly at Millie. Aunt Vicky had no apparent feelings for Millie and so the little girl wondered what would happen to her now. If Aunt Vicky didn't want her, perhaps she would be happy to let Millie go and live with Marie and Jim, she thought hopefully.

The ambulance and the doctor arrived at about the same time. They all disappeared into grandmother's bedroom. Eventually the ambulance men left, and the doctor came out. Just then Aunt Vicky arrived home and flew into the house, having seen the ambulance driving off down the road. When the doctor told her that her mother had died in her sleep, Aunt Vicky screamed and had hysterics. The doctor took her sobbing up to her room and gave her a sedative. Irene rang the undertaker, who came an hour later and took grandmother's body away.

Irene took Millie into the kitchen, pulled her on to her lap and hugged her. Her own eyes were full as she grieved for her employer, and she dabbed at her eyes with a tissue. Millie felt sad but she could not cry. She was so used to sad events reoccurring in her life that she simply coped by going into a blank, detached state. This is how she had coped with all the tragic things that had happened to her so far. It was like a door would close on her pain and leave behind it a kind of raw emptiness.

She had only known short periods free of stress in the big house with Sofia and Nabila, and now while living here with her grandmother. Those quiet periods had been interrupted every time by tragic or horrifying events or bad people, and so Millie had no idea what a normal child's life should be like. She vaguely remembered the happy times when she lived with her mother, but that was so long ago now that Millie sometimes thought it was just a lovely dream.

Irene gave Millie her tea in the kitchen and sent her to bed early, a little unnerved by Millie's detached, closed-in attitude. She wondered if Millie would ever be like a normal British child. She always had a slight aura of foreignness about her, and her reactions were more like an adult than a child. Millie was fond of her grandmother, Irene knew, but the child had not cried at all, and Irene found this very unsettling.

Millie went upstairs and got ready for bed. As she went to the bathroom, she heard Aunt Vicky crying in her bedroom. Millie wasn't tired and sat by the window looking out at the garden. She watched Jack still wandering around outside in the evening gloom, his white coat standing out against the dark shrubbery. The little dog would miss her grandmother very much.

When he wasn't in the garden, he lay either on grandmother's bed or on a little blanket by her bedside. Aunt Vicky never took any notice of him, and Irene had to take care of him, feeding him and brushing his wiry coat.

When she was in bed, Millie heard Irene locking up and a few minutes later she heard Jack whining and scratching at her bedroom door. She let him in and got into bed. Jack jumped up and cuddled up to her. Millie put out her light, and stroked Jack. He sighed and laid his head on her chest. Millie thought about her grandmother dying quietly, all alone in her room and then she cried, her tears falling on Jack's fur.

Chapter Eleven - School

The next morning, Aunt Vicky came downstairs with puffy, red-rimmed eyes. She did not speak to Millie and Irene tactfully took the child into the kitchen to have her breakfast. After a cup of coffee, Aunt Vicky started telephoning people to arrange the funeral. For the next few days, she stayed shut in the study on the telephone, and she ignored Millie completely. Irene felt very awkward about this and tried to keep Millie occupied in the kitchen. Her teacher, Mrs. Bellman, had been told by Vicky that her services were no longer needed. Millie wished she had had a chance to say goodbye and to thank her teacher. Irene said she would telephone Mrs. Bellman and give her a message from Millie.

Two days before the funeral, Vicky told Irene to pack Millie's clothes into whatever suitcases she could find. Vicky looked defiantly back when she saw the housekeeper's questioning face.

"I have arranged for Amelia to go to a good boarding school. She needs to get a proper education. You may tell Amelia this if she is in her bedroom."

"Isn't she to come to the funeral?" asked Irene.

"No. I don't want her at the funeral. All Mother's friends will be there, and they will be too curious about her. It isn't suitable at all. A driver is coming to fetch her this afternoon." Aunt Vicky gave Irene a stern look, defying her to argue the point.

Irene considered arguing for Millie being allowed to stay for the funeral at least. She looked at Vicky's hostile expression, decided she really had no right to oppose her employer, and went to do as she was bidden. She found Millie in her bedroom drawing at her desk.

Irne sat by Millie and took hold of her hand. "Amelia, your aunt has decided that you are to go to school, and I am afraid she has arranged for you to go today. I have been told to pack your things."

Millie looked at Irene in total shock and her face went white.

"Can't I go to Grandmother's funeral first?"

Irene shook her head, feeling tears coming.

"What school, where is it?"

"I don't know," said Irene. "I am sure it will be a nice school and you will likely be happy there. You will have friends your own age and lots of activities. I think you usually share your bedroom with another girl or two, so you won't be alone there."

Millie looked even more shocked. She had thought Irene meant she was to go to the local school.

"I don't understand. Won't I live here anymore?"

Irene sat on the bed and held her arms out to Millie, who went to her to be hugged.

"No, sweetheart, you are going to a boarding school. That means you will sleep at the school. Aunt Vicky went to boarding school when she was your age and so did your mother. Your aunt probably thinks it is the best thing for you. She and your mother lived at the school in term time and came home for the holidays."

Millie nestled closer to Irene, but she did not cry. She thought about how life would be living here without her grandmother. She understood that Aunt Vicky would not want her around and she knew it had only been her grandmother who had wanted her. She decided that being in a school might be better than living with an aunt who disliked her, but she would miss Irene and Jack.

Irene said, "Come along, let's get your things packed. You can help me to make sure I don't forget anything," and she kissed Millie tenderly.

"Irene, when you find out where the school is, will you tell Marie and Jim where I am. If it is not too far away, perhaps they can come and visit me there."

"That's a lovely idea. I am sure they will be happy to visit you if they can. I will telephone them as soon as I know where you are."

Irene found two suitcases and they packed most of Millie's things carefully. She took the book and the teddy that Jim and Marie had given her, her mother's teddy and some pictures of her mother. Irene had found frames to put them in.

After lunch, which she ate in the kitchen with Irene, Aunt Vicky called Millie into the living room.

"Sit down, Amelia. No doubt Irene has explained to you about boarding school. Your mother and I went to a similar one. It is a small school, just for girls, and they know that your education has been neglected but not why. I advise you not to tell anyone about your previous life, they might be unkind to you because of it. You have an opportunity to get a good education and, if you are sensible, you will make the most of it. Your grandmother has set up a trust fund, that is a special bank account, to pay for your education. You are extremely lucky that she did that. Most girls would be grateful for the chance you are being given. I hope you will behave yourself and remember that your grandmother wanted you to have this opportunity."

Vicky continued, "A driver will be coming to take you to the school this afternoon. The school has undertaken to provide you with all the uniform and equipment that you will need. I suppose you probably expected to go to your grandmother's funeral, but the term at the school has already begun so I think it better that you go now."

Aunt Vicky looked at Millie, a strange expression on her face.

"I am going away myself after the funeral and will be travelling for some time. I cannot stay here without Mother."

Millie bowed her head, she had been growing fond of her grandmother herself and would miss her, but she could understand that Aunt Vicky would miss her mother more, and she almost felt sorry for her. She was too afraid of her aunt to speak. She wanted to say something sympathetic but could not find the words.

Aunt Vicky turned her back to Millie and said, her voice breaking, "Go along now, and make sure you are ready to go."

As Millie left the room, she saw her aunt had started to cry.

The driver arrived. Irene, and Jack came out with Millie to say goodbye. As the driver put the cases into the boot, Irene asked him where the school was, and he wrote down the address for her on a bit of paper she had brought out in her apron pocket.

"There you are, Millie, I know where you are going, and I will write to you soon. I will also telephone Marie and Jim and tell them where the school is. It is not a huge distance from where they live, and I am sure they will visit you if they can."

"Thank you, Irene. Thank you for being so kind to me."

She hugged Irene and picked up Jack to give him a hug too. She looked back at the door, wondering if Aunt Vicky would come out to say goodbye, but she didn't.

Millie got into the front seat of the car next to the driver, and they drove off down the drive. Millie looked back as they drove off and saw Irene was waving and mopping her eyes with her apron.

"Well, nice to meet you, Amelia, my name is Bill," said the driver, "Off to school then?"

Millie nodded. She looked at the driver, he had a nice, friendly face. He was wearing a shiny black suit and a tie. He was so portly that the buttons strained across his chest to keep his jacket closed. He had no hair on his head, but large tufts of hair sprouted out of his ears and nose, which fascinated and horrified Millie in equal measure.

"First time you've been to boarding school?" said Bill.

"Yes," said Millie, "I've never been to any school before. I had a lady, Mrs. Bellman, who came to the house to teach me."

"You were a lucky girl, weren't you? Mind you, you will enjoy it at Elliot House. It is a small school, quite near the sea, and there are activities outside school hours."

Millie thought that this school was starting to sound quite nice. Maybe she would like it there.

"Do you know the school?" said Millie.

"Oh, yes," said Bill. "I live on the school grounds, in a bungalow, with my wife. We both work for the school. My wife helps in the kitchen, and I am the caretaker and driver. Quite a few of the girls live close to the school and I take them home in the school bus at weekends, or at holiday time. I also drive girls to the doctor and the dentist in the village, if need be, with the school nurse usually."

It was quite a long drive, but Bill kept Millie amused telling her funny jokes and stories and singing silly songs. Eventually Millie fell asleep. When she woke up, they were driving along a narrow road by the sea. The sun had given way to darkness, and the moon was shining down on the calm sea. Millie suddenly remembered the night they had driven out of the city of Beirut and how the moon had seemed to be following as if it wanted to see into the car. It seemed to be doing the same now. To Millie the moon seemed like a familiar friend, and she loved to see its cool, silvery light shimmering on the rippling waves of the sea.

The car stopped in front of a large pair of wrought iron gates between brick pillars. Bill got out to open the gates, drove the car through, then closed them behind the car. Millie could see a large red brick building at the top of the drive, flanked on each side by long low buildings. They drove up to the front of the house and then to the right, through a brick archway, and stopped at a door at the back.

"Out you get, Amelia, we're here now," said Bill.

Millie got out, feeling very apprehensive, and Bill lifted her cases out of the boot. A tall, thin lady came out of the door, a broad smile on her rather angular face. She had a set of large horsey teeth and was dressed in a grey skirt and cardigan over a white frilly blouse. Her hair was cut in a plain and practical style, but she had a kind and gentle manner.

"Hello, you must be Amelia. I am Miss Gideon. I am your House Mistress and also the English teacher."

Miss Gideon took Millie by the hand and took her in the door.

Before them was a long, wide corridor, painted cream at the top and maroon at the bottom. The walls were lined with landscapes and seascapes. Miss Gideon took Millie down the corridor and pointed out different classrooms leading off each side of the corridor. Millie listened carefully, but soon lost track of which room was what. In the middle of the corridor, it opened into a large square hall with a wide, elegant staircase. Portraits of dour people in strange clothes lined the staircase. They mounted the stairs and Miss Gideon led Millie along a wide corridor, similar to the one below. They went right to the end of the corridor and into a long hallway. Off this hallway were lots of smaller rooms. Some of the doors were open and Millie could see girls about her own age sitting on beds, in armchairs, or writing at desks. Some of them looked up curiously as they passed.

Miss Gideon took Millie into a room near the end of the corridor. It had two of everything in it. Two beds, two small wardrobes, two desks, two armchairs, and a bedside cabinet with a lamp beside each bed. A large window lay between the beds, with cheerfully bright curtains. Sitting on one of the beds, her knees up supporting a book, was a plump girl, her hair in two untidy plaits, and a well-chewed pencil between her teeth. She had round, brown eyes over plump red cheeks. Her nose was small and snub, sprinkled liberally with freckles.

"Amelia, this is Jacqueline, but she prefers to be called Jackie," said Miss Gideon. "Jackie, this is Amelia, your new roommate."

Jackie sat up and grinned a bit wolfishly. "Hi, Amelia," she said.

"Actually," said Millie, with a quick look at Miss Gideon, "I like to be called Millie."

"Do you, dear? Your aunt didn't mention that to us," said Miss Gideon vaguely. "Very well, Millie it shall be."

Bill puffed up the corridor, carrying Millie's cases, which he put down next to the empty bed.

"Jackie, be a dear and show Millie where to put her things, and then bring her down to supper."

"Yes, Miss Gideon," said Jackie, and the teacher left the room. Bill winked at Millie and gave her a thumbs up as he followed her out.

Jackie showed Millie where to put her things, and Millie unpacked. She thought Jackie looked rather fierce and Millie could not make up her mind if she liked her or not. She had never talked to another girl her own age, so chatting with another child did not come naturally.

Jackie sat on her bed again, and watched Millie put her clothes in her wardrobe.

"How come you have arrived in the middle of term?" said Jackie.

"Well, my grandmother just died, and my aunt is going away so there was no one to look after me except Irene, granny's housekeeper. I don't know why I couldn't just stay with her." Millie's voice wavered a little and Jackie guessed that she was probably feeling sad about her grandmother, so she didn't ask any more questions.

Jackie took Millie down to the school dining room for supper. The cavernous room was an echoing hubbub of noise and chatter as a room full of girls ate their supper. Millie received a few curious glances, but Jackie took her to one end of a crowded table where there were two free chairs and sat between Millie and the other girls.

After supper Miss Gideon came over and patted Millie on the shoulder.

"Everything all right so far?" She smiled at Millie, and Millie smiled tentatively back. She liked Miss Gideon. "I think it might be a good idea to have an early night tonight and have a fresh start tomorrow to get to know everybody."

She took Millie back to her room, with Jackie following behind. When the two girls were in bed, Jackie told Millie that Miss Gideon had asked her to take Millie around with her the next day to make sure she didn't get lost or miss any lessons. A while later Miss Gideon popped her head round the door and told them to put out their lights and go to sleep.

Millie lay in the dark, her eyes open, thinking about the events of the day. She laid her cheek on the soft Teddy that Marie and Jim had won for her. She wished she had been able to go to her grandmother's funeral. Granny had been her only relative, at least the only relative who appeared to care about her. Her aunt had made it clear that she had no feelings for Millie at all.

Millie could not understand it. Surely, she should be a little bit interested in her dead sister's child but, for whatever reason, it seemed her Aunt Vicky had been quick to shunt her off to school the very first minute she could, before Millie's grandmother was even buried. Millie had been prepared to love her aunt, but it had proved impossible, and the feeling of rejection hurt. She hoped that Irene managed to tell Marie and Jim where she was and that they would visit her if it were allowed.

Jackie did not try and talk to Millie and, as the sounds of the girls in the rooms either side of them gradually died down, both girls fell asleep.

The next morning, Millie woke up to the sounds of girls laughing and slippered feet going up and down the corridor. It was much noisier than she was used to, but it seemed quite a cheerful noise. Jackie yawned, stretched and climbed ungracefully out of bed. Her hair was like a bird's nest, and she stumbled off to the bathroom with her towel and washbag. Millie grabbed her own wash things and followed her, anxious not to be left behind.

Millie had no uniform yet, so she put on a skirt and

jumper and followed Jackie down to have breakfast. After breakfast Miss Gideon came to fetch Millie and took her to the secretary's office. They gave her some spare uniforms until they could purchase her some new ones. Miss Gideon gave Millie some pens, a ruler and eraser, all safely put in a new pencil case. She gave Millie a piece of paper with her timetable printed on it and explained to Millie what each item was. Apart from Reading and Arithmetic, all the subjects on the timetable were completely strange to Millie. She began to feel very anxious but kept her worries to herself.

Miss Gideon took Millie back down the corridor and into a classroom full of girls. There was another teacher at the front of the room writing on the blackboard. Millie was told to sit at a desk by herself at the back of the room. She saw Jackie across the room sitting next to a tall, lanky girl with a haughty face. Jackie gave Millie a small wave and then got on with her work. Millie tried to work out what the lesson was all about but was completely mystified.

Half an hour later a bell rang, and all the girls stood up and hurried out the door. Jackie motioned to Millie to follow her, and they hurried to another classroom where Millie was relieved to see Miss Gideon at the front of the room. This was an English lesson which Millie had more success understanding, but it was much more advanced than the lessons she had received from Mrs. Bellman, and Millie realized nervously that she was going to struggle in this school. She was not used to sitting on a hard chair for so many hours of the day and, by four o'clock that afternoon, Millie was completely exhausted and trying hard not to yawn. Her mind was spinning with trying to absorb facts that she could not comprehend.

After tea, Jackie told Millie that she was free to do what she liked until supper time. She could watch television in the sitting room on their floor or read quietly in her room. Jackie said that they had no lessons on a Saturday or Sunday. They wore their uniform in the week but could wear their own clothes if they wanted to at weekends. She explained that some girls went home at weekends, but most only went home in the holidays, or half-term. She told Millie that they could have visitors at the weekend, with the school's and parent's permission. Millie was pleased to hear this.

Jackie asked Millie questions about where she lived and about her family. Millie remembered Aunt Vicky's warning and so she simply said she had lived abroad with her mother who had died, and then she had been sent to live with her grandmother, and now she had died too.

Jackie told Millie that her parents lived in Germany where her father was in the Army. She only went home in the summer holidays, and all the other holidays were spent with her aunts and uncles. Millie asked Jackie if she were happy in the school. She didn't answer for a minute, then she said, "Army kids get used to being away from their parents. I have been here for two years, and I am used to it now. I wish I could have stayed with my mother, but my father believes army kids are best off at boarding school. There are some compensations; at weekends we can go pony riding or have dancing lessons."

Millie liked the idea of learning to dance and hoped perhaps she could go pony riding too. Jackie promised to ask Miss Gideon about it the next day.

By the time the weekend came, Millie was quite exhausted with trying to make sense of all the lessons and the constant presence of so many people, and the need to understand a whole new set of rules which are an essential part of a school. Saturday arrived at last, and Millie was thrilled when, after breakfast, Marie and Jim arrived. Miss Gideon had telephoned Aunt Vicky to ask if Millie could have visitors, but only Irene was home. The housekeeper had crossed her fingers, hoping that her statement would not come back to haunt her, and said that she was sure that Aunt Vicky would be happy for Millie to go out with Marie and Jim at any time.

Happy to see Millie again, Marie and Jim took her out for the day. They had lunch in a cafe after driving down the coast road to a seaside town a few miles away. They asked Millie if she were happy in the school and about her grandmother dying. Millie answered them as best as she could but could not help tears springing in her eyes.

"It is all so strange, and I miss Irene and Jack. I can't do all the lessons and the other girls know what to do and I don't. I don't want to stay there. Can't you rescue me like you did in Tripoli?" Millie knew in her heart that they couldn't do that, but she was so miserable and being with her friends, who she knew loved her, lowered her resistance. Tears poured down her cheeks.

Marie and Jim looked at each other. Marie put her arm around Millie and kissed her cheek tenderly.

"I know it is all strange now, but you will get used to it. I know that school was not part of your old life but getting an education is a really good thing and will help you when you are grown up. All children in Great Britain have to go to school. You know we cannot take you away from the school, that would be against the law. Your aunt is your legal guardian, and we cannot challenge her decisions."

Millie dried her tears and looked at her friends. "I know, but I wish I could live with you."

Marie bit her lip as she stroked Millie's hair. "We can't come every weekend, but we will come as often as we can. If your aunt will agree, you can come to us for holidays too. I will ring Irene and see what she says," said Marie. They hugged Millie when they dropped her off back at the school and reminded her that she could call them any time.

Chapter Twelve - Inheritance

Within a few weeks, Millie became accustomed to being at the school. She was very much behind the other girls in many subjects, and she experienced some very unkind teasing because of it. She didn't retaliate and gradually the other girls got bored with teasing her and left her alone.

She occasionally had nightmares, usually involving snakes hiding in coats or in cupboards or some other mundane place. The nightmares would fill her with panic, and she would wake up suddenly, sweating with fear, but she managed not to scream aloud or disturb Jackie.

Initially, Millie got on quite well with Jackie but because she had to avoid talking about her past life, it had the effect of making Jackie feel that Millie was a bit secretive. She was accustomed to being close friends with other girls and exchanging confidences – and Millie avoided all intimate conversations. After a while, Jackie gave up trying to be friends with Millie, spending most of her time with her existing friends, so Millie was often left alone.

Millie had no experience of dealing with other children and she listened to their conversations about their lives and families but had no corresponding experiences to exchange. She had spent her formative years with two simple uneducated women, Sofia and Nabila, who accepted their narrow domestic lives without question. Millie wanted to be friends with the other girls but had no idea how to go about it.

Gradually, through a lot of hard work and some extra tuition, Millie started to catch up with the other students. She learnt to ride a pony during the weekends and absolutely loved the ballet dancing classes. When she was dancing, that was when she felt truly happy. She knew that her mother had been a dancer, and she felt a bond with Rachel because they both enjoyed the same thing.

Irene wrote to Millie to tell her that Aunt Vicky had gone abroad and that she had given permission for Millie to go out for the day with Marie and Jim, but that she had to return to home to stay with Irene for the holidays. She said she had written to Marie and Jim to tell them this.

As the years passed, Millie caught up with the other girls in many respects, but she was always somewhat an outsider. She never made a special friend at the school and had an undeserved reputation for being unfriendly. Still, Miss Gideon wrote good reports to Aunt Vicky, telling her that Millie worked hard and behaved very well. She passed some of her exams creditably for a child who had missed so much school.

Millie went home for the holidays, driven back by Bill. Aunt Vicky was never there, but Irene was always thrilled to have Millie back. Jack was ecstatic and leapt up and down, catching his claws in the material of her skirt.

Irene would let Millie go out with Jack on a lead, to take him for a walk in the surrounding countryside. Sometimes she would walk into the nearby village and chat to the lady who served in the village shop when she was buying sweets. Millie wondered why Aunt Vicky never came home when she was there on holiday. Irene told her that she came home occasionally, stayed a week or two then went off travelling somewhere else. Irene said that Aunt Vicky had been tied to the house while her mother was alive. Irene reckoned that Aunt Vicky, now that she had inherited money from her mother, was "making hay while the sun shines."

When Millie turned thirteen, Aunt Vicky arranged to send Millie to a bigger boarding school. It was another all-girls school, but much nearer home. There were no riding facilities, but she could still have dance classes. Millie was able to board during the week and go home every weekend. Irene was glad about that as she got lonely and bored living at the house all alone while Millie was at school. Millie loved being able to go home at weekends and she and Irene and Jack were contented together.

Millie settled well at the new school and made a few friends there. She worked hard at her lessons, driven by the stubborn need to impress Aunt Vicky and in the vain hope she would unbend towards Millie. As time passed, Aunt Vicky came home less and less, and never when Millie was home.

One weekend, the taxi driver dropped Millie off at home, and she ran into the house to call for Irene but stopped short when she saw Aunt Vicky's suitcases dumped in the hall.

Irene came bustling into the hall. "Oh, you're home, dear. Pop your case down and come into the kitchen for a cup of tea."

Millie went into the kitchen and Irene closed the door behind her.

"Your aunt has some news. She has met a man in Switzerland, and she is getting married again. I am so upset. She is putting this house up for sale. She says she never wants to come back here to live ever again."

"What will happen to me?" said Millie anxiously.

"I don't know yet, Amelia, but don't worry. I am sure your aunt will sort something out for you. She says she will tell you herself. Drink your tea and then go down to the study to talk to her. Don't let on that I've told you about the house."

Millie nodded. She sighed as she dunked her biscuit in her tea. Nothing in her life stayed the same for long. She could never count on anything staying the same.

She went down to the study and tapped on the door. Aunt Vicky called for her to go in. Her aunt was looking very sleek and well-groomed, sitting on the sofa with her legs elegantly crossed. Her hair was cut in a flattering style and a large glittering diamond gleamed on her ring finger. Vicky looked Millie up and down without saying anything for a while and then motioned for her to sit down opposite her.

"Well, Amelia, you have become quite grown-up. Irene tells me that you have been behaving well at home and I have good reports from your school. I am glad to hear it, and your grandmother would be pleased."

"You have probably heard from Irene that I am going to sell this house. My mother left this house half to you and half to me. As I am your legal guardian, I have decided to sell the house and put your half of the money into the trust fund my mother set up to pay for your schooling. I intend to give Irene some money, and she will go and live with her sister."

"The house will go on the market tomorrow and, of course, Irene and you will live here until it is sold as it may take some time. All the furniture will be sold as well, so when Irene tells you the house is sold, you must make sure to pack up all your own personal things. Irene has offered to store anything you can't take to school at her sister's house. Irene has also offered to have you to stay with her in the holidays and she will be paid for that."

"The money in your trust fund will be yours to do what you like with when you reach eighteen. Until then you will have your education paid for and receive an allowance each month. Three people are trustees of the trust fund other than me. It is unlikely I will come back to England after I am married, so in my absence, they will become your legal guardians."

Aunt Vicky handed Millie a small leather notebook and indicated the front page with some names written on.

"This book is for you. Keep it safe. I have put my address in Switzerland in it and the names of your other trustees. Two of them were Mother's solicitors, and the other was Mother's bank manager until he retired. They are willing to continue to act as your guardians and trustees for the time being. If you have a problem, you can contact any one of the three. You will only have to wait three years to have control of the money in your trust fund. I hope you will be sensible and use it to go to university or to buy a house, and not fritter it away. Have you any questions you want to ask me?"

Millie was busy thinking, her head down. She was surprised but pleased to hear that she would inherit some money when she was eighteen and that she would not be dependent on her aunt, but it still hurt her that her only living relative was so cold and detached. How different things could have been if her aunt had been as loving and giving as her mother, Rachel, would have been, had she been alive. These thoughts made her sad and angry at the same time.

Millie looked at her aunt with a somber expression and said, "I just want to say that I hope you will be very happy in your marriage. I wish I knew why you don't want to see me happy, too. I have done nothing to you to make you dislike me, yet right from the day I came here, you have treated me coldly. But, despite that, I really hope that you will be happy."

Without another word, Millie turned and went out of the room, closing the door quietly behind her, leaving her aunt feeling chastened and rather guilty for a few moments. Then Vicky tossed her head and told herself that just because her sister was careless enough to leave her child uncared for in a God-forsaken country, this was no reason for Vicky to have to take her place. She had given the child a home, an education and she would receive money on her eighteenth birthday. Vicky considered that this was more than sufficient.

Millie went out to sit in the garden and she closed her eyes to let the sunshine warm her face. She thought about what her aunt had told her. She was glad Irene was to get some money. She thought about the money she was to inherit from her grandmother when she was eighteen; there were three years to decide what to do with that money. She went back in the house when the sun started to go down and sat in the kitchen with Irene.

"Where is your sister's house, Irene?"

"Janet lives in Norfolk," said Irene. "She's a widow and lives in a lovely bungalow near the sea. She has always said that she wants me to go and live with her when I retired, so I think I will now."

Millie said, "Oh, I am so glad you have somewhere nice to go. I have been worrying about you."

Irene smiled and patted Millie's hand affectionately. "I will take Jack with me too. He's very old now and your Aunt Vicky doesn't want him. I have been thinking about you too, Amelia. I want you to come and stay with my sister and me in the holidays, if you want to that is. I don't think your aunt is bothered about what you do now, so you could always go and stay with Marie and Jim now, can't you?"

Millie nodded, "That is very kind of you, Irene, and I would like to come and visit you very much, if your sister wouldn't mind, that is."

"Oh, Janet would love it, I am sure. Her children have all grown up and moved away. Her son lives in Australia, so she has never even seen her grandchildren except in photos. She always says she misses having youngsters about the place."

"I would like to go and stay with Marie and Jim too, but I think they will probably be off on their travels again soon," said Millie.

"Well, when Aunt Vicky has finished with the telephone, you can go and call them to see what they say."

"Yes, I will do that. It will be strange not to be able to come back to this house again."

Folding her apron between her fingers, Irene sighed sadly, "I feel that too. It has been my home for a long time. I had a happy life here with your grandmother. I will be fine living with my sister, Janet, but it can be difficult with two women in one kitchen, you know. It reminds me of how your mother and Aunt Vicky used to squabble when they were around your age. Different as chalk and cheese, they were. I loved your mother. She was always so lively and happy. Always singing and dancing around the place. She was a kind and thoughtful girl. She used to come into the kitchen and help me just like you do. Vicky never did. I was always just a servant to her."

Irene paused a moment and then she smiled at Millie.

"Your grandmother and Aunt Vicky never knew it, but your mother wrote to me once, from Paris it was. I have the letter upstairs. Next weekend, when you come home, I will give it to you because in the letter, she talks about a man she was in love with. I think he may have been your father, judging by the date she wrote it, and the date you were born. Maybe you could write to him and ask if he could be your father. I always meant to give you this letter when you were old enough."

Irene started to cry and plucked a hankie from her apron pocket to wipe her eyes. Millie gave Irene a hug, a feeling of elation rising in her. She might have a father and perhaps she might be able to find him! She had never given her father much thought. It was a thrilling idea, but maybe he hadn't wanted a child and that was why he had never been part of her life. She would write to him anyway. After all, she had nothing to lose.

Millie went back to school on Monday morning without seeing her aunt to say goodbye. Over that week, Aunt Vicky packed up all the things she wanted to keep from her mother's house and arranged for them to be shipped to her new home. An estate agent was summoned to measure up the house and take pictures for a brochure. A "For Sale" sign was nailed up by the front gate. When Aunt Vicky was finished with all the arrangements and her things crated up ready to be shipped, she packed her suitcases and said her good-byes to Irene.

The next weekend, Millie came home to find some empty spaces where Aunt Vicky had taken antique furniture and ornaments that she had wanted to take with her to her new home. Irene made dinner for them both and afterwards they sat in Irene's bedroom to watch her little television, something they never did when Aunt Vicky was there. Irene pulled a letter from her pocket and gave it to Millie.

"Here is the letter I told you about, the one your mum sent me saying she was in love with a man. Be careful what you say when you write because this man may not be your father. Also, he may have a wife and family after all these years. You would not want to upset them, would you?"

"Oh yes, you are right, I would not have thought of that. I wouldn't want to make anyone unhappy because of me. Thank you for pointing that out. I will have to think very carefully what I am going to say. When I have written it, I will show it to you to see if you think it is okay. Anyway, he may have moved and not be there anymore. Is his address in the letter?"

"Well, she puts an address at the top of the letter, and she says she is living with him. But I never heard from her again, and I never got a reply to the letter I wrote to her. But, even if he is not at the same address, you will know his name. Perhaps that will help you find him one day."

Millie took the letter. It had a return address in Paris

on the top left corner. Millie opened the letter and read:

Dearest Irene,

I hope you are keeping well.

I am living in Paris now, as you can see, and I am very, very happy. I am madly in love with a WONDERFUL man called Guy Broussard. He is a journalist and works freelance for lots of different newspapers and magazines.

I have just moved into his apartment with him. His family owns the whole house. His parents live on the ground floor. His brother and his wife have the first floor. Guy and me have the second floor. It was once the servant's quarters, so the rooms are quite small, but the windows open on to dear little balconies with wonderful views over Paris. I love it here in Paris so much.

I am dancing in a big show with lots of other dancers, and don't worry, I get to keep my clothes on! Although there are other dancers in the show that don't. We wear beautiful costumes covered in sparkling fake jewels. We have lots of ostrich feathers on our heads and attached to our bottoms, like big, exotic birds.

Sometime Guy has to go away on assignments, and I am very lonely when he is not here. I am afraid that his family does not approve of me. His mother wants Guy to marry an aristocrat, not a lowly dancer. When he is here, they are polite, but when he is away working, they are a bit hostile. I think they want to drive me away, but – no chance – I adore Guy and would walk through fire for him.

I think he loves me as much as I love him, but time will tell!

Take good care of yourself.

Much love

Rachel

Millie folded the letter and put it back in the envelope. The date on the top of the letter was about a year before she was born. That meant that Millie had been conceived three months after the letter was written. It seemed likely that Guy was her father, but she couldn't be sure. She would write to him and phrase the letter very carefully.

It was strange to read her mother's writing. Her letter radiated the happiness of being in love. Millie wondered what had happened to separate them. Maybe her mother had told Guy she was pregnant, and perhaps he had not wanted a baby. She decided to take her time drafting a letter to Guy over the next week at school and to show it to Irene the next weekend to see if she forgotten anything or had not been tactful enough.

When Millie came back the next Friday evening, Irene told her that several people had viewed the house and seemed quite enthusiastic.

"Your aunt is going to sell all the rest of the furniture when she receives a firm offer for the house. She had it valued when she was last here. Why don't you come round the house with me and choose some things for you to keep? After all, your granny left the house to you too. I can take them with me when I move to my sister's house and store them for you in her garage. She doesn't need a car where she lives, and she will be happy to store things for you until you get a place of your own."

"I would like that, Irene. Thank you for thinking of it for me. I would like something that was my mother's, perhaps the little desk in my room. I would also like something to remind me of Granny. Maybe some photographs of her and of my mother."

"Well, we will go through everything this weekend in case a sale goes through sooner rather than later. By the way, I telephoned Marie and Jim to tell them the news and they want you to call them. They will be happy to have you visit for weekends and holidays

194

whenever you want. They are planning to spend the school holidays on their boat this summer. I think they are going to France so you will have to get a new passport. I will help sort that out for you with your guardian if you want to go. It will be lovely for you to go with them on their boat, won't it?"

Millie was pleased that Irene had telephoned her friends for her. She felt embarrassed to do it herself as they might have volunteered to have her, even if they didn't really want to, if she had asked them herself.

After they had supper, and were sitting cozily in the living room, Millie showed Irene the letter she had written to Guy Broussard, her possible father:

Dear Mr. Broussard

I am writing to you in the hope that you will remember my mother, Rachel Randall.

I believe you knew her about sixteen years ago in Paris. From there I do not know where she went but when I was three, she was living and dancing in a show in Beirut.

Sadly, she disappeared, and her body not found for some months. She had been murdered. No one knows who killed her. I am trying to find out what happened to her in the years after she left her family here in England and up to the time she moved to Beirut. As part of that search, I am trying to find out who is my father. If you have any knowledge which might be useful to me, I would be glad if you could contact me at the above address.

Yours sincerely,

Millie (Amelia) Randall

Irene read the letter through carefully. "I think that is just right. You are telling him all he needs to know but not actually saying you think he might be your father. If he suspects he is your father and is happy about it, he will let you know.

What address are you thinking of using? I suggest using my sister's address as Marie and Jim might go off on one of their trips and you would not get any reply until you get back. If a reply went to my sister's house before this house is sold, then she will forward it on to us. What do you think?"

Millie hugged Irene tightly and said, "Thank you, Irene, that's a really good idea, if you are sure your sister won't mind."

The next day Millie walked into the village to post her letter. As she put it in the letterbox, she hoped very much she would get a reply.

Chapter Thirteen - Paris

A week or so later, in a suburb of Paris, a young woman happened to be leaving the house as the mailman approached the door. She took the letters from him and sorted through them for those addressed to herself. She set aside her own letters and then noticed the one from England addressed to Mr. Guy Broussard. She examined it carefully, frowning thoughtfully, then she tucked the letter amongst her own letters and put the other letters on the table in the hall put there for this purpose. She put her own letters in her purse and left the building to walk to the Metro.

She was on her way to her job in a bank, just off the Champs Elyseés. When she reached her office floor, she went into the kitchen where other employees were making coffee. She waited until the others had gone out of the room then she got out the letter from England and opened the envelope in the steam from the kettle. She went to her desk, and, when no one was nearby, she removed the letter from the envelope.

She was a small but elegant young woman with dark brown hair, cut in a swinging bob reaching her shoulders. She had a heart-shaped face, almond-shaped green eyes and pale skin. Her nose was a little large and her mouth full-lipped and pouting. She frowned as she read the letter.

She went to the photocopier in the corner of her office and made two copies of it. She folded the original back into its envelope and applied some glue to stick it back down. She folded the copies and tucked them into her purse, with the original letter.

"Mademoiselle Broussard, please come into the meeting now," a voice called from another office and the young woman got up and left the room.

At the end of her working day, Mademoiselle Natalie Broussard returned to her home, the top flat of her family's house. This flat had once been the home of her Uncle Guy but was now hers. Her mother and father lived in the apartment below, which had the biggest and most spacious rooms. On the ground floor was the apartment of her grandmother, a widow who was a very stern, unforgiving old woman, very much the matriarch of the family. Old Madame Broussard ruled her children and grandchildren with a rod of iron. They had always bent to her will, apart from her youngest child, Guy. Natalie was clever enough to seem to defer to her grandmother, but in fact she did just what she liked, avoiding unnecessary confrontations.

Natalie returned home and, as she entered the front door, saw that the morning's post was still on the table in the hall. She slipped the letter from England out of her purse and put amongst the other letters. She climbed the stairs up to her parent's apartment and went in.

"Mother, Father, are you at home?" she called. There was no answer, so she went out and up to her own apartment upstairs. She hung up her coat, kicked off her shoes and flopped down on the sofa. She got out the photocopies of the letter from England and read it through again.

Natalie had been a very small girl when her Uncle Guy had lived in this same apartment. She and her brother Benoit lived downstairs with her mother and father. She remembered Rachel who had come to live with Uncle Guy for a while. Natalie had liked Rachel very much. She would play games with Natalie and Benoit and was always patient and kind. When she had seen the letter was from England, she thought perhaps it was Rachel writing at long last.

For some reason that Natalie could not understand at the time, her grandfather and grandmother disapproved of Rachel. Natalie's parents took their cue from the older couple and were cool with Rachel, too. At the time, Natalie had been angry with her grandparents and ashamed of her parents for following suit, but now she understood that her grandmother was an extremely snobbish woman, who looked down her nose on most of her fellow humans and was probably too old to change her ways. However, she was still ashamed of her parents because they were too quick to let her grandmother dictate to them. Even today, now she was a very old woman, her grandmother still ruled the household. Natalie had been determined, while still young, that she would get a job and become independent of her grandmother's threats to cut her out of her will.

Her Uncle Guy had moved out of the family house shortly after Rachel had gone away. He had gone to Canada to work as a journalist and had done very well there. He had obtained a job as a Foreign Correspondent on a Canadian Television News channel. He had traveled all over the world reporting on wars and insurgencies until the terrible day, five years before, when he had been caught in crossfire in conflict between local tribes in Africa.

He had been taken back to his home in Canada as soon as his medical condition had stabilised and had been confined to a wheelchair ever since. He could no longer work as a roving reporter and now he wrote novels, mostly thrillers. These, along with the insurance compensation he had received, provided him with enough income to live on and to pay for his care. He refused to accept any help from his parents, or his brother but always kept in touch with his niece, Natalie and her brother, Benoit.

*   *   *   *   *

Guy blamed his parents and his brother for driving Rachel away. His girlfriend had tried to come to terms with his parents' cold and hostile attitude to her, and at first she had appeared to cope with it. Over time, she had become more and more subdued. She would not say what had upset her, but he knew it had to be his parents or, more likely, his mother.

One day he had come home from work to find that Rachel had packed her things and gone. He had hurried to the nightclub where she was a dancer to be told that her contract had finished and that Rachel had left, although the management had wanted to renew her contract. She had told no one in the show where she was going, and when Guy contacted her agency, they said Rachel had told them she didn't want anyone to know where she had gone.

He had returned home and demanded to know what his mother had said to upset Rachel. His mother said, in her usual haughty way that "nothing she had done could have upset Rachel." Guy did not believe this as he knew that his mother had never refrained from strongly criticising anyone or anything of which she disapproved. He had asked his father if he knew of anything that had upset Rachel, and he had denied knowing of anything. Guy's brother and sister-in-law said they knew nothing, but Natalie told him she had heard her grandmother raising her voice to Rachel and that she had heard her crying.

Guy had spent weeks frantically searching for Rachel and questioning all her friends and everyone she worked with. No one would admit to knowing where she had gone. Guy decided that he could not stay living in the same house as his mother. He applied for a job in Canada and when he was successful, he packed all his personal possessions and moved there. He kept in touch with Benoit and Natalie, but with no one else in the family as he was sure that their attitude towards Rachel was the cause of her leaving.

Madame Broussard knew why Rachel had gone. She had gone up to speak to Rachel when she knew Guy was not at home. She told Rachel that "she was not the sort of girl that Guy should marry, that he should marry someone of his own class, not some common stripper working in a nightclub." She told Rachel that were Guy to marry, Rachel he would be disinherited and she said that any children from their union "would be no better than mongrel dogs and not welcome in the family."

This onslaught of verbal evil devastated Rachel and she was even more distraught because she had just discovered that she was pregnant. She believed that Guy would "do the right thing" and marry her if he knew about the baby but could not bear that he might feel forced to marry her and he would be disinherited and estranged from his family as a result. She felt that she could not stay in the same place as that horrible old woman a moment longer.

She had only her clothes as she was used to moving on when a dancing contract came to an end, so she packed all her things quickly. Travelling light was a necessity in her profession. She took her cases down in the lift, having telephoned for a taxi, and left. She took a train to Monte Carlo where she had a gay choreographer friend, Gary. She was sure that he would let her stay with him in his apartment in Menton, a small town a short distance from Monte Carlo, near the border with Italy.

Gary was thrilled to see Rachel again, and happy to let her stay with him. He was an extremely kind and generous man. For the first part of her pregnancy, while she could still dance, he gave her a job in one of his shows. She saved her money carefully and had a small amount of savings by the time she got too large to dance. Then Gary employed her as a wardrobe lady and dresser in the show. In this way she passed the remainder of her pregnancy.

When her baby girl was born, Gary stood by her like the good friend he was. When the baby was a few months old, and Rachel had got her figure back, Gary recommended Rachel for a job working with a contact of his who was to stage a new show in the Casino in

Beirut.

Rachel was given her fare to Beirut as part of her contract, and the baby, Millie, travelled free as she was so small. Rachel had enough money saved to rent a small apartment, and the wardrobe lady of the show helped her find a local woman, Sofia, to live in and look after Millie while she worked.

Working in Beirut had its problems and dangers. The other dancers warned Rachel to be very careful around local men who did not – overall – have much respect for non-Lebanese women. Some of the blonde dancers wore even dark wigs outside of work to avoid unwanted attention from men. Rachel took their advice and was as careful as she could be.

There was a great difference between the show in Beirut and Rachel's previous workplaces. The show was spectacular and the dance routines enjoyable, but the lack of respect shown to the dancers and showgirls was very noticeable. Sometimes the stagehands would brush their hands over the dancer's bodies as they passed in the dark spaces backstage. There was no use the girls complaining to the management; they were indifferent.

Rachel was paid well, but never felt completely safe in Beirut as she had done in Paris and Monte Carlo. Each night after work, she hurried to her car and drove straight home to her apartment in a pleasant block with a security guard guarding the reception.

She relied heavily on her nanny, Sofia, who spoke no English but did speak basic French, as most Lebanese did at that time. Rachel could speak French and so they could communicate well. Rachel became extremely fond of Sofia and Millie adored her. Sofia was a good cook and Rachel and Millie both loved the Lebanese dishes she cooked. As Rachel worked nights, she would sleep late each morning but, in the afternoons, she spent all her time with her child.

When Sofia went out to shop, she was sometimes waylaid by her son Hassim who would harass her for money. She had told her employer about her son and sometimes Rachel had seen him when she left the apartment to go to work. Hassim constantly hung about waiting for Rachel and seemed to become obsessed with her. He hassled her to go out with him, but Rachel always refused and avoided him when she could.

Chapter Fourteen – Natalie and Guy

Natalie read the letter from Millie Randall and concluded that the girl might be her uncle's child. She remembered how Guy and Rachel had been so much in love and felt great anger towards her grandmother. How tragic that Rachel had been murdered. She wondered what her grandmother would do with the original letter she had left in the hallway. She suspected she would return it unopened or destroy it.

Natalie was a very strong-willed young woman and never let her grandmother get the better of her, but her shy brother Benoit was unable to stand her constant criticism and simply avoided her. She read the letter through again and decided she would write to her Uncle Guy and send him a photocopy (after keeping the other copy for herself). She felt he should know that Rachel had died and that, if Millie might be his child, he had the opportunity to do something about it. She wrote a letter to her Uncle Guy and took it to work with her the next day. She put a copy of Millie's letter in with her letter and posted it.

When the letter arrived in Canada, Guy Broussard opened it with a smile. He always enjoyed his niece's letters as they were full of cheeky comments of whatever mischief his mother was up to at the time. She was either in clashes with her neighbours or writing letters to the newspapers decrying the state of the country and the entire population. Natalie had a way of describing his mother's offences in a very humorous fashion and, over the years, he had begun to forget just how very monstrous the old lady's behaviour could be.

He read Natalie's letter sitting in his wheelchair by the window. Then he unfolded the copy of the letter from Millie and, when he read about the dreadful way Rachel had died, he was devastated. He had never stopped loving her. He had been certain she loved him back, and when she had left in such a mysterious way, he suspected his mother of being involved. Why hadn't Rachel discussed her unhappiness with him? Even if his mother had been the cause, he would have moved to another apartment with Rachel if that had been the price of her happiness. He would happily have given up everything for Rachel's sake, but she had not given him the choice.

He reread the letter, and it gradually dawned on him that Rachel had almost certainly been pregnant with his child when she left. If so, she might have been more than usually vulnerable in the face of any verbal abuse from his mother. He checked the time, calculated that it was evening in Paris and dialed his niece's telephone number.

Natalie answered and Guy said, "It's me, your favourite uncle."

"My *only* uncle," said Natalie laughing with joy to hear his voice.

"I got your letter, and it seems I might be a daddy."

"That's what I wondered," said Natalie. "How do you feel about that?"

"Well, I am truly sad to hear that Rachel had such a tragic death, but very intrigued to hear that I might have a daughter."

"I'm glad to hear it. I thought you would be. What are you going to do?"

"Natalie, can you take any vacation time and meet me in England? I can get to England on the plane by myself okay, but it would be nice to have you for company. I need a driver too, and help with the chair and all."

"I will ask at work tomorrow and ring you in the evening. I am sure it will be okay, but it might be next week before I can get away. Is that okay with you?"

That is marvellous, *chéri*. I will wait to hear from you."

Chapter Fifteen - Nabila

In Lebanon, Nabila had found her cousins' home near Tripoli. To her relief, they had welcomed her and Ali in and generously offered to support them both until Nabila found a new job. It took some months, but in the meantime, Nabila helped by taking care of the family vegetable garden and helping around the house.

Ali had grown but he still had the mind of a small child in a hefty young man's body. He still clung to Nabila's skirts. He was unaware of his strength and because of how he had attacked Hassim, Nabila worried that he might use it at the wrong moment, so she kept him away from people as much as possible. Her cousins tolerated him because of her, but she knew they would prefer him not to be around. As he had grown, his disability became more noticeable and people shied away from this huge young man with a strange misshapen face, his mouth hanging open to one side and drool dangling from his lips.

Eventually Nabila's cousins heard of a job in a village close by. An older man with no relatives, who was slightly disabled after suffering a stroke, needed a housekeeper to take care of him and his home. It was arranged for Nabila to go to meet the man and she took Ali with her. If her new employer would not accept him, she could not take the job.

She found her potential employer sitting in his garden. He was a slim, handsome man with silver hair.

"I am a hard worker, sir," Nabila said, "and I have looked after a place that was bigger than your house."

The man frowned. He might be a little frail, but he was extremely proud of his house and walled garden with many trees growing there, oranges, lemons, figs and apples, also date palms and banana trees. The house was large, built round a shady courtyard surrounding a square pool with a small fountain and with the larger part of the garden beyond the trees. Bougainvillea bushes cascaded their pink and purple blossoms from the courtyard to the balcony of the upper floor and bright geraniums flowered in terracotta pots. It was a delightful place to sit and allow the tinkling water to sooth his spirit.

Nabila noticed the frown and quickly said, "Of course, this is a much lovelier house and I have never seen such a beautiful courtyard. The other house was larger, but the owner lived abroad and never came home. A house does not live if no one is there."

The man, Khalil Massoud, smiled at this remark and nodded agreement.

"Tell me about your son." Mr. Massoud looked at the boy with pity. "Where is his father?"

"My son was born like this. He is a man in body, but a child in his mind. He will never grow up now. He is very strong and helps me willingly in the garden. His father abandoned us many years ago, and we have nothing to do with him. He was a cruel man."

Mr. Massoud felt sorry for Nabila having to take care of such a peculiar looking boy all on her own. He felt some sympathy for Ali as his own illnesses had robbed him of his formerly active life. He decided to give her a job on a trial basis.

"I will give you the job of looking after me and my home on the condition that, if it turns out you are not suitable, then you will be given one month to find another place. Is that acceptable?"

"Oh yes, sir, that is perfect," said Nabila with great relief. "I could always go back to my cousins' house until I find another job. I am grateful to you."

Mr. Massoud nodded kindly. "Now here is some money. I will call you a taxi and you can collect your belongings and come back in the taxi. Will you be able to do that? A local woman comes in to bring me some food. I will tell her that she no longer needs to come after today. Your rooms are to the side of the kitchen. You will have a bedroom and a small room to sit in. Is that enough?"

Nabila nodded happily. She was looking forward to living and working in this beautiful house and garden.

Later that evening she arrived back with her belongings. She had nothing apart from a few clothes for her and Ali. Luckily her rooms were furnished, and she did not need anything else. Mr. Massoud had eaten his meal and was sitting in his wheelchair in the courtyard garden.

Nabila made Ali stay in their bedroom while she went to speak to her new employer. "Do you need any help this evening, sir?" she asked him.

"I am able to walk a little and can climb the stairs. I do not need any help in that regard. I only use my wheelchair during the day to conserve my strength. I only need you to clean the house, cook my food, and keep the courtyard tidy. I have a man to help with the heavy jobs in the garden and to work on the house when something needs repairing. Help yourself to any food that you need. You may go to your rooms now, but I would be happy if you could take a jug of cool water up to my bedroom."

Nabila did that, then wished Mr. Massoud goodnight. They soon settled down to a routine. Nabila was able to persuade Ali to stay in the kitchen most of the time, but he insisted on accompanying her into the garden.

Mr. Massoud was very pleased with Nabila. She was a good cook and was very efficient at cleaning the house in a quiet, inconspicuous way. His house started to look as clean and homely as it had not done since his wife had died, and Mr. Massoud was contented.

Nabila would go to the market in Tripoli once a week by taxi. It was not necessary to go more often as the garden provided many vegetables and there was a refrigerator in the kitchen. Nabila loved this as she had never had one before. It was so nice to know that food was still fresh and healthy to eat for more than a day or two.

Time went by in complete contentment for Mr. Massoud and Nabila. Ali was calm because his mother was happy, and they lived in peaceful surroundings. Sometimes Nabila would think about Millie, and wonder if she was safe, and if she had found her family. She worried that perhaps she had been found by someone as unpleasant as Hassim, and fervently hoped that she hadn't.

One evening, after Ali had fallen asleep, Nabila went to take Mr. Massoud's jug of water upstairs and then went to bid him goodnight. He was sitting in the courtyard, his head thrown back, gazing up at the moon and the stars.

"Come, sit for a while, Nabila. Look at the stars, they are very bright tonight. They are so beautiful."

Nabila sat and looked at the stars. They were indeed very beautiful. She felt a little sad that night, wondering where Millie was. Mr. Massoud noticed her sad face and asked her what troubled her. She told him about

Millie and Sofia and about the child's mother disappearing. She told him about Hassim and how he had sold Millie to a man for a night and about the beating the child had suffered. He nodded his approval when she explained how they had escaped. She did not dare tell him about Ali hitting Hassim with a stone, in case he thought the boy was dangerous. She had tears in her eyes when telling him how she had lost Millie in the marketplace, and how she had searched for hours and hours.

Mr. Massoud listened carefully and with great interest.

"What nationality do you think the child was? And you say she had papers in her case that were her mother's?""

"Sofia said that Millie and her mother were English. She did have the papers with her when we got separated"

"I have an English friend who lives in Beirut. He might be able to find out if the child reached the safety of her family. I will write to him tomorrow."

The next day, he sat with Nabila while he wrote the letter, checking that he got the facts as clear as possible. Nabila posted the letter the next time she went to the market.

One day, while Nabila and Ali were walking round the marketplace in Tripoli buying food, she was utterly shocked to see Hassim getting out of a taxi on the other side of the market. She grabbed Ali by the sleeve and hurried him into a shop selling women's clothes. She sat her son on a chair hidden by some hanging robes. She peeped out between beads hanging in the doorway to discourage flies. She saw Hassim walking round, gazing around him intently as if he were searching. Could it be that he had found out Nabila and Ali had come to Tripoli?

She watched Hassim for several minutes as he walked round and round the marketplace scanning the faces around him. It certainly looked like he was searching for someone. Her heart constricted with fear. The shopkeeper asked her if she wanted anything, and she pretended to look at the clothes nearest the window so she could keep her eye on Hassim. Eventually he got back into his friend Ahmed's taxi, and they drove away.

Nabila pretended to look at some more robes for a while and then, smiling apologetically at the shopkeeper, she took Ali's hand and hurried home. When she got home, Mr. Massoud noticed the anxious look on her face. She told him about seeing Hassim in the town, and how he seemed to be searching. Mr. Massoud frowned. He was very fond of Nabila by now and wanted to make sure she was safe.

"When you need to go to the market, you can go to Al Minyah. It is almost as close as Tripoli and it is less likely he will look there."

Nabila thanked Mr. Massoud. She thought that was a good plan and she smiled a broad, happy smile of relief at her employer. He smiled back; glad he had made her smile again.

Some days later Mr. Massoud received a letter from his English friend. He read it out to Nabila:

My dear friend Khalill,

I was so glad to hear from you after so long, and very intrigued by the request you made.

I have investigated with a friend at the British Embassy. It seems that, sadly, some months after the child's mother disappeared, her body was found in woodland, and it seems that she had been murdered. No one knows who the murderer could be.

When it was discovered that Rachel Randall had a child, a search was made for her without success. When she got separated from your housekeeper in the marketplace, an English couple found her. They got in touch with the British Embassy in Athens and the child was reunited with her mother's family.

That is all I could find out. I hope this reassures your housekeeper that the girl did indeed find her relatives. If you wish, I will forward any letter Nabila might want to write to the girl care of my friend at the Embassy.

Affectionately

Bernard Johnston

Mr. Massoud folded the letter. "It sounds very much as if the child is safe and back with her family. Does that make you happier?"

Nabila nodded happily, her eyes shining. She could not have hoped for a better result for Millie.

"Would you like me to write a letter to Millie from you?"

Nabila nodded, and the next night they sat down together, and Mr. Massoud helped her write a letter in English to Millie:

Dearest Millie

I am so happy to discover that a kind rescuer helped you to find your family. I have been very worried about you ever since we lost each other in the marketplace.

I am living here at the address above with my employer whose friend discovered that you were safe. My employer is writing this letter for me. I am glad you are not here as I saw Hassim recently and he seemed to be looking for someone. Maybe he is still looking for us? I will not often go to Tripoli again as I am frightened of him finding us again.

Mr. Massoud, my employer, is a kind man and Ali and I are very happy living here in his beautiful home. I was very sad to hear about your poor mother, but I am glad you found your family.

If you would like to you can write to me at the address on this letter. I hope one day we shall see each other again.

With love from your friend

Nabila

Mr. Massoud enclosed the letter with another to thank his friend, Bernard, and Nabila posted them at the post office in Al Minyah. They did not receive a reply and after a few years they stopped hoping to hear from Millie.

Mr. Massoud and Nabila were very happy living together. Because she took such good care of him, and he was so very content, he started to regain some of his former strength. After some months he did not need his wheelchair anymore. After two years of contented life together Mr. Massoud asked Nabila to marry him.

She thought for a while and then she said, "Nothing would make me happier, but what about Ali?"

"Ali is happy here and does not trouble me at all. When we marry, you will sleep upstairs with me, of course, and he shall have the room next to us. We shall encourage him together to accept that. Will you say 'yes' now?"

"Yes, yes, please. I will be a good wife to you." Tears of happiness filled Nabila's eyes as she had grown to love Mr. Massoud very dearly.

"My dear, I know that. That is why I am asking you and I will take good care of you and Ali."

Chapter Sixteen - Sailing

A letter was delivered to Irene's sister's house in Norfolk. It was the letter Millie sent to Guy Broussard. Someone had written on the letter in black ink, in large decisive script, "NOT KNOWN AT THIS ADDRESS, RETURN TO SENDER."

Millie received it at school a few days later, enclosed in a letter from Irene. She said she was sorry that Guy Broussard had obviously moved away and not left a forwarding address. After all these years it was to be expected really. Irene hoped that Millie was not too disappointed.

Although Millie was extremely disappointed, she was not really surprised. It would have been too easy to find Guy Broussard living in the same place so many years later.

It was nearly the summer holidays. Marie and Jim were planning to go sailing down the coast of France for the whole six weeks and asked Millie to go with them. She jumped at the chance to go as the house sale had finally gone through and Irene was busy packing all the things that they were to take to her sister's house. The date had been set for three week's time and Millie asked Irene if she minded if she were not around to help.

"Not at all, Millie. If you are not here, I can just get on with it. You go on and have a good holiday. Marie and Jim can take you back to school and, in future, you can come to stay at my sister's house in the holidays, if you want to, of course."

Millie packed her things and said goodbye to the house. She had been grateful to have a home provided for her, and to be given an education. She remembered that she had not been completely happy there, however, as her Aunt Vicky had always made her feel like an interloper.

Marie and Jim came to pick her up and they drove off happily, waving goodbye to Irene, who stood on the doorstep smiling. They drove to where the boat was moored. The local boatyard had given her a thorough overhaul, and she was all shipshape and gleaming. They carried all their gear aboard and stowed it safely away. They went to a local restaurant for supper and then slept on the boat.

The next morning, they set off down the estuary using the boat's engine. Millie sat up on the prow of the boat, taking photographs with the camera Marie and Jim had given her for her last birthday. When they got near the open sea, the sea became rougher and Jim reminded Millie to put on a life jacket. They sailed up past the Isle of Wight into the open sea. They crossed the English Channel to France and entered the port of Cherbourg for the night.

That evening they went ashore to a local restaurant, one that Marie and Jim knew specialised in sea food. Millie had a wonderful Dover sole, with a delicious green salad and *pommes frites*. Marie and Jim shared an enormous lobster, getting covered in butter as they sucked every last scrap of meat out of the shellfish.

They all had a dessert and over coffee, Jim said to Marie, "Where shall we go next?"

Marie glanced at Millie. She had heard all about the letter to Guy Broussard, and how it had been returned. "Why don't we go up the Seine and have a look at Paris?"

Millie looked at Marie. "I know what you are up to. We shouldn't waste our holiday time on a fool's errand."

"We can have a look at the sights of Paris at the same time. Have you ever seen the Eiffel Tower, or Montmartre?"

"No, I haven't," said Millie, "And I would love to, but it's not sailing, is it?"

Jim said, "Why don't we just spend a week on this "fool's errand' and then we will concentrate on having a wonderful time sailing south. There are some interesting places to see down the coast. For instance, there are some fascinating megaliths near Carnac."

They talked it over for a while and decided to go to Paris, on the proviso insisted upon by Millie that they spend no more than a week and see all the best sights of Paris as well.

The next morning, they set off and found a boatyard on the Seine just outside Paris to moor the boat. They slept on the boat that night and in the morning packed enough clothes for a few nights' stay in Paris. They asked the boatyard owner and he directed them to the metro from where they could travel into the city center. They left the metro near the Louvre and walked around until they found a reasonably priced hotel. The hotel was in an old and crumbling building and the décor was old-fashioned and rather threadbare. The floors in the bedrooms sloped precariously, but the bed linens were clean and the staff polite and helpful.

They went out to eat and wandered around happily in the balmy evening air. All the pavement cafes were busy and as they passed each one, they heard people talking and arguing amiably as they ate. They eventually found a table in a restaurant and had a delicious meal.

The next morning, they bought a map and plotted their way to the address where Guy Broussard had lived with Rachel, Millie's mother. After a short journey on the Metro and a five-minute walk, they found the address. It was a very elegant house with a very large and imposing front door, but judging by the three doorbells, the house was divided into apartments. They were intrigued to see that all three bells had a small hand-printed label underneath, and all three were in the name of Broussard!

"'Not known at this address', indeed!" said Marie indignantly. "Something's fishy about this."

Jim rang the bottom doorbell, and a bell echoed far back in the building. Eventually an elderly maid answered the door. Jim, who spoke good French, smiled politely and asked if Monsieur Broussard was at home. The maid answered that the old Monsieur was unfortunately dead, but his son, Monsieur Broussard was at home, and she indicated the middle bell.

"Who is there, Thérèse?" A voice called sharply from the depths of the house.

"A gentleman is calling for Monsieur, Madame," answered the maid.

"Ask him to enter and have him wait in the hall. Then go and get Monsieur."

The maid beckoned them into the hall and bade them wait by a table just inside the door. She went up to the next floor and returned with a silver-haired man in his late forties or early fifties.

"My name is Henri Broussard. How may I help you?" said the man, looking them over curiously.

Marie spoke up, as Millie said nothing. "We are looking for a Mr. Guy Broussard."

The man looked anxiously behind him at the apartment door that the maid had gone through and closed behind her.

"Come with me up to my apartment. We can talk there."

They followed him up the stairs, and he showed them into a beautiful apartment, with large windows overlooking the street.

"Please sit down," he said indicating some chairs, "and tell me what you want with my brother."

Jim turned to Millie, "I think you should tell this gentleman about your mother yourself."

Millie cleared her throat nervously, "Before I was born, I believe that my mother, Rachel Randall, lived here for a time with Guy Broussard. I know she left, although she was very much in love with him. I don't know why she left. A few months later I was born, and eventually we went to live in Beirut where she worked. I didn't know when I was a child what she did, but I have since been told that she was a dancer."

Millie took a deep breath, "I am trying to find out why she left Guy, where she went then, and why she ended up in Beirut. I am hoping to find out who my father was, because..." Millie paused for a moment. "Because, sadly, my mother was murdered, and I am now an orphan unless I can find my father. I was hoping that

Guy Broussard would be able to help me find my father."

Henri Broussard regarded Millie closely. "I suppose you think that Guy is your father."

"I don't know," said Millie. "I only know that she became pregnant while she was living here in this house."

"My brother was a journalist and was shot whilst on an assignment in Africa. He is now confined to a wheelchair and writes books to make a living. He left this house when he discovered your mother had run away, and he has never come back. I believe he is in contact with my son and daughter, but they are both away at present. If you give me your address, I will ask my daughter to send it to Guy. If he desires to do so, then he may contact you. Is that acceptable to you?"

Millie nodded, and she scribbled Irene's address on a sheet of paper provided by Henri.

"I am sad to hear that your mother was killed in such a terrible fashion. It is even more tragic if she were pregnant with Guy's child when she left. He was devastated to find her gone and blamed our mother.

He left home shortly afterwards and remains estranged from us to this day."

Henri Broussard continued, "you look very like your mother, but I can see a resemblance to Guy. Except for your colouring, you also resemble my daughter a little. I think it is very possible you are Guy's daughter. I think he will be happy to find he has a daughter. His accident has meant he is unlikely to have children and he has never married. If you are indeed his daughter, I will be honoured to be your Uncle Henri."

With this, he bent over and kissed Millie gently on each cheek. His kindness brought tears to Millie's eyes. Henri Broussard had always felt guilty about the way his mother had treated Rachel and that he and his wife had tolerated the old woman's unkindness. Henri chatted about his family, mentioning Natalie and Benoit.

Millie, Marie and Jim said goodbye and left. As they passed the apartment on the ground floor, they noticed a beady eye observing them from the slightly open door.

They went for a coffee in a pavement café. Marie spoke first. "Well, Millie, it seems you may have a father, an uncle, two cousins and an unpleasant old granny."

"It seems so," said Millie. "I am going to wait until I hear from Guy Broussard before I get too excited about it. Now, are we going to the Eiffel Tower or not?"

They went to the Eiffel Tower and all the other sights that they had planned to see. They had seen everything they wanted to see in four days, so they returned to the boat and set sail south down the coast. Millie had a wonderful time spending the rest of her holiday with Marie and Jim, sailing and sightseeing.

Now and again Millie's thoughts turned to Guy Broussard and whether he would contact her. She supposed that his mother must have returned her letter with "address unknown" written on it. This suggested that her paternal grandmother was not likely to be glad to have a new grandchild. If she had indeed been unkind to her mother when she was pregnant, then Millie wanted nothing to do with her either.

Chapter Seventeen - Recriminations

As Millie, Jim and Marie left the Broussard house in Paris, Natalie was in London waiting at the airport for her uncle's flight from Canada to arrive. He was brought out into the airport riding on a special buggy with a flashing light, his wheelchair folded up behind with his suitcase.

"Travelling first class, I see, Uncle." Natalie threw her arms round her uncle's neck. "It is so good to see you again. It's been far too long."

"It's great to see you again too, Natalie. You've become a very beautiful young lady."

They went to find the estate car that Natalie had hired in the airport. Natalie helped her uncle into the car, put his luggage and the wheelchair into the trunk and they drove off towards Norfolk. They reached the town where Irene lived with her sister and decided to find a hotel before they arrived at the house. They checked into a country house hotel with a lift. They drove to the address on Millie's letter with the aid of directions written down for them by the hotel receptionist.

Eventually they found the address, a neat, white bungalow with green painted shutters. Natalie parked the car and got out her uncle's wheelchair. They went up to the freshly painted front door and rang the doorbell. Hanging baskets either side of the door, planted with pink and purple petunias, swung gently in the breeze. A ginger cat sat curled up peacefully sleeping amongst the lavender bushes growing against the house and bees hummed industriously among the flowers.

Irene opened the door. "Can I help you?" she said with a smile, drying her hands on her apron.

"We are here to see Miss Millie Randall."

"Oh, I am so sorry… She is away on holiday in France at the moment."

Natalie and Guy looked at each other and burst out laughing, while Irene looked bewildered.

"I had a letter forwarded on to me by my niece here. It is a letter from Millie sent to my old home in Paris. I live in Canada but when Natalie, who lives in Paris, sent me the letter, we decided to come here together to find Millie and now you say she is in Paris. This is quite amusing, isn't it?"

Irene quickly realised that this was Guy Broussard who was quite possibly Millie's father.

"Oh, do come in. I am pleased to meet you. Millie will be so sorry to have missed you."

They went in, struggling to get the wheelchair over the doorstep. Irene took them into her sister's cosy sitting room, liberally decorated with knick-knacks, and introduced them to her sister Janet, who bustled out to make some coffee.

"When do you expect Millie back?" said Natalie.

"Well, they left yesterday and planned to sail down the coast of France for the next six weeks of her summer holiday. I am not expecting to hear from her before then."

"Oh, what a pity, we just missed her. Uncle Guy, what shall we do?"

"I think we shall fly to Paris, and I shall question my mother again about what she said to Rachel. I am sure she was most certainly the cause of Rachel leaving me."

"I know Millie was most disappointed when the letter she wrote you was returned unopened with 'Address Unknown' written on it in black ink," said Irene.

Guy and Natalie looked at each other. Guy's mother *always* wrote in black ink.

Guy smiled at Irene, "If you should hear from Millie, perhaps you would be kind enough to give her my phone number in Canada, also and Natalie's home number. I shall be in Paris for a few days. Please tell her that we will both be extremely thrilled to meet her at any time. I will be able to tell her everything I know about her mother."

They thanked Irene for her help and thanked Janet for the coffee. Both women came to the door to wave goodbye. Natalie drove them back to the hotel and, after a nearly sleepless night for Guy, they flew to Paris the next day.

Natalie had left her little car at the airport, so she drove her uncle into Paris.

"Uncle Guy, will you stay with Grandmother?"

"No, I will take a room at the hotel down the street. It will be impossible to ask hard questions of Maman if

I must rely on her for a place to sleep. I need to be independent of her."

They arrived at the house and Natalie parked her car in her usual place. She helped her uncle into his wheelchair and pushed it to the front door. They entered and Guy wheeled his chair to his mother's apartment door and knocked. His mother's maid opened the door. She had come to work for his mother after he had left, so she did not know him, however she could see a family resemblance.

"Monsieur?" she said.

"Is my mother at home?" Guy said politely.

"Pardon, monsieur, I will tell Madam you are here."

Guy's mother called from inside, "If that is my son, tell him to come in."

The maid held open the door and Guy wheeled his chair in. He turned to Natalie who lingered in the doorway, "I will call you later, Natalie. Please could you call the hotel and make me a reservation." Natalie nodded and left.

Guy's mother got up from her chair and came over to kiss him on each cheek, but Guy held up his hand.

"So many years since we have seen you. I am pleased to see you again. You look well," said Madame Broussard

"Maman, you look well yourself. I will not apologise for the length of time since we saw each other. You know well the reason for my leaving, and why I have stayed away. Also, traveling for me is not an easy thing."

"Well, you are here now, and that is the important thing. I will telephone your brother; we must have a family dinner in celebration."

"Exactly what are we celebrating, Maman?" said Guy sarcastically. "Are we celebrating the fact that you drove Rachel away from me? Are we celebrating the fact that I suspect she was carrying my child when she left? Or the fact that, knowing I can no longer father a child, you have recently returned a letter written to me, not you, from Rachel's child, having written that my address was unknown on it? Which of those things do you deem worthy of celebration?"

Madame Broussard blanched and looked down at her hands as Guy spat these words at her angrily. She tried hard not to show any emotion, but her hands trembled. She raised her eyes and looked at Guy. Her voice was a little unsteady as she spoke, "How did you know about the letter?"

"That is not important, Maman. I demand to know exactly what you said to Rachel to drive her away. You ruined her life and you ruined mine. If you had not driven her away and broken my heart, I might still be living here in Paris and not stuck in this chair. I only went to Canada and took the foreign correspondent job because I had no Rachel to come home to."

"I would have married her and settled down to raise a family right here in Paris. She ended up in Beirut working as a dancer and was murdered. So, inadvertently maybe, you also ruined her daughter Millie's life, because she grew up without a mother or father and suffered dreadfully because of her mother's death." Guy leaned forward as he spoke to his mother, his voice harsh, but quiet and cold.

His mother put her hand up to her mouth, and her eyes grew big.

"I...I did not mean for such things to happen. I only wanted her to go away and for you to be married to someone more suitable, someone of the same class.

She was just a common '*danseuse*', no good family or breeding. I did not know she was expecting your child. She did not tell me that."

"Which goes to prove that what you did say to her was very cruel indeed to make her run away from me knowing she was pregnant," said Guy.

His mother took a handkerchief from her pocket and dabbed at her nose. She did not answer.

"Maman, I ask you again, and I demand you give me a truthful answer. Exactly what did you say to Rachel?"

His mother straightened her back and looked back at him imperiously.

"I said only what I considered was the truth. I said that she was not the kind of girl that we wanted to join the family as your wife. I may have said something about her being a common stripper working in a nightclub, which is virtually what she was. I told her that if you married her, you would be disinherited and that any children from such a marriage would be no better than crossbreed dogs. She made no attempt to argue with me. I do not apologise for what I said to Rachel as I believed it to be true. Your brother had unsuitable 'liaisons' when he was young but had the good sense to marry the proper type of girl. However, I am sorry if my actions have ruined your life. That was never my intention. I was trying, in my own way, to prevent the ruination of your life."

Guy sat back in his chair. He was shocked to the core that his mother had said such cruel, grotesque things to his Rachel. His head dropped on his chest and tears filled his eyes. How hurt she must have felt, carrying his baby and having that child called a 'crossbreed'. She must have thought that to leave was the only thing to do. She must have thought that her child would not be welcomed in this family, and she would have caused Guy's disinheritance if she stayed. If only she knew that his so-called inheritance consisted of his share of the house and a paltry sum of money, neither of which he wanted or needed. His poor darling, soft-hearted Rachel. He wondered where she had gone.

His mother coughed, and spoke, "Are you sure this girl is your child?"

Guy looked at his mother with distaste. "The dates of her birth suggest that she is. I am leaving now. You needn't trouble yourself to provide a celebration dinner.

There is nothing to celebrate. I am ashamed to have a mother who is such an impossible snob and who could be so brutal to such a gentle person as Rachel. I am ashamed that I brought her into this house to be treated so abominably. If I had known what my own mother was capable of being, she would have never stepped over the threshold. I shall not return here again while you are alive."

Guy turned his chair and left the room. The maid was just outside the door and helped him out into the street. He went down the street and entered the nearby hotel. He asked the receptionist if his niece has reserved him a room. She assured him that she had and handed him the room key. He went up to the room in the lift and telephoned Natalie.

"Hello, Uncle, where are you?"

"I am at the hotel, in Room 10. Would you be a darling and bring up my bag later?"

"Of course, I will. What did Grandmother say?"

"Natalie, you will not believe it. She was so cruel to the poor girl that I am not surprised she ran away. I wish I had never brought her into that house. She might still be with me today and Millie might have had a proper, happy childhood. I feel so sad and depressed about it all."

"I will come over and take you out for dinner, Uncle. You must not be alone now," said his niece sympathetically. As quickly as she could, Natalie went to the hotel and took her uncle to a good restaurant. They talked while they ate, and Natalie managed to comfort her uncle.

"Uncle Guy, you should try to forget what Grandmother did. You know that Millie wants to meet you. You can invite her over to visit you in Canada. She could even live with you and finish her schooling in Canada and have a proper parent for the first time since her mother disappeared. Why don't you write her a letter at Irene's house to invite her to come and live with you, or if she prefers, just to have a holiday?"

Guy thought about it. "That is a wonderful idea. She could have a good life with me in Canada. I will write the letter tonight. Now, I must go back to the hotel. I have booked a flight back home tomorrow. Are you free to take me to the airport?"

Natalie said that she would make sure she was free the following day and she went back with him to the hotel lobby.

"Can you manage now?" she asked him.

"Yes, I can manage fine now. They have a lift. I will see you at 10.30 in the morning." Natalie kissed her uncle goodnight and walked home. She dropped in to see her grandmother. The old woman was sitting in her armchair, gazing into space. She glanced up at her granddaughter and looked away. She looked chastened and sad.

"I have been a foolish and stupid woman all my life. I see that now. I have followed the ways taught to me by my own parents and have never before questioned the right of what they taught me. Please go away, Natalie, leave me alone. I have no heart to talk to anyone tonight."

Natalie said goodnight to her grandmother and went upstairs to her own flat. She was glad she had managed to comfort her uncle. It was a pity that they had not found Millie on their trip to England. How ironic that Millie was in Paris looking for her father when he was in England looking for her. The next day she drove her uncle to the airport, and they kissed goodbye fondly.

"You know you too are always welcome to come and stay with me as long as you like, don't you?" Guy said to Natalie.

"Yes, Uncle, I know. If Millie does come to stay with you, I will come over for a visit, so that I can get to know her too."

Chapter Eighteen – The Fixer

In Beirut, Hassim was doing well. For most of his life he had hung about on the fringes of those people who make money out of the weaknesses of others. Over the years he made himself quietly useful to anyone who needed a rival dealt with or even killed. He discovered that once you had killed a person, it got easier to do it each time. Over time he made many useful contacts and, because he never quibbled about how much he was paid, quite powerful people in the criminal world started to trust him and gave him increasingly better jobs. In time he was able to afford to rent a decent apartment and to buy a decent car.

He started to get occasional work as a security guard and general 'gofer' for an extremely wealthy arms dealer called Kamel Khoury, a man who mixed with some of the richest people in the world. Khoury was a wheeler-dealer, a finder and a fixer, involving himself in shady business transactions, often involving weapons, on behalf of his wealthy clients, protecting them so that their hands were always seen to be clean.

Kamel Khoury was not an attractive man. He was rather short and portly, although he did have large lustrous eyes. He had a large family; a beautiful French wife, who had been a dancer before their marriage and who had borne him five children. Several relatives lived with them in his massive compound in the hills south of the city.

Hassim was given the job of driving some of the lesser members of the family when they went into the city. He carried out these duties well and enjoyed the status of being on the fringes of Kamel Khoury's exotic life. When he was guarding or driving one of Mr.Khoury's immediate family, he occasionally had need to go inside the main house. This was situated in the center of the compound inside high walls and electric gates guarded by an armed guard stationed in a gatehouse.

The main house was the height of luxury and ornate European style. Each of the five children had their own enormous bedroom, each decorated in a different style to suit the child. The children spent most of their time in a big playroom and nursery where they were ministered to by a team of starchy British nannies.

Elsewhere in the grounds were smaller apartments for the lesser family members and for the most senior staff. There was a huge, professional kitchen manned by a French *chef de cuisine* and his team of under-chefs. When anyone in the family wanted food, they telephoned the chef who could produce restaurant quality food at short notice. The chefs also cooked ordinary Lebanese food for the staff and other family. These meals were served in a canteen-like room off the kitchens.

Hassim was sometimes permitted to eat in the staff canteen, and to walk in part of the grounds, away from the house. He sometimes caught a glimpse of Mrs. Khoury. She was still extremely lovely, even after giving birth to five children. He listened to the staff surreptitiously when they chatted about their employer and his family. They were very respectful of Mr. Khoury and admired him for his power and wealth. They were less respectful of his wife, Jeanne, and seemed to see her as just a brood mare.

Jeanne Khoury was a lonely person. Her husband made little effort to consider her happiness. He thought that a woman as blessed as she was, thanks to her husband's industry of course, should be content to live a life of luxury which did not require her to do any physical work. Apart from looking after her husband's needs and looking beautiful for him, she had nothing to do.

Mr. Khoury was very wealthy and powerful, but he was not high born or from a good family. He was a self-made man and therefore, although rich people used him for business reasons, Kamel Khoury and his wife were not welcomed in real high society despite his extreme wealth and power. Jeanne therefore had almost no social life and as a foreigner she was doubly restricted in who she could mix with. With her children almost out of her reach, she led a lonely and aimless life.

Hassim developed a fascination for Jeanne Khoury. Sometimes he was given the job of following her car whenever she went out. Hassim's job, along with other men like him, was to shadow Jeanne everywhere she went, ostensibly to make sure she was safe, but also to make sure she was not enjoying assignations with other men. Jeanne was too astute not to know that she was followed about for this reason. She had no intention of giving her husband a reason to divorce her. She would wander around the shops, dark glasses hiding her identity, enjoying the relative feeling of freedom, being outside the walls of her plush and luxurious prison.

Another of Hassim's jobs was to hang about at the airport, watching to see any VIPs who arrived and or departed. He was to note who among Mr. Khoury's business rivals they associated with. Mr. Khoury had succeeded in his business by knowing exactly who was doing business with whom at any given time. Hassim became quite successful at this job. He was quick to learn new names and adept at listening to other people's conversations. He reported back all the information to Mr. Khoury's right hand man, a Glaswegian thug with a talent for creative accounting called Gordon Meldrew.

Gordon Meldrew reported back favourably to Kamel Khoury about Hassim, and gradually he became part of Mr. Khoury's trusted bunch of former criminals and small-time gangsters which made up his team of bodyguards. Hassim was proud of the rise in his status at long last, and of being associated with a man of the calibre of Kamel Khoury. His boss often travelled abroad, sometimes with his family and their entourage, sometimes just with a close circle of men, including

Gordon Meldrew as always. Hassim was never part of this group, although he believed that someday he would be.

When Mr. Khoury travelled with his family, they stayed quietly at top hotels. When he travelled without his family, his social life was much more exciting, involving nubile and extremely obliging girls and much riotous partying. Hassim hoped that, if he kept his head down and his nose clean, one day he would be included in such events. In the meantime, he hung round the nightclubs and casinos, and hassled the dancers to go out with him. Very occasionally he got lucky.

Chapter Nineteen - Canada

When Millie arrived back from her holiday in France, Marie and Jim took her straight back to school. She telephoned Irene to tell her about the holiday and about finding her father's family home. Irene told her about her father and cousin coming to find her and Millie was stunned. What an amazing coincidence, she was looking for her father in France and he was looking for her in England!

She asked Irene many questions about her father and cousin: "What did he look like? Was he nice? And her cousin, did she look like Millie?"

Irene answered all her questions positively. She said that she could see a resemble to Millie in both her father and her cousin. Millie was really intrigued. What would it feel like to have a father? Would she feel anything for him, meeting him for the first time after all this time.

Irene promised to put the contact numbers that Guy had given her in the post the very next day. When the letter arrived, Millie looked at the numbers and tried to work out what the time difference was between

Canada and England. She asked one of her teachers who explained it to her and gave her permission to use the telephone to call Canada.

That evening, she dialed Guy's number in Canada. The number rang for a while and then an answer phone message came on, "This is Guy Broussard's number. I am not at home at present. Please leave a message and your number, and I will call you back."

Millie said a little shyly, "This is Millie Randall. Irene told me that you came to England to see me. I am back at school. If you want to call me, it will have to be between six and eight-thirty in the evening as that is the only time that we are allowed to have personal calls. Well, er, goodbye."

Later that evening, when Millie was drying her hair after a shower, one of her classmates came to fetch her to the shared telephone in the corridor. Millie picked up the receiver and said, "Hello?"

"Is that Millie? It is Guy Broussard speaking. I am so happy to be talking to you at last."

"Irene said you had come to England to see me, and that you had received a copy of the letter I sent you."

"Thanks to my lovely niece, yes, I did. Millie, I loved your mother very much. If I had known how cruelly *my* mother had treated her, I would have taken her away. I knew my mother was snobbish, but I had no idea how low she would sink. I am so terribly sorry that she drove your mother away."

There was a brief silence on the line before Guy continued. "Millie, I think perhaps I am your father. Actually, I am sure I am. Rachel and I were living together when you were conceived, and I would bet my life that she was not involved with anyone else. She loved me deeply, I know that. I wish she had told me that she was expecting a baby. I would have been so happy about it."

Millie leaned her head on the wall as she listened, tears rolling down her cheeks. If only her mother had not run away from Guy, they could have all lived together happily. Her mother would not be dead, and Millie would have had two parents.

"Millie, say something," said Guy gently.

"I am sorry, talking about it makes me dreadfully sad. I am glad you are happy to have a daughter, but I wish my mother was still alive to know it." Millie was crying very hard by now.

"Millie, listen to me. I think we need to get to know each other. Would you like to come to Canada to see me in your next holidays? Just tell me you want to, and I will arrange for a plane ticket."

Millie blew her nose and said, "I would like that, but I think I have to ask my legal guardians if I can go."

"Give me their names and numbers and I will sort it out with them. Millie, we have been kept apart for all these years. It might be that you cannot think of me as your father. I want you to know that whatever you come to feel for me in time, I will always be there for you if you ever need anything, anything at all. I want to try to make up to you for all that my mother's meanness has stolen from you."

"Thank you," said Millie. "I would like to visit you."

After that first tense call, Guy telephoned Millie every week. Sometimes he asked her questions about her life in Lebanon, but Millie did not want to talk about it on the telephone. She wanted to feel love for her father, the same as she felt for her mother, but it did not seem to be happening. Perhaps this was just because they were just speaking on the telephone. Perhaps it would be different if they met in person.

Guy arranged for her to visit during the Christmas holidays. He asked Irene to contact Millie's guardians and one of them called her to see if she believed that Guy was her father. She replied that she was sure that he was. Irene had suggested to them that it might be better for Millie if her cousin Natalie was there also. Guy thought that was an excellent idea and arranged a ticket for his niece too.

The term went by very slowly, but eventually the Christmas holiday arrived. Marie and Jim had volunteered to drive her to the airport. Marie was so excited that Millie was finally going to meet her father, more excited than Millie was herself. She felt strangely low key about meeting her father for the first time and she could not work out why.

The flight was very long, and Millie was exhausted when she finally arrived in Montreal. Natalie was at the airport to meet her in a hired car, holding up a notice with Millie's name on. The two girls spotted each other at the same time. Apart from the difference in their colouring, they could be looking in a mirror. They both smiled at the same time and felt an instant bond of affection.

"Millie, I am so happy to meet you at last." Natalie threw her arms round her cousin and kissed her on both cheeks, French style.

Millie smiled back, "I am so glad you are here. I am a little nervous about finally meeting my father."

"Uncle Guy is a darling. He is the dearest person in the world although I have not seen much of him over the years. He has always kept in touch with me and with my brother Benoit, despite his problems with Grandmother. Benoit is longing to meet you also but did not want both of us to desert our parents at Christmas time."

Natalie kept up a constant chatter all that way to Guy's home. Millie was grateful for this as she was getting more and more nervous about coming face to face with her father for the first time. She looked out of the window at the snowy landscape, although the roads were fine. The snow ploughs had heaped huge, dirty piles of snow alongside the road on either side.

Finally, Natalie drove the car into a covered parking place in front of her uncle's single story house. She could see a face looking out of the window and as soon as they got out of the car, the door flew open and Guy was there, sitting in his wheelchair, smiling a welcome.

"Come in, come in, both of you. Get out of the cold quickly."

The two girls grabbed Millie's luggage and dashed inside. They closed the door and Millie looked around the room. A fire burned cheerfully in the spacious living room. The furniture was minimal and spaces between things were wide to allow space for Guy's wheelchair. There was a low-level kitchen area off the living room and two bedrooms. One was for Guy with a specially adapted bathroom off it and the other was a spare room, furnished simply with two single beds, for the girls to share. It had a bathroom across the hall.

Millie looked at her father, sitting in his wheelchair, an anxious look on his face. This was her father. She had hoped to feel an instant connection with him, but she felt only curiosity. A sliver of disappointment and hurt pierced her heart. How she had longed to feel the love for her father that she had felt for her mother. She brushed those feelings aside and smiled at Guy.

Her father had noticed the emotions flitting over his daughter's face and his heart ached for her. The poor child, she had been so let down. He resolved to be there for her even if she never came to love him.

Natalie showed Millie the room they were to share, and the two girls unpacked their things quickly and then Guy ordered a takeaway.

"I am sorry, I am not much of a cook," said Guy with a smile. "As I am usually writing all day, I get absorbed in what I am doing and forget to eat. I have a couple of ladies who take turns coming in to cook for me and to keep the place tidy. I also have a physiotherapist come in most days to help me keep fit. I am afraid I am relatively housebound, but I hope Natalie will drive you about to see the sights while you are both here."

Millie smiled, "That will be lovely, as long as you don't mind, Natalie?"

Natalie shook her head, "It is good to be here with Uncle Guy, but we must take advantage of the chance to see something other than his ugly face." Natalie grinned cheekily at her uncle.

They all laughed at that, Guy was anything but ugly, but he was able to laugh at himself.

After they eaten, Natalie tactfully said she needed a nice long shower and an early night. She wanted to give Guy and Millie a chance to get to know one another. Guy pulled his wheelchair up to the fire and motioned Millie to sit in the chair opposite him.

"First of all, Millie, why don't you call me Guy. If you ever want to call me Dad, I would be really happy about that. But, as we both know, I wasn't there when you needed me, and when your mother needed me too. I will always regret that, but we have to look forward now and try to make the future better for us both. I would like to know what life has been like for you. I guess things have been really tough for you, but I don't know any details. Are you able to talk about it?"

Millie looked at him, she chewed her lip thoughtfully. It was difficult for her to talk about some of the things that had happened to her, but if she were not willing to try to talk honestly with her father now, she reckoned that the time might never come again. She decided to tell him the truth. After all, her grandmother and her Aunt Vicky had not really wanted to know the truth. That had hurt Millie very much and so she had tried to bury the past. Perhaps it would be a relief to tell Guy exactly what had happened.

She told him everything she could remember, how bewildered she had been when her mother had disappeared. She described her time with Sofia and then with Nabila and Ali in the big house. She told him about the dreadful time that Hassim had taken her to the white house in the city and what the man had done to her. Guy was distraught at hearing that Millie had been abused and beaten in that dreadful way when only a small, defenseless child and his eyes filled with tears. This started Millie crying too. Guy reached forward and put his big, warm hands over his daughter's small ones.

"Can you go on or is that enough for one night?"

"No, I am okay, there is not much more to tell now."

She told him about Nabila trying to make Hassim stop hitting her, then hitting and kicking Nabila and how Ali had hit Hassim on the head with the stone. She described how they had hidden in the basement and that the next day they had run away to Tripoli. She told him how she had become separated from Nabila and Ali in the marketplace and how she had hidden down by the quayside. She described hearing Marie and Jim talking as they walked downy the quay, and how the way they spoke reminded her of her mother. She said how grateful she was to Marie and Jim as they had taken care of her and become her good friends. She told Guy how she had been taken to her grandmother's house and that she still didn't understand why Aunt Vicky had seemed to resent her.

Millie explained how Mrs. Bellman taught her to read and write and the awful day she had found her grandmother dead. She described being sent off to boarding school and not being allowed to attend her grandmother's funeral.

"That's about it now," she said. "I am at another boarding school now and will inherit some money from my grandmother when I am eighteen. I have three trustees and one is my legal guardian. They pay my school fees and my allowance into the bank and they take care of my inheritance money. I don't know exactly how much it is, but Aunt Vicky said I should buy a house with it so it must be quite a lot."

Guy sat for a while absorbing all she had told him. This poor girl had missed out on her so much. She had been denied the innocent childhood that she would have had if she had been looked after by both her parents. He frowned grimly. His mother had a great deal of unhappiness to answer for.

"I am so sorry that you had to face such awful experiences by yourself, Millie. I wish I could go back in time and change things, but I can't. All I can do is to be a good father to you now. Of course, you may have made plans for your future already, but I would like to be a part of your life from now on. I am prepared to sell this house and move to wherever you would like to live. If you would like to, perhaps we can arrange for you to come and live here with me for a while, for as long as you want, and go to school here. Then you can choose whether or not you want to make your permanent home with me. At least you would not be in a boarding school, you would be able to come home each day to a home. What do you say?"

Millie looked at Guy. She felt she could trust him, and she liked him, but she had no feeling of him being her father yet. She supposed perhaps it was because he was a man. She was wise enough to know that she had only ever felt love and affection from women so far in her life. She did like Jim, but her trust and affection was mostly directed at Marie, not her husband.

"I would like that. I think that, because your house is arranged to suit you and your chair and everything, it would be better if I came here so that we can get to know each other. We will have to convince my legal guardians, but I am pretty sure my Aunt Vicky doesn't care what I do. Why not say it is just for a year to start with and see how we go?"

Guy agreed and he said, "I know you want to know more about your mother and the time she lived with me. We will talk about that another time as I can see you are tired. I don't know how we can find out about where she went after she ran away from my home. Where does it say that you were born in your passport?"

"It says I was born in Menton, in the south of France."

"Menton, you say? There is a casino in Monte Carlo. Perhaps she knew someone in the show there. I will make some calls tomorrow and see what I can find out. Okay?"

Millie nodded, then yawned hugely.

"You are tired, why not go to bed now? Good night, Millie. Sleep well," said Guy

Millie went off to the bathroom to clean her teeth and tried to get ready for bed without disturbing Natalie, who was fast asleep.

The next morning, both girls woke late. They got up to find a friendly lady cleaning the house and a lovely smell of fresh coffee. There was no sign of Guy. The cleaning lady, Myra, told them he was with his physiotherapist in his room. The girls had breakfast and Myra told them she would be shopping for food. She asked what they liked to eat, and she would stock up the refrigerator. Natalie gave her a long list of foods to buy. "I am a good chef," Natalie told them proudly. "I am French, so of course I can cook."

Natalie went to tell Guy that they were going out to explore and would be back later. They went to the "Underground City," a mall under the *Place Ville Marie*. They had a wonderful morning trying on clothes and laughing at each other. Natalie was a very lively girl and great fun. Millie was reserved at first: she had never had a close female friend other than Marie. Natalie understood how Millie was feeling but was relentless in her efforts to make Millie laugh. She smiled triumphantly when she had finally made Millie giggle.

Natalie bought them both matching black fake fur-lined jackets. "For the cold" she said. After shopping, they went back to Guy's house to have lunch. For the next week they followed the pattern of going out in the day and spending time with Guy in the evening. Guy had to write in the day as he had a publisher's deadline to meet.

He made some telephone calls while they were out. Several calls were to Millie's guardian and trustees to obtain their agreement for her to come and live with him for a year at least. They agreed with the proviso that Millie's education should not suffer. The other calls were to friends back in France to ask them to try to find out where Rachel night have been in Monte Carlo around the time Millie had been born.

They celebrated Christmas together. Natalie cooked Christmas dinner but dispensed with the traditional English Christmas puddings and cake. Guy and Natalie drank wine, and Guy allowed Millie some, also in the French tradition. She had not tasted wine before and found it rather sour.

One evening Natalie excused herself early, "I have some girly maintenance to attend to. Goodnight to you both." She smiled and disappeared into the bedroom.

Guy and Millie pulled their chairs up to the fire.

"I had a call from some friends in Paris today," said Guy. "They have been checking some things for me about your mother. Apparently, a gay man, who was a choreographer in the show in Monte Carlo, had a friend staying with him at the time who was pregnant and who gave birth to a little girl. This guy took good care of your mother, and after you were born, he helped her to get the job in Beirut."

"Can we actually talk to this man?" asked Millie.

"Unfortunately, no. It seems he died of AIDS about five years ago."

"Oh, that's so sad," said Millie. "I would have liked to thank him for being kind to my mother."

Guy winced, he would never get over the guilt of his mother's unkindness to Rachel, his lovely, gentle Rachel. Her life had been such a tragedy after she had left him. They sat for a while talking about Rachel and Millie wanted to know all about their time together. Guy had lots of photographs of them as a couple and they sat together, tears in both their eyes looking at the pictures of Rachel, alive, happy and in love. Millie had begun to warm to Guy. Their love for Rachel was a bond between them, and it was a base upon which to start to build a relationship.

"The only thing I need to find out now is who killed her," said Millie.

"I don't know how we can find that out," frowned Guy. "I have no contacts in Lebanon and surely you wouldn't want to go back there?"

"No, I don't ever want to go back there. It is a funny thing, Guy, but I have feeling that I will find out somehow, some day, when the time is right."

Millie flew back to England the same day as Natalie flew back to France. Natalie had to go back to work, and Millie was going back to fetch her things from her old school and to pack more belongings to move to Montreal to start her life with Guy.

Millie went to stay with Irene and told her about going to stay with Guy for a year to see how they got on. Irene was pleased for Millie but assured her that she was always welcome to come back to stay with her and Janet at any time if she ever needed to. Janet agreed and reassured Millie that she always had a home with them. Millie hugged both women gratefully and promised to keep in touch.

She flew back to Montreal ready to start the next term. Guy's cleaning lady, Myra, took her to her new school to register on her first day. She was able to take most of the subjects she had been studying in England. There was also a drama department that Millie was keen to join and Guy had already arranged for her to take lessons at a dancing school near his home. She had been very touched that he remembered that she had said she loved her dancing lessons at boarding school.

Millie settled quickly in her new school and was pleasantly surprised that all her classmates were warm, outgoing young people and very friendly towards her. The first few weeks flew by as Millie got to know her classmates, and she and Guy rarely had time to chat. For the first time in her life, Millie was having fun with people her own age and she was relieved to find that she felt comfortable with some of the boys as well as the girls. Soon she was meeting groups of friends after school and at weekends.

Guy was very impressed with the way she settled down, but he was a little worried about the hectic social life Millie was getting involved in. He had hoped that they would become close in a father-daughter way, but Millie flew in and out of the door in a flurry of school, dancing lessons and social events and he saw little of her. He wanted to be responsible for her and to be a real father, but he was slightly constrained by the fact that he had not been there for her and Rachel when they had needed him.

He could no longer drive and so she had to get about by bus, taxis or in the cars driven by her young friends. This worried Guy as he could remember being a young man with his first car only too well. He tried to make sure Millie was always safe and with someone responsible, but she waved away his concerns. She assured him she knew who was safe to drive with and who wasn't.

Three months went by like a flash and Millie was due to celebrate her sixteenth birthday. Guy asked her if she would like something special for her birthday present. Millie thought hard. "I think I'd like a bicycle. Would that be all right?"

Guy smiled, "Of course it is, but it won't be much use to you in winter when it snows."

"I know," smiled Millie. "Very useful in the summer though."

Guy did not know it, but Millie had a serious crush on a boy at school called Antoine who went everywhere on his bike in good weather. She hoped she might bump into him now and again, although not literally. Millie got her bicycle for her birthday, and she kissed Guy when she thanked him.

Antoine had noticed Millie too. She was so different from other girls; she was mysterious and intriguing. She did not indulge in the usual flirty behaviour of other girls her age. She did not look coyly up at boys, flick her hair, or pout her lips as other girls did. Her expression was usually quite serious but when she smiled, she smiled with her whole face and endearing dimples appeared in her cheeks. She listened carefully to what people said and when she looked at someone, she gave them her whole attention. She was so different to other girls that Antoine hesitated to approach her, but he could hardly take his eyes off her. He noticed that Millie sometimes was looking back at him too, but nothing changed in her expression, and he could not judge if she liked him or not.

Several times in the next few weeks Guy was worried when Millie was late home after her dance class. He asked her to telephone if she was going to be late, and she said she would. However, the next time she was late she forgot to telephone.

"Millie, I am glad you are having fun at last, but I do need to know where you are, and if you are going to be back late, I wish you would telephone," said Guy firmly.

Millie pouted. She was finally having some fun and now Guy was trying to stop her. She flounced off to her room and slammed the door. Guy wheeled his chair down the corridor and demanded that Millie open the door.

"No, I won't! Leave me alone!" shouted Millie.

Guy thought for a while and decided to leave her alone for the moment. He was utterly perplexed. Millie had seemed to be too quiet and well-behaved when he first met her but in the space of a few weeks she had changed completely. He had no experience of being the parent of a teenage daughter and he had no idea how to cope. He decided to telephone Natalie to get her advice.

He told Natalie what was happening, and he was taken aback when she laughed.

"Uncle Guy, I think that it is very good news that Millie is starting to behave like a normal teenager. She was much too quiet and passive before. It is only her hormones acting up, Uncle, and I don't think you have much to worry about. She is probably in love with a boy."

"Good Lord," exclaimed Guy. "What have I let myself in for."

Just then Millie walked into the living room and heard what Guy said. She burst into tears and ran back into her room, slamming the door again.

Natalie laughed when he told her what happened. "Uncle, dear, I think I need to come for another little holiday. I think you need someone to hold your hand."

"Would you, Natalie, dear?" said Guy with relief. "I think someone needs to explain the birds and bees to Millie."

"Sadly, I think she does know something about it, Uncle, but perhaps not the right things. But you are right, she knows little about how to deal with rampant teenage boys. I will come as soon as I can organize it."

Guy went down to Millie's room and knocked on the door. "I am going to bed soon, Millie. If you want to talk, I will be up for another half an hour."

Millie never appeared, so he went to bed. The next morning Millie was quiet at breakfast time. Guy made her some toast and a cup of tea. She sat, hugging the mug in her hands, not speaking.

"You know, Millie, I think you are right to be cross. I have not been around to be your father and you have managed to survive some dreadful events all on your own. It must seem like I am trying to spoil your fun, but really, I'm not. You see, Millie, I have missed out on being a father just as you have missed out on being a daughter. I am just learning what a father feels like, and you have no idea how worrying it is to finally find your daughter and then start to worry about losing her."

Millie looked up at him, a smile starting to tug at the corner of her mouth. "I am sorry, I am just having such a good time. I have never been with people my own age before who seem to like me just as I am. I did not mean to worry you. I have had to look after myself till now, and it felt for a moment like Aunt Vicky. She hated me to be happy and enjoying myself. She even tried to stop me seeing Marie and Jim sometimes. I hated her for that, but I was too scared to say anything in case she sent me away."

"Oh, you poor little soul. Of course, I want you to have fun and I am glad that the other kids are being friendly. All I want you to think about is that there are dangers everywhere, not just in Lebanon. You still have to watch out for yourself here too. This is a big city and not everyone here is as nice as your friends. There are bad people here too. I would like it if you had your fun, but just let me know where you are and which friends you are with. Is that okay?"

Millie said she would in future and dashed off to school. That afternoon, before Millie got home from school, Natalie rang.

"Uncle Guy, I can't come to visit just now. Grandmother has had a stroke and is in the hospital."

"Is it serious?" said Guy.

"Well, yes, I think it is extremely serious. If she does survive, and that seems unlikely, they say she will probably be brain damaged. We won't know for a few days probably."

"Do you think I should come over?' said Guy.

"No, Papa say that you should wait. She is in a coma, and she won't know you are there. You should not interrupt Millie's schooling unnecessarily."

"Maybe you are right. I will wait to hear from you."

Guy put the telephone down and sat thinking. His mother had not been the warmest of parents and she had behaved unforgivably towards Rachel and Millie, but she was still his mother. He was sad that she had missed out on such a lot of happiness by being such a cold, snobbish woman.

He heard Millie's key in the lock. She came in and dumped her schoolbag on the floor.

"What's the matter, Guy? You look sad. I came straight home just to please you," she teased.

Guy smiled at her. He told her about his mother. Millie pulled a sour face.

"I am sorry, Guy, I can't feel sad for her. She is a horrible person, and I really don't care if she lives or dies."

Guy was shocked at her bluntness, but he understood. Millie had no reason to feel any sympathy for his mother. She had, after all, felt no pity for Millie's mother. Three days later Natalie called to say that her grandmother died without regaining consciousness. Guy and Millie had discussed what they would do in that event. They had decided that they would both fly back to Paris for the funeral.

"You won't have to go to a hotel, Uncle Guy. You can stay in Grandmother's apartment. It is on the ground floor and suitable for your wheelchair," suggested Natalie.

They flew to Paris the next day and Natalie met them at the airport. Natalie loaned Millie a black coat as she had no suitable black clothes. The whole family was going to the funeral and Millie was glad to meet her other cousin, Benoit, for the first time. He had brown hair a little darker than her own and very pale skin. He wore glasses and was a quiet, bookish young man but he smiled shyly at Millie.

The funeral was held in a large ancient church. Many people were there, most seeming very haughty and snobbish to Millie's eyes. They looked down their noses at people around them. She stood behind Guy's chair hoping that no one would notice her or expect her to talk. Natalie seemed to understand how she felt so she talked to everyone who came over to give their condolences so that Millie was left alone.

Afterwards they went back to the house and Natalie's mother, Denise, laid on a dinner in their enormous apartment on the first floor. Guy went up to the apartment in the ancient creaky lift, but there was no room for Millie in there with him, so she ran up the stairs. Denise and Henri, Guy's brother and sister-in-law, were kind to Millie but not overly demonstrative. Millie did not mind at all; Guy and Natalie were family enough for her. She did not realise that all the years of living under the old grandmother's overbearing thumb had affected Denise and Henri too. They had almost forgotten how to be relaxed and open.

Guy went to the solicitor's office with his brother to find out what was in his mother's will. Guy was surprised to find that his mother had left him her own ground floor apartment. His brother, Henri was to have the first-floor apartment he already lived in. There was very little money in her estate. Henri had been supporting his mother financially for years without telling anyone. What little money she had left was to go to Henri, which Guy considered fair. She had also left the top apartment jointly to Natalie and Benoit,

Thankfully all the family were happy with the contents of the will. Henri asked Guy what he was going to do with the apartment. "Why don't you come back to France and live in it? It would be ideal for you and for Millie. You can write your books anywhere. You will have people close by if you need anything and Millie will get to know her family," said Henri.

Guy smiled at his brother, it was a generous thing to say, especially as Guy had been away for so many years.

"I will give it some serious thought. It does sound a good idea, as long as all the family agree with you," and Guy looked at his sister-in-law, Denise. She smiled back quite warmly.

"I think, Guy, that there has been too much distance between the members of this family for far too long. We have the opportunity to do things differently now."

Millie was the only one who was not happy about this idea. She was having fun in Montreal and there was Antoine too. He was just beginning to take notice of her, and now her father was talking about coming back to France. Millie had had to struggle to learn English properly and to catch up in an English school. Then she had to adjust to a French-language school in Montreal.

The language would not be a problem in France, but switching schools again would take her away from her friends… and Antoine… She didn't say anything as she thought she would discuss it later with Guy. Later that evening, when Millie and Guy were back in the downstairs apartment, Guy asked Millie about the idea of coming to live in France.

"I can understand that you would like that," said Millie a trifle grumpily, "but, Guy, I have only been in school for a few years and had to learn to speak English and better French as well as catch up with the other girls. It would be hard to adjust to another school." Millie had reckoned that this would be a good enough reason to deter Guy from moving back to France.

"But you could always attend one of the English-speaking schools, such as the American School. I am sure there is more than one high school in Paris that teaches in English. Anyway, it could take a long time to sell my house as it is specially adapted for a wheelchair user. I don't suppose it will sell for months."

Millie pouted; this conversation was not going the way she wanted at all.

"Well, I could always go back to school in England and come over to Paris to visit you in the holidays." Millie wondered how Guy would take to that suggestion.

Guy looked at Millie closely. He knew that she was enjoying the freedom of her life in Montreal, but he could not help feeling concerned that she was going a little wild. He realised that the teenage years could be difficult but had underestimated how much it would worry him. He saw moving back to France and the stricter regime that young people were accustomed to might mean that Millie might be protected from her own vulnerability. He was very worried that she was too new to the freedom that teenagers had in Canada and might not be able to handle some of the situations that she might encounter. He wondered if she could handle a boy trying to have sex with her. She might either be upset because of having been mistreated as a child or, with her lack of sophistication, she might confuse lust for love.

"I tell you what," Guy said to Millie, "we'll go back and think it over for the rest of term and then, if we decide to come to Paris to live, then we will put my apartment up for sale. What do you think of that idea?"

Millie had no good reason to say no. After all, she could understand her father wanting to be around his family after all the years of estrangement. They flew back to Canada and Millie went back to school. Antoine had missed her while she had been away and asked where she had been. She told him that she had been to her grandmother's funeral in Paris.

"Oh, I am sorry," he said sympathetically.

"Don't be," said Millie. "She was a horrible old woman who made a lot of people unhappy. I was quite glad she died."

Antoine laughed, rather shocked and embarrassed. "Wow, you really didn't like the old gal, did you?"

"I had no reason to like her. She separated my mother and father before I was born. Because of her, my mother died, and I had a really bad time. She robbed me of my mother, my father, and a normal life. Why would I be sorry she died?"

"When you put it like that, no reason to be sorry at all."

Millie smiled at Antoine, "Enough gloomy talk. Let's go down to the coffee shop, I could murder a latte and a cake"

By the end of term, they had become girlfriend and boyfriend, spending as much time as possible together. Millie never took him back to the house or introduced him to Guy, she wanted to keep him a secret as she was afraid Guy would say she was too young for a boyfriend and her feelings for Antoine were a delicious secret she didn't want to share just yet.

During the holiday, Millie went out a lot, telling Guy she was out in a group but in fact she was often alone with Antoine. They went to the cinema, and to a pop concert. Most of the time they just walked and talked. Millie told him a lot about her life in Lebanon but could not talk about the man abusing her. She tried to shut that event out of her mind.

Antoine kissed her often but never tried to touch her anywhere private. As they spent more time together, their kisses became more ardent. One day he asked her if she wanted to come to his house to listen to some music. She agreed as she trusted him. When they got to his house his family were all out. She looked round the living room, it was a messy and homely room. The sofas were of the saggy, comfortable sort and plants stood in every corner.

Antoine took her up to his room, a typical teenage boy's bedroom, posters on the wall, a computer on a desk in the corner and an untidy, unmade bed. Antoine smoothed his bed cover a little. There was no chair in the room except his computer chair, so they sat on the bed. Antoine put on some music, then he put his arm round Millie and kissed her tenderly. She kissed him back.

Their kisses got more and more passionate and then Antoine slid his hand up her sweater and caressed her breast. Millie could hardly breathe, it felt so wonderful to be wanted and loved by the boy she cared for.

Antoine got more and more aroused and put his hand on her thigh. A little flicker of panic pierced Millie's heart. Antoine slid his hand up her skirt and inside her knicker leg. Millie could not help herself reacting, panic overcame passion. A horrible image of the tall, thin man's face, and cold, snake-like eyes as he had attacked her, came into her head. She pushed Antoine away and shouted, "No, no!"

"Hey, it's okay. We don't have to do anything you don't want," said Antoine. Millie's eyes were wide and wild, and she seemed not to see him. Her extreme reaction puzzled him.

"Millie, Millie, it's okay. Don't be upset. I won't do that again."

Millie struggled into her coat. "I want to go home, sorry, I'm sorry! I've got to go."

"Okay," said Antoine. "I'll walk you home."

"No, it's okay," said Millie tearfully. "I'll be all right. I just want to go home."

Millie left and walked quickly home. Guy was in his room writing when she went in, so she could go to her room without having to talk. She took off her coat and lay on the bed.

Tears streamed down her cheeks. She didn't understand her own reaction. She had been hoping that Antoine would take notice of her, and she had been thrilled that he had wanted her to be his girlfriend. She had really been enjoying their kisses but, when he had touched her in that way, a wave of revulsion had come over her and she had been transported instantly back to that hot, sweet-smelling room in Beirut. She had not seen Antoine's nice, honest face; she had seen instead the snakelike eyes of the man who had stolen her innocence when she was just a little girl.

Millie turned her face to the pillow and sobbed her heart out. Antoine wouldn't want her to be his girlfriend now. She had ruined everything. How could she face Antoine again? He must have thought she was weird. When Guy knocked on her door later that evening to ask if she wanted to eat, she told him she didn't feel well and just wanted to sleep. The next morning, she came into the living room with a pale, sad face.

"You don't look well, Millie, why don't you stay home today?'

Millie poured herself a glass of juice, "I think I will. I have a bit of a headache. By the way, Guy, I don't mind if you put the house up for sale and we go to live in France."

Guy looked at her with surprise, "Are you sure, Millie?"

Millie kept her expression normal while her heart broke inside. "Yes, I'm quite sure. Go ahead and put the house up for sale."

Millie went back into her room and shut the door. There was no point staying in Canada now. She had ruined things with Antoine. He would not understand, and she couldn't explain to him why she acted as she did; she hardly understood it herself. She adored Antoine, she trusted him, but she had acted as if he was trying to force himself on her. He wouldn't want to know her now. She laid on her bed and cried bitterly.

Guy put the house up for sale and, to his surprise, received several offers within days. It seemed that houses adapted for people in wheelchairs were in great demand. The sale was agreed with the highest bidder and when Millie went back to school, she told all her friends she was going to live with her father in Paris.

Antoine was listening when she was telling them and tried to catch her eye. He wanted to talk to Millie to reassure her that they could take it slower if she wanted, but she avoided talking to him. He decided that if she wanted to leave Canada, she had gone off him and very reluctantly he left her alone.

The days flew by till the day came to leave the house in Montreal. Guy had sold most of the furniture with the house and all they had to pack up was their books and personal stuff. Most of this was collected and shipped off to France. Guy's physiotherapist lady, Jane, drove them to the airport and kissed Guy sadly goodbye. She had carried a secret yen for him for a long time and was sad to see him leave.

They landed in France, tired and emotional after the long flight. Natalie met them at the airport in a large taxi to accommodate all their bags and Guy's wheelchair. They arrived at the house and were happy to see that a lot of changes had been made. The front door had been painted a glossy black, and the hallway was now sleek and modern. They went into the ground floor apartment and were thrilled to see that it had been completely redecorated.

All the old-fashioned furniture and carpets were gone and the smooth wooden floors had been stripped and sealed. Modern furniture had been installed and the kitchen and bathrooms had been refurbished to suit Guy and Millie. The two bedrooms had also been redecorated. Millie's was a pretty, feminine room done out in cream with coffee and lavender accents. Millie loved it immediately. Guy's bedroom was neat, streamlined and masculine. His bathroom was en-suite, as it had been in Montreal, and adapted for his disability. Millie had the use of the other bathroom.

"Natalie, this is all wonderful, but it must have cost a fortune," said Guy, gazing about him with approval.

"Ah," said Natalie with a smile. "Papa thought the old décor might remind you too much of the past. All Grandmother's furniture was antique, and he sold it for a great deal of money. This money he gave to me and asked me to change everything to suit you both. I have tried my best to arrange it as I thought you would like it. But there is still some money left over so we can buy some more things, such as pictures, if you want. Papa has also had the lift updated. Grandmother would never agree to it while she was alive. I have to say that changing things has done us all good. We are all much happier and Maman and Papa have quite come out of their shell. They are out all the time, going to the theatre and the opera. They have even booked a cruise for the very first time and will be leaving next week."

Guy was impressed. His brother had always seemed too quick to appease his mother and he was glad that he was finally free of her demoralising control.

"Thank you, Natalie, for doing such a fantastic job with the redecoration. I am most impressed. You could make a career of interior design. It is marvellous, isn't it, Millie?"

Millie kissed her cousin's cheek, "It is all fantastic and makes us feel so welcome. I was rather dreading living in this apartment with all your grandmother's things around. Now it feels like a different place. Thank you so much! You are a darling."

Natalie was so pleased at their approval and kissed them both.

"I'll leave you now to settle in and I will come back later. We will all go out for a celebration dinner together."

Millie unpacked their clothes while Guy got on the telephone to get Millie into a good school where French and English were taught equally. He was successful and told Millie that she could start the following Monday. Natalie and Guy would go with her the next day to register and to show her where it was. She could get to the school on the Metro, but they would go by taxi the first time as Guy wanted to make sure the school would be the right place for his daughter.

While they waited for the family to come to take them to the restaurant, Millie went into her room and sat in her chair looking out of the window which looked out over a courtyard at the rear of the building. An old woman sat in the courtyard knitting. Some pigeons strutted round her feet and fluttered up and down to a high wall and into a tall tree on the other side of the wall. It was nice to see some greenery from her window.

In her solitude, she thought of Antoine. She still had strong feelings for him and sighed. She knew she would probably never see him again and that made her dreadfully sad. She rested her chin in her hands and tried hard not to cry.

They had a good time at the family dinner. Everyone was in a relaxed mood, and they all felt that it was a new beginning as a family. Millie felt included in the general feeling of goodwill and began to think that perhaps she would enjoy being part of a family here in Paris. She felt a bond with Natalie and her cousin's warm acceptance made her feel welcome.

Chapter Twenty – Paris Again

Millie settled in her new school, but the standard was higher than in her school in Montreal and initially she struggled. She had to have some extra tutoring to help her to keep up. Her school friends did not enjoy the freedom to do what they liked as her friends in Canada had. She missed the informality of her life there and her moody behaviour pushed Guy to raise his voice at her sometimes.

She enrolled in a dance class, partly because she enjoyed dancing, but mostly to have an excuse to be out on her own after school hours. The other young people at the dance class were more like her Canadian friends, open and friendly, and she often joined them after class for a coffee. They all liked Millie and she started to go about with them in the evenings, even when they had no classes. They often met up at weekends as well but never stayed much past ten o'clock in the evening as their families did not allow it.

One of the girls in the dance class was a Russian girl called Valentina. Her burning ambition was to become a Bluebell Girl in the *Lido de Paris* show. She was tall and willowy and had a beautiful elfin face, so

Millie told her that she was sure to be successful. Valentina was only seventeen, too, and her parents hoped she would change her mind before she became eighteen and was able try for a job at the *Lido*. They wanted her to become a classical ballerina.

"Why don't you try for a job at the *Lido* too?" said Valentina to Millie.

Millie said, "I haven't had enough dancing lessons. I am not nearly as good as you."

"You are very beautiful, and you dance very well. You are nearly tall enough. Maybe you will grow a bit in the next few months."

"Well, if I do, I'll apply for a job when you do, okay?"

The two girls quickly became close friends. Millie would go to Valentina's home, a rather dingy, poky flat in a back street. Valentina's parents worked long hours. Her father was a cutter in a bespoke tailor's and her mother worked as a waitress. They had left Russia because they wanted their daughter to grow up in freedom and to be able to choose her own career. She could have trained to be a ballerina in Russia, but her options and freedom were greater in Paris.

Valentina sometimes came to Millie's home, and she was a overawed by the luxury of the apartment. She was surprised when Millie told her that she had only known her father for a year. She told Valentina all about her life up till she had gone to live with her father, leaving out the part about the horrible man who had abused her so cruelly. She never wanted to tell anyone but her father about that. It disgusted and horrified her to think about it. She imagined that if she told people about it, they would look at her with the same horror and disgust that she felt about it herself.

Time passed with Millie going to school, then going to her dancing lessons and spending all her other free time with Valentina. Guy was usually immersed in his latest book. Writing took all his concentration, and he was content when he did raise his head from his PC that Millie seemed to be well, happy and behaving herself. Valentina was not allowed out late by herself and so Millie was always home at a reasonable time.

On Sundays, the whole family had a meal together up in Henri and Denise's apartment or in a local restaurant. Natalie was always lively and cheerful and good at keeping the conversation going. After her success at refurnishing Guy and Millie's apartment she had asked her father if she could go back to college to study interior design. He had agreed eagerly. Henri had always thought that working in a bank was not the right job for his daughter; It was his mother who had arranged it. She had asked an old family friend who was a director at Natalie's bank to give her a job. Natalie had been unable to refuse the position without causing extreme embarrassment to her grandmother. She had made the best of her job but never enjoyed it. She was thrilled to be able to study a subject that she found inspiring and which she felt she had a talent for.

Natalie and Millie got on very well but there was quite an age gap between them, so they did not spend much time together. While Natalie was working full time she was not around when Millie was in the house, but when she started her interior design course, she was home during the day more often and would take Millie out on shopping expeditions to the boutiques where young people bought their clothes in *Boulevard St Germain* and *Les Halles*. Millie was not particularly fashion conscious, generally to be found wearing jeans and long-sleeved tee shirts, but Natalie bought her some more innovative clothes, and she gradually evolved an interesting style of her own.

Millie's golden, brown hair was long and hung in coils down her back. Most of the time she wore it in a high ponytail. She would wrap colourful scarves round the bands holding her hair up and let the long ends hang down with her hair. Millie had no valuable jewellery and did not want any. She liked bold colourful necklaces and bracelets made of beads, or Indian costume jewellery, the more inexpensive the better. She had rather a hippie style that reminded Guy of Rachel, quite painfully at times. One time, she was shopping with Natalie in a market selling vintage clothing, and she came home with a long sheepskin coat that was the image of one that her mother had worn. She had asked Guy if he liked it and he said that he did, with tears in his eyes. Millie looked so like her mother when she wore it.

Guy was sometimes disappointed that he and Millie had not become closer over time. She had never called him "Father" or "Dad" – although he would have loved it if she had. He supposed it might have been different if he were not tied to the wheelchair or did not have such a time-consuming profession. When he started to write, he got so involved in his plot that he could look up what seemed a short time later to find the whole day had passed, and he had forgotten to eat lunch again.

Sometimes he asked Millie if she was happy. She would always smile and answer that she was. Guy had to be content with that. He felt that he did not have the right to ask more than that she do her best at school, which she did, or to come home at a reasonable time, which she was careful to do since they had been in Paris. He could not help feeling that Millie did not appear to want to be closer to him. They shared their apartment like a couple of roommates, not father and daughter, and he could not help thinking that this was not right, but he did not know what to do about it.

When Millie turned eighteen, she received a letter from her legal guardians telling her that her legacy was now her own to use as she wanted and that she no longer needed to have a legal guardian. They suggested that she leave the money where it was for the time being until she needed it for buying a house, for instance, and they would arrange for her to receive the interest from the money as an income if she required it. They assured her that it had been invested very carefully to bring her the highest return possible without too much risk, and they included a statement of where and how it was invested.

Millie showed the letter to Guy and asked him what she should do. He recommended that she do as her guardians suggested. He said that she could open a bank account in Paris and arrange to have some of the money transferred into the account and she could have a debit card so that she could draw out money when she needed it. He also suggested opening a deposit account and arranging for a regular amount to be paid into it from her bank account as he didn't think she would need to use much of it. He said he would continue to give her cash to spend if she needed spending money and so her money would still be there in the future if she needed it.

Natalie went with Millie to open the bank account as Millie's French was still not good enough to read contracts. It gave Millie a good feeling to know that she had enough money to one day buy her own house if she needed to, but she did not want the responsibility at her age. She was quite happy to live with her father in the apartment for the moment.

When the school term finished, Guy asked Millie what she wanted to do after the summer holidays. Did she want to go to college and what did she want to do when she finally left school? Millie was non-committal, and said she wanted to think about it. Guy said she should take all the time she wanted. In fact, both Millie and Valentina knew what they wanted to do. She and Valentina had written to the *Lido de Paris* nightclub asking for the chance to become dancers in the Lido dance troupe, giving their dance teacher's name as a reference. They kept it a secret from both their families as they were not sure such a career would be approved of.

Eventually they each received a reply from the *Lido* asking them to come for an audition. Their dance teacher told them she had given them both a glowing reference, and as she had been a former Bluebell girl herself and knew the requirements, they had given the girl's letter serious consideration after telephoning their teacher to check on them.

They attended the auditions with several other girls, still keeping it a secret from their families. To their joy and pride, they were both offered jobs as dancers in the world-famous Bluebell Girls dance troupe, started by Margaret Kelly. They left the theatre in high spirits and went home to inform their families.

Valentina's family were a little disappointed that she was not going to try to be a ballerina as they had hoped, but when she said that she was thrilled to get the job, they were happy for her. She would be earning more money than in a *corps de ballet*, so it was easy for them to be happy for her. Things were not so easy for Millie. Guy was desperately disappointed that Millie didn't want to carry on studying or go to university.

"I think you could get a degree and have a proper profession, Millie. You can only dance when you are young. What if you get injured, or maybe can only get a job in another country? You will not have a profession to fall back on."

Millie scowled, she did not like having cold water poured on her dreams.

"I can still teach dancing. You forget, I have plenty of money and if I cannot dance, I still can live on the money."

"That's true," admitted Guy reluctantly, "but that money is for your future and a profession will mean you have a way of making a living after you are no longer young."

Millie got angry and shouted at Guy, "Why did everyone encourage Natalie to follow her dream and go back to studying and you don't want me to do what I want to do?"

"No, no, Millie," Guy was getting flustered now as Millie had raised what seemed a very valid point. "I don't want to crush your dreams. You have never said before that you wanted to dance for a living. I just thought it was a hobby, just something you liked to do in your spare time."

Millie spoke quietly now, "Dancing is what I do, dancing is what I am. Just like my mother. You were happy enough for her to be a dancer. Well, why can't you be happy for me to be a dancer?"

Guy was silent. He could not think of a single good argument to that.

"Just promise me that you will continue to live here at home with me. I will try to be happy for you to be a dancer. Truthfully, I am very proud of you for getting a job in the best dance troupe in the world. I suppose I am worried that you will get offered a job in another country eventually and I will lose you as I lost your mother."

Millie narrowed her eyes. He had done a quick about turn and she suspected he was still not happy about her being a dancer.

"There's no reason for me to leave home. Valentina got a job there too and we can share a taxi home each night. I will be very quiet even if it is late and won't disturb you"

"When do you start work there?" he asked.

"We have to go for class next Monday morning. We will have to learn all the routines and they will fit us with costumes. They said we would be dancing on stage in a couple of weeks."

She smiled at Guy, "Please be happy for me. I have dreamed of being a dancer ever since I first had dancing lessons at boarding school in England. When I am dancing it is the only time I am really, truly happy. Can't you understand that?"

Guy held his hand out to her. He so wished he was not trapped in this chair and could just hug her.

"I do understand, darling. You must do what makes you happy."

Natalie was happy for Millie and even Benoit was quite taken with the idea of a Bluebell girl for a cousin. Henri and Denise tried hard to appear to be pleased but were secretly very glad that their own children were pursuing 'more respectable' careers.

Millie started work the next Monday. Natalie drove her and Valentina to the theatre where they were to rehearse. They had a dance class first to warm up and then spent the entire day learning the dance routines. Several other girls and young men started on the same day. They were all filling vacancies left by dancers who had taken jobs in other similar shows in Las Vegas.

The girls danced hard all week but were given the weekend off to rest. The next week was more of the same and the girls were exhausted but completely happy. They were allowed to sit in the stalls and watch the rehearsals when they were not dancing. The costumes were incredible, lavish concoctions of sparkling sequins and ostrich feathers, dyed in gorgeous colours. In between the dance numbers there were speciality acts. These were acrobats, a magician and some jugglers.

When one of the lavish dance numbers finished, a curtain would fall, and the acts would come on to perform in front of the curtain. Behind the front curtain the scenery for the next dance number would be changed. Sometimes an act would be made part of the dance numbers. In a number with a Greek theme, two statuesque male acrobats, dressed in nothing but a g-string, and gold greasepaint, did a slow sensual balancing act, demonstrating their extreme athleticism and balletic grace.

Millie and Valentina gradually made friends with other dancers. Valentina was rather disappointed to learn that the male dancers, who were extremely handsome, were all either married or gay. They worked extremely hard and were soon ready to start in the show. They had been fitted with their costumes and shown how to apply the heavy stage makeup and the necessary false eyelashes so that their faces could be seen at the back of the huge auditorium.

Guy and the whole family arranged to attend on their first night. The two girls were hard to spot under all the feathers and heavy makeup, but eventually they worked out which one was Millie and which was Valentina. Valentina's parents could not afford the cost so Millie paid for them as a thank you for their hospitality to her.

The two girls soon became accustomed to the routine of dancing in the show. They had one night off a week and, because they were working so hard physically, they usually slept all day. Guy saw even less of Millie than he did before, and it worried him that they seemed to be drifting ever more apart.

Because the two girls were working at night, they did not keep up their old friendships with their school friends. They were dependent on each other and the other dancers in the show for companionship. The conversations backstage was often rather racy, and Millie and Valentina became accustomed to hearing and ignoring things that would bring a blush to the cheeks of a stevedore. Show business was a refuge for people, often very talented, whose morals would outrage normal society if they knew about it. Seeing people walking about in a state of almost complete nudity soon became a completely normal thing to both girls.

Sometimes they were invited to parties thrown by other dancers after the show. They would all pile into taxis and squeeze in great numbers into someone's apartment. The drink would flow, and the talk would become naughtier as people got more inebriated. People did take drugs of various sorts, but the girls would decline if they had been offered them. They were not pressed to try them and were much too scared to experiment.

One time they were at a party in an older man's apartment. Someone started to play a pornographic film. Valentina wanted to watch it, but it really upset Millie and she had to leave. It reminded her of being beaten and abused, but she did not want to explain this to Valentina. Her friend reluctantly agreed to leave the party with Millie, and they called a taxi to take them home.

The months flew by, but although dancing was hard physical work, Millie absolutely loved it and she was truly happy. Because of their working hours, they spent less and less time with their families and more and more time with the other dancers in the show. One night, after the show, the two girls were introduced to a very sleek, well-groomed Italian man. His name, he said, was Alessandro Fortunelli. He was representing the producer of a show in Las Vegas, and he wanted to offer them both a job in a new show to start in five months' time. He asked them how long their contracts had to run, and they told him they finished in three months' time. He asked them to come to his hotel the next day and he would meet them in the restaurant and buy them lunch.

They went to the restaurant and saw Mr. Fortunelli sitting on his own at a table in the window. He smiled and raised a hand to indicate they should sit down at the table. "Good afternoon, ladies. I am very glad you decided to come. Please call me Sandro, not Mr. Fortunelli. Now, please order whatever you like and, after we've eaten, we'll talk."

They ordered and enjoyed their lunch very much. Sandro was very amusing company. He kept them enthralled with stories of the big stars who were featured in the Las Vegas shows and about all the big hotels down the Las Vegas Strip. He described the fantastic revues put on at all the largest hotels. He told them about the "high rollers," the gamblers who won and lost huge sums at the gaming tables. He made Las Vegas sound like a vibrant and exciting place. Over coffee, Sandro leaned back in his chair and smiled in rather a feline way at the girls.

"So, have you given my offer any thought?"

The girls looked at each other. They were very tempted. Las Vegas was the place that all the dancers in their show wanted to go to. They could not easily turn down such an offer, but they were sure their families would be unhappy about them leaving Paris.

Valentina said, "We both want to, very much. It is just that our families will be upset."

"I understand," said Sandro, "But they have lived their lives and made their choices. You have your own lives to live. I think you should do what you want to do. I suggest you talk it over and call me tomorrow with your decision. Here is the telephone number of my hotel. I will wait until midday tomorrow to hear from you. After that I will soon be leaving to fly back to the USA. Is that okay with you girls?"

Valentina and Millie nodded and thanked Sandro for their lunch. The two girls went back to Millie's house and shut the door to Millie's room behind them.

"What shall we do?" whispered Millie.

"I think we should go," said Valentina. "It's a chance we might never get again. There are so many shows in Las Vegas we need never be out of work again."

"I know my father will be very sad to see me go," said Millie doubtfully.

"Look, Millie, he had his career. He went off to Canada, didn't he? This is your time now. Don't you think that you have had enough bad luck? It is your turn to have good luck, excitement and to achieve as much as you can in your career. A dancer's career is often a short one, so you cannot afford to turn down a spectacular offer like this one."

"I suppose you are right. This opportunity may not ever come again." Millie gave her friend a hug. "I will only go because you are going. We will be together there, won't we?"

Valentina smiled, happy now she had persuaded her friend into going. "We will do everything together. Nothing will separate us."

Valentina went home to tell her parents and Millie sat in her room, trying to get the courage to tell Guy. The two girls were going to meet before they went to work and to drop a note off at Sandro's hotel telling him that they wanted the job, and to leave him their telephone numbers. Millie went to find Guy. He was in his study, working on his latest book.

"Can I interrupt you, Guy?"

"Yes, of course Millie. Is anything the matter?" He had noticed her serious expression.

"No, nothing's wrong. In fact, it is the opposite. Something wonderful has happened, but I don't think you will like it."

Guy's heart sank. *"What was she up to now?"* he thought to himself.

"Valentina and I have been offered a job in the biggest show in Las Vegas. Our contracts finish in three months and then, if we accept the offer, we will go over to America to rehearse. We have talked it over and we have decided we want to take the job."

Guy sat, his head down. He had expected that one day Millie would have to move elsewhere in pursuit of her career but had hoped it would not happen as soon as this. He had no right to try to stop her. He decided not to fight it as he did not want her to turn against him. Even if she went away to work for a year or two, the chances were that she would come back to Paris again afterwards if they had stayed on good terms.

"Darling, I am so proud of you. It is a wonderful opportunity for you, one that your mother would have loved to have had. Take the job, if you are sure about it, but promise me one thing. Please will you remember that if things are not happy for you in America you will always remember that your home is here for you, just waiting for you to come back to."

Millie rushed over to his chair and leaned over to hug him.

"Thanks, Dad, for being so understanding." She whirled away to rush off to telephone Valentina to discuss how to write their note to Sandro accepting his job offer.

Guy sat in his wheelchair, his eyes moist with unshed tears. He had longed to hear her call him Dad, and now she had, but only because she was relieved that he was letting her go without an argument. How ironic that was. What was that old saying about your children, "If you want to keep your children's love, let them fly free." He hoped that she would always come back to him.

Chapter Twenty-One – Las Vegas

Sandro had been very glad they had decided to take his offer and had delayed his flight hone for long enough to talk to them the details of the job, like salaries, and to make sure he had their addresses to send their contracts to. He said they should sign the contracts, return one copy to him and he would send them their air tickets a few days before they were due to travel. He offered to arrange temporary accommodation for them at a motel near the casino until they could arrange to rent a house or apartment. The girls gratefully accepted his offer of help with their accommodations.

The last three months of the girl's contract in Paris passed quickly. The management of the *Lido* were sorry to see the two girls leave but understood their desire to go to Las Vegas. Guy and Natalie were both desperately sad to see Millie go.

The day came for them to leave. Valentina's father had offered to drive them to the airport. The girls each had two large cases and squeezed them into Valentina's father's car. Millie was in the back seat squashed by luggage. The two girls were incredibly excited. Valentina was so excited she couldn't sit still or keep quiet. She babbled on and on, her father grunting unhappily in the front seat.

They reached the airport and unloaded the cases. Valentina's father loaded them on to a baggage trolley and then hugged and kissed his daughter goodbye. Valentina burst into tears and Millie had to push the trolley as Valentina was crying too much to see where she was going. Once they were inside the airport terminal Valentina cheered up. They checked in and, once free of the heavy cases, happily roamed around the Departure Lounge shops and drank coffee and ate pastries until their flight was called.

The flight was long, and they had to change planes in Chicago. The second flight was about four hours long and by the time they reached Las Vegas, the two girls were tired and tetchy with each other. Jet lag added to the tension between them.

As they left the air-conditioned airport, the hot desert air hit them like the heat from an oven and they felt as if they couldn't breathe. They found a taxi and asked for the Cactus Inn, the motel that Sandro said he had booked for them. They drove down the Strip and at first there was not much to see other than sand but after a few minutes they saw huge skyscraper hotels on either side of the road. They passed the grand Dunes Hotel with the tall figure of a smiling Ali Baba outside. He stood smiling with a colourful turban on his head and striped baggy pantaloons. Millie and Valentina loved him.

The taxi turned off the strip and into a motel shaped like a Spanish *hacienda*. In front was a desert-style garden of palm trees, cacti and spiky ground cover underneath. They checked in and a bell boy loaded their cases on to a cart and pulling it behind him, showed them to their room. It was like a small apartment with a bedroom containing twin beds, a living area with a TV, a settee and a small kitchen at one end. In the small but well-equipped bathroom was a shower over the bath. It smelled a bit stuffy, but the bell boy showed them how to regulate the air-conditioning. They unpacked some of their clothes, fell into bed and slept.

The next morning, Millie woke up before Valentina. She peeped out of the curtains. The day was already hot and sunny. Whilst she was showering, she heard Valentina stirring. When they were both dressed, they walked to the motel coffee shop. They sat down in a leatherette-covered booth by the window and immediately a waitress brought a glass of iced water each and two mugs. She smiled and gave them a menu and asked if they wanted coffee.

The two girls nodded and examined the menu. Valentina was disappointed not to see her favourite chocolate brioche, but they were both starving so they had bacon and eggs with toast. Every time they finished their coffee the waitress topped their mugs up. They were a little surprised at this until the waitress said with a smile that top-ups were free.

After breakfast the two girls had the day to themselves, so they tried walking along the Strip. It was incredibly hot for early in the day, so they soon turned round and went back to the motel to enjoy the air-conditioned coolness.

They watched TV for a while and began to feel their excitement subsiding. At lunchtime they went to the coffee shop again and ate lunch, having a salad this time. The waitress was friendly and asked if they had seen the pool at the back of the motel. They hadn't, and after their meal they went to look for it. It was quite a large pool with loungers set around it. Several other guests were sunbathing, and the men looked at the two attractive girls with interest. They had both brought bathing costumes with them, so they returned to their rooms to change, then sunbathed for an hour or two. One or two of the men tried to chat them up, but they pretended to be asleep.

They went back to their rooms and as they passed Reception, they were handed a message from Sandro. He apologised for not calling them earlier as he had been tied up in meetings. He invited them to go with him that evening to the show at the hotel where they were going to be working and arranged to pick them up at seven thirty.

Sandro drew up in front of the hotel that evening in a black Mercedes. The two girls got in, Valentina at the front and Millie in the back. They were both wearing long dresses with light jackets as Sandro had suggested. The night was much cooler although still deliciously balmy. Sandro explained that it was inside the buildings in Las Vegas that they needed a jacket as the air-conditioning everywhere was so fierce you could easily feel quite chilly.

Sandro seemed pleased to see the girls again. He was very attracted to Millie, although she was the quieter and less forward of the two. Valentina was a beauty but a little too attention-seeking for his taste. Millie had an air of mystery about her that he found very compelling. He had guessed that the outgoing Valentina was the leader of the two of them and probably used being the centre of attention. If he wanted to get close to Millie, he decided he would have to bide his time until they were both settled, and Valentina had other people to take Millie's place as her sidekick.

He was a patient man, used to getting his own way. He would play the game however it needed to be played. Playing the game was his hobby really. He liked to set himself a challenge, and he had decided that his latest challenge was to get Millie under his spell. He was married and had three children, but he considered that having affairs with the girls that he found for his employers was part of the rewards of his job.

Once he had a girl in his thrall, he usually lost interest in them almost immediately. He only went after girls that he thought would be hard to get, and they almost invariably became clingy and demanding as soon as he had conquered them. Sandro enjoyed charming girls, but he never actually developed any feelings for them. They were so easy to dupe that he really had no respect for them at all. He didn't see it as robbing a girl of her innocence; he merely saw it as proving that they were all fundamentally stupid and deserved what they got.

The two girls were under twenty-one and should not have been allowed to go into the showroom in the audience as in those days you had to be twenty-one to be where alcohol was served, but Sandro was an important man in the hotel, and no-one asked to see the girl's ID. He poured them each a glass of champagne and raised his glass.

"Here's to a wonderful time in Las Vegas for you both."

They clinked their glasses and drank. Millie had never had champagne before and liked it a lot. So did Valentina. The show was wonderful. The girls were starry-eyed at the fantastic sets, the incredible costumes and marvellous music. Showgirls strutted about with enormous ostrich feather head-dresses on, even more elaborate than those they were used to wearing in the *Lido in Paris*. The stage was huge and absolutely full of people: showgirls, boy and girl dancers, soloists, and in between the numbers the most fantastic and talented variety acts did their performances.

When the show was finished both girls were starry-eyed from the show and too much champagne. Sandro drove them back to the motel and parked his car. He walked them back to their room and kissed them both goodnight. First Valentina on the cheek, and then as Valentina bent to unlock their door, he kissed Millie on the lips. He was surprised as she jerked back away from him. He could see she was a little drunk, so he thought nothing of it.

"You should both learn to drive as quickly as possible," he said. "It is impossible to live in Las Vegas if you can't drive. Why don't you book some lessons as soon as possible? Rehearsals start tomorrow but you will have the mornings free."

They said goodnight and stumbled into their room. They were still not adjusted to the different time zone and were sleepy as well as affected by too much champagne. Millie went into the bathroom. She had been surprised when Sandro had kissed her and had not been able to avoid reacting. In spite of his smile, Sandro's eyes had been rather coldly focused on her during the evening and it had reminded her for an instant of the man who had beaten her. She had not thought of Sandro that way, he had seemed to her to be of her father's generation, not her own. She hoped he would not do it again. Perhaps, she thought, he had been affected by the champagne as well.

That night, she dreamed the old dream of snakes appearing out of her clothes. This time they appeared out of the bedclothes when, in her dream, she lifted them to get into bed. They coiled themselves around her arms and she struggled to get free of them. She woke with a little scream as she struggled to escape from the dream. She was afraid she had disturbed her friend, but Valentina didn't stir: she had drunk the champagne very freely and was deeply asleep, snoring gently.

Millie lay awake for a while. The euphoria of the last few weeks was gone, and she suddenly felt very apprehensive about the future. Perhaps that she had been impulsive in taking this job in Las Vegas where she knew only Valentina. She thought about Guy and was sad that they had not become as close as she had hoped they would. She felt great affection for him but not actually love as she imagined a child would love their father. Perhaps it was necessary to grow up with a father to have that special bond that she imagined between a daughter and her father. She had expected to feel the love for him that she had felt for her mother, but so far it had eluded her, and she felt a huge sense of loss. She turned over and as she snuggled down, she resolved to telephone and write to him often. Perhaps one day that bond of love that she knew they both craved would appear.

The next morning, they looked in the Yellow Pages for a driving instructor and made an appointment for the next morning. Then they called a taxi and drove to the casino where they were to work. Sandro had indicated the backstage entrance the evening before, and they entered it carrying their bags of rehearsal gear. A stagehand pointed the way to the stage, and they went through the flats at the side of the stage where a group of dancers in rehearsal clothes were warming up and practicing steps. A plump, effeminate man with receding sandy hair and a grey scarf wound round his throat came over to them, smiling in a friendly way. He introduced himself as the show choreographer

"I'm Pete... Pete Nash. I guess you are Valentina and Millie from Gay Paree. Just give me a few minutes and you can show me what you can do. I am sure you will be great; Sandro is rarely wrong, but I would like to judge for myself. Is that okay with you girls?"

Valentina and Millie smiled and said it was okay with them. Another dancer showed them to a dressing room so they could change their clothes and put on rehearsal gear.

They went back into the auditorium and sat in the stalls to watch the other dancers rehearsing. Eventually Pete motioned them to go up on stage and all the other dancers went and sat in the stalls.

"Why don't you just do a bit of one of your old routines from the *Lido*?"

Millie and Valentina had a short discussion about what to do and then danced in unison, repeating one of their numbers from the *Lido* show. When they had finished, Pete called them to come down to where he was sitting.

"You are both very good, and your style is almost identical."

"Well, we did learn to dance at the same dance school, and we have done the same routines for a long time," said Millie.

"You will join the general corps of dancers but in one number in the new show I have a duet spot for you girls dancing together but like a mirror image. Do you think you could do that?"

Both girls said yes, they could, and they were thrilled.

Rehearsals were scheduled for six days a week for the next two months. Most of the dancers rehearsing the new show were also dancing every night in the current show, which was a tough physical workload for anyone. Millie and Valentina were lucky that they didn't have to work at night but due to their youth and the fact that they couldn't drive yet, they were rather limited in what they could do.

As they got to know the other dancers, they did get invited to people's apartments on their day off. Their hosts were generous and made sure they got lifts from other dancers. One evening they were at a party given by one of the dancers, Annalise, who had also come to the USA from working in Paris. Annalise also had been recruited to come to dance in Las Vegas by Sandro Fortunelli. She looked at the two girls curiously.

"Did he make a pass at you girls? I hope you resisted the temptation, although I know how tempting it can be, because our gorgeous friend Sandro is very, very married."

"Oh no," said Valentina, "He was a perfect gentleman." Millie kept quiet.

"That's good," replied Annalise. "Just remember in case he tries it on, which he will almost certainly do, that he is married to a devout Catholic. Divorce is not on the cards. He also has kids."

"You needn't worry about us. We have no intention of getting involved with any men just yet," said Valentina.

All the other dancers at the party laughed, "Yeah, right. That won't last long."

Valentina pouted and Millie bit her lip, remembering how Sandro had kissed her. She started to worry in case he might try to pursue her. She decided to avoid ever being alone with him.

Sandro often hung about during rehearsals and Millie was kept busy making sure he never got the chance to talk to her alone. She could tell he was interested, he smiled at her a lot, and she caught him looking at her from the corner of her eye. Valentina was oblivious and often talked to him, but he never tried to get her alone at all. She was quite disappointed as she fancied him a lot. She did not intend to sleep with him but was quite prepared to flirt.

The two girls had driving lessons every chance they could and after three weeks the instructor said he thought they were ready to take the driving test. The test was quite simple and both girls passed quite easily. Millie used some of her trust fund money to buy a small car. Valentina didn't have enough money to buy a car straight away and would have to save up. They both loved the independence of being able to get about on their own without bothering friends or calling taxis.

Millie insured them both to drive the car and they drove about looking for a furnished apartment to rent. They found a nice apartment on the edge of the town, with two almost identical bedrooms. Millie paid the deposit and the first two month's rent. Valentina would pay the next two month's rent when she was earning enough to contribute. Valentina was grateful that Millie had a little money as they would not have been able to afford such a pleasant apartment if Millie was as poor as she was.

The apartment building was a big rectangle with apartments on two floors overlooking a small pool and courtyard garden. Surrounding the apartments was a rather bleak outlook of sand and the occasional patch of bristly weeds. Far in the distance lay the rocky peaks of La Madre mountains.

As they now had a car they could go exploring. There were two or three shopping malls, but they were more interested in the shops in the big hotels. They went to a different hotel on their days off, browsing the arcade shops and choosing a coffee shop for lunch. They were young and had soon adjusted to the Las Vegas way of life, but Millie secretly was rather disappointed in the place. Apart from the glamour of the shows and one or two of the oldest streets of the city where the trees were well established and the houses old and elegant, she thought it was a bleak and ugly place. Just sand, rocks and more sand although it came to life at night when all the hotels and casinos were lit up with neon fantasies. Millie could see the lights gave the impression of glamour but, under the superficial gloss, she felt that Las Vegas was rather a tawdry place. On the Strip, the main street through Las Vegas, she saw dozens of street walkers plying their trade, dressed in an overtly sexual fashion that made her just feel sad that girls had to make their living in that way.

Chapter Twenty-Two – Trip to LA

Sandro came to one of their rehearsals and watched them dancing. He came up and sat by them when they took a break and offered to take them out for the day on their day off. He suggested driving to Los Angeles and having a meal at a magic club he knew. He said they could stay at a hotel and then drive back the next day in time for rehearsals. Valentina was excited by the idea, but Millie felt worried about accepting. She asked Sandro if they could get back to him in a few minutes and then she dragged Valentina off to the dressing room.

"What's the matter, Millie. Why can't we just say we'll go?"

"Valentina, you know he's married and has children. I don't think we should accept any more invitations from Sandro," said Millie anxiously.

"Don't be ridiculous," said Valentina scornfully. "We are just going out for the day, and if we stay over, you and I will sleep in the same room so we will be quite safe. Look, Millie, I understand what you are saying. I tell you what, how about we spell it out before we go.

No funny business. If he agrees, we go. Is that okay with you?"

Millie thought for a while, then she smiled. "Okay, if he agrees, we'll go."

The girls went back to the front stalls where Sandro was sitting by himself.

"My friend here won't go with you unless we spell it out. We girls will sleep together and neither of us will sleep with you. You okay with that?" Valentina smiled sweetly at Sandro.

Sandro replied smoothly, but untruthfully, "Of course, I had no intention of anything else. I'll pick you up at seven am."

The girls were ready outside their apartment on time and Sandro drove up in his Mercedes with a squealing of tyres. Valentina got in the front seat and Millie settled herself in the rear with their overnight bags.

They drove out of town and along the highway running through the desert. The scenery was quite dull, just the usual rocky hills, sand and cacti instead of trees. Sandro chatted about Los Angeles and said he hoped they would make good enough time to have a drive round Beverly Hills to see the gorgeous houses of the rich and famous. Valentina chatted happily and did not notice that Sandro was constantly looking in the rear-view mirror at Millie. She caught his eye a few times and then studiously avoided doing so again. There was an unspoken question in his eyes and Millie was not sophisticated enough to handle the pressure this put on her. Although she felt he was not to be trusted, she could not help being attracted to him as he was an extremely handsome man with a marvellous physique and seductive brown eyes.

They stopped for coffee and a snack in Barstow and travelling on, they reached the outskirts of Los Angeles in the early afternoon. The two-lane road widened into the San Bernardino freeway until it was five or six lanes wide in each direction. The speed limit was fifty-five miles per hour and all the lanes of the freeway were full of cars, crawling slowly along. Sandro drove into Beverley Hills and drove round the beautiful streets with lofty palm trees on each side of the road. All the gardens were lush with tropical greenery. The opulent homes, in all kinds of styles from fake Tudor cottage to Spanish hacienda, stood well back from the road, many behind large security gates.

Sandro drove to a hotel called the Carlyle Inn and they checked in. Sandro had reserved two rooms and handed one of the keys to Millie with a rather sardonic smile. She took the key and blushed shyly. They went to their rooms which were next to each other, and Sandro smiled and said, "Get dressed up, girls, I am taking you to dinner at a very special place. I'll be ready to go in an hour. Is that long enough?"

Both girls smiled and nodded, and they each went into their respective rooms. When they were ready, Sandro drove them to Sunset Strip. He turned up a hill off Wiltshire Boulevard and stopped outside an old Victorian mansion. They got out of the car and a car hop came and took the car away to park it.

"This, ladies, is the Magic Castle. It is a club for magicians, but I am acquainted with the owner, Bill Larsen, and I come here every time I come to Los Angeles. The food is delicious, and the entertainment is great."

The 'maitre d', an elegantly dressed man who took care of reservations and showing people to their tables, came forward.

"Mr. Fortunelli, how good to see you again. Can I

show you and these lovely young ladies to your table now?"

"I think so, do you girls want a drink first?"

Valentina and Millie shook their heads, looking about them with interest. The club was decorated like an old Victorian house might be. There seemed to be an old-fashioned lift in a corner of a large landing. Its wrought iron bars were closed, and it was dark inside. Several people moved forward to see if the lift was working when suddenly a man dressed in a gorilla suit jumped out of the darkness. Everyone leapt back in shock, treading on each other's feet and then laughing at being caught out. They were shown to their table in the restaurant and sat down. Sandro ordered some wine and helped them to order, suggesting things he thought they would enjoy.

Their food came quickly and was delicious. Sandro poured them some wine and they chatted happily as they ate. Millie tried hard not to drink too much wine but soon lost track of how much she had drunk. Another bottle appeared without the girls noticing. They refused dessert as they had to watch their figures.

After they finished their meal, Sandro took them

round the club. There was a room with a piano, haunted by Irma, the ghostly pianist, that played requests. In another room, magicians were performing close-up card tricks. The girls watched closely and could not see how the tricks were done. They enjoyed this immensely and thought the magicians very clever.

At the end of the evening, when they were standing outside in the cool of the evening, Sandro helped the girls on with their jackets. As he helped Millie into hers, his hand lingered on her neck, and she shivered. The car hop bought the car and they got in.

"Well, did you enjoy yourselves?" said Sandro.

"It was great," said Valentina.

"It was really marvellous. Thank you very much for taking us," said Millie politely.

"You're very welcome," said Sandro. "Now, it is still early. Shall we have a nightcap in the bar?"

Valentina was keen but Millie less so; however, she didn't want to leave her friend alone with Sandro. They sat in a comfortable booth and Sandro ordered a bottle of champagne for the girls and a whisky for himself.

"So, tell me how you are enjoying Las Vegas? Do

you like your apartment? It is better for you now that you can both drive, isn't it?"

"Oh yes," said Valentina. "It is lucky that Millie has her own money, or we would not have such a nice apartment. It is nice not to have to wait to save up for a car and nice place to live."

"I am sure you are right," said Sandro, looking curiously at Millie. He did not know she had money.

Millie frowned a little. She did not like people knowing about her private affairs. She was not sure why this was. She was a little annoyed with Valentina for talking about it but she knew she should blame herself for she had never told Valentina not to talk about her money. She resolved to mention it as soon as they were alone.

A man came into the bar and sat down at the piano. He played show music and sang in a mellow voice. There were several parties sitting around chatting happily, and the girls relaxed. They sipped their champagne and managed to drink the whole bottle. Valentina had drunk much more than Millie and she got a bit loud and giggly.

"I think perhaps we should go to bed now, if you

don't mind, Sandro?" said Millie, worrying that her friend was beginning to draw stares. She was also aware that she had drunk too much herself.

"Perhaps you're right," said Sandro with a smile.

They left the bar and got into the lift. Valentina was beginning to sway about and was slurring her words. Sandro had to help Valentina to stay upright and by the time they reached their bedroom door she was only upright because Sandro was virtually carrying her. Millie unlocked their door and helped Valentina over to one of the two large double beds in the room. He laid her down on the bed and she fell immediately asleep. Sandro wrapped the bedspread over her and turned to smile at Millie.

"I think Valentina had a little too much to drink, don't you? I can see that the same is not true of you. Are you afraid of enjoying yourself?"

Millie looked up at him seriously. "I never like to be in a position of being unable to take care of myself. I have been at the mercy of people in the past and I will not be in that position again willingly."

She surprised herself by speaking like that, it was too near the truth, but she must be a little under the influence of the wine and champagne to admit it. She was feeling an intense attraction between herself and Sandro, and it frightened her.

Sandro put his hand under her chin and looked into her eyes. "You have been badly hurt in the past, am I right? Why are you afraid of me? I have no intention of hurting you."

Millie moved back and his hand dropped away. "I am not afraid of you, but you are a married man. That makes you off limits to me. I can't speak for Valentina. She is more impulsive than me, but I could never forget that you have a family."

"That is very honourable of you, Millie, but don't you think my family is a matter for my conscience, not yours?"

Millie shook her head. Sandro moved closer and leaned forward and kissed Millie on the lips. The wine and champagne made her head swim and she found herself in his arms. She closed her eyes and did not resist as he kissed her tenderly.

"Come next door so we can talk without disturbing Valentina," Sandro whispered in her ear.

He put his arm around her and drew her into the corridor, then into his room next door. He closed the door and put his arms around her. Millie was unable to resist him, the alcohol was affecting her very much now. He kissed her softly and gently, then gradually his kisses became more passionate. Millie started to feel very aroused and kissed him back. She found herself on the bed and her head was swimming. Sandro removed her clothes very skillfully and pulled back the covers on the bed. Millie was close to sleep now and did not hear him undress or feel him slip naked into the bed beside her.

He stroked her back and his hands moved gently round to her breasts. Millie moaned with pleasure. A little voice tried to remind her she was doing wrong, but his hands moved lower, and she was lost. He was a skillful and experienced lover and he brought her to a pitch that he knew meant she was past refusing him, then slipped gently inside her. She moaned again and again, and he started to move faster and faster carrying Millie away in a blur of pleasure. Millie suddenly realised what was happening and tried to resist but Sandro was too strong and too carried away in his own pleasure to notice she was resisting him.

He reached his climax and became aware of her again and was surprised to see that she was crying and gasping with distress.

"What's the matter, Millie darling? Didn't I give you pleasure?"

Millie tried to stop crying. "I didn't want this to happen. What about your wife and family?"

Sandro pulled back and said coldly, "My family is not your concern. I don't want you to mention them again."

"It's wrong, it's wrong what we've done. I wish we hadn't done it."

"Millie, you are being silly and over-dramatic. We have just made love, there's no harm done."

Millie realised she could not say anything. She had been in the wrong to come into his room. She got up and slipped on her clothes.

"I'm sorry, I think I had better go back to my room now. Valentina might need me."

Sandro got up and put on his robe.

"Okay Millie. If that's what you want. Here's the key to your room."

He didn't try to touch her again and Millie left his room. Hearing the key turn in the lock behind her. She went into her room and saw that Valentina had not moved. Millie went into the bathroom and had a shower. What if she got pregnant? She had been a fool; she should never have had so much wine and champagne and she vowed never to make that mistake again. She dried herself and went back into the bedroom. She roused Valentina enough to get her clothes off and then tucked her under the covers. She hung up both their clothes carefully and then got into the other double bed.

She stretched out under the cool sheets. She had to admit that until she had sobered up that she had been enjoying making love with Sandro very much. She was sorry she had made love with Sandro because he was married. Millie knew that, without the influence of the alcohol, she would never have done it. She must make sure she didn't drink too much again, especially with Sandro, especially as she was very attracted to him.

Until now Millie had thought that, because of the man who had abused her and her reaction to Antoine, she would never enjoy having sex with a man. Sometimes Millie had wondered if she would ever enjoy making love with a man, as she knew from talking with other girls that making love could be wonderful, and now she had enjoyed it. In fact, until tonight, the thought of ever having sex filled her with repulsion.

She remembered how she had been with Antoine in Montreal. She had enjoyed his kisses and then, when he had touched her intimately, she had reacted badly. She wished she hadn't done that as she still had strong feelings for Antoine. She thought of him often and wished that life had not taken her away from him. Millie could not understand why she had resisted Antoine but had not resisted Sandro and had let him make love to her. It could only be the wine and champagne; she knew she must beware of the same situation happening again.

The next thing Millie knew, the telephone was ringing beside her bed. She picked up the receiver.

"Good morning, Sweetheart." It was Sandro, his voice warm and intimate. "We need to set off in an hour if we are to get you back in time for rehearsal this afternoon. I'll see you in the coffee shop in half an hour." The line went dead.

Millie woke up Valentine and told her they had half-an-hour to get down to the coffee shop if she wanted any breakfast. Valentina got up grumbling and headed off for a shower. Millie packed both their bags and when Valentina came out of the shower, she went in for a quick wash and to clean her teeth. They came down to the coffee shop in good time and Sandro smiled warmly at them both. Millie felt rather embarrassed, but Sandro acted like nothing had happened.

They set off for the long drive back. They chatted for a while, and then Sandro turned on the radio and they listened to the usual Californian Country and Western radio music. The girls were a bit late back for rehearsals but because they arrived with Sandro, who was an important man in the hotel, no one said anything to them.

The weeks continued and rehearsals became more intense. The tension mounted as the opening night of the new show got nearer. The girls were busy every day now, rehearsing in costume, having adjustments made by the seamstresses and falling into bed each night exhausted.

They saw Sandro around the hotel and, when he

met them, he always kissed them both on each cheek, European fashion, but said nothing about the night he and Millie had made love. Millie was glad about this but puzzled. She knew he had been attracted to her and had thought she might have to rebuff his advances, but he never made any.

Chapter Twenty-Three – Echoes from the Past

The old show closed a week before the opening of the new one to get the sets and lighting for the new show set up. They had to rehearse with the new scenery and sometimes there were delays when there was a technical hitch.

All the dance numbers in the show were spectacular. The choreographers in Las Vegas were the best in the world and Pete Nash was the *crème de la crème*. The costumes were so lavishly decorated with ostrich feathers and heavy beads that they were quite difficult to dance in. The headdresses were heavy, and the girls took time to get used to dancing in them.

Opening night finally arrived. The tension backstage was horrendous, and tempers were flaring everywhere. It would become routine after a few days, and everyone knew it was a great show but there was still that terrible dread that something awful would go wrong that they had not been prepared for. However, with just a few little faults that the audience never noticed, the first show went off well and Millie and Valentina were on a high all evening. They found it all immensely exciting.

Their duet was incredibly successful. It consisted a huge mirror frame in the centre of the stage and their routine was a slightly humorous one. They each danced across the mirror frame as if they were the reflection of the other and then one would do a tiny movement differently and the other would do a double-take and look back to see the other copying her exactly. Both girls were dressed in matching wigs and dresses and to start with the audience thought they were really looking at a girl dancing in front of a mirror, but then one "reflection" would peep round the mirror frame when the other wasn't looking.

Millie and Valentina loved their routine, and it showed in their dancing. Both adored the euphoric feeling they got when the audience roared their approval. Their solo number was a great success, and the feeling of achievement carried them through the rest of the evening on cloud nine.

After the show, the management had laid on a party in a big room in another part of the casino for all the cast and the crew. There was a bar and a buffet, and all the dancers flocked in and started eating and drinking with abandon. Millie stuck firmly to orange juice. Valentina was off chatting to people in her usual outgoing fashion and Millie stood on her own. A beautiful older woman, wearing a lovely peach-coloured evening gown and flawless make-up, came over to Millie. She looked at Millie's face closely.

"Excuse me, dear," she said in an English voice tinged with American. "My name is Dinah Farley. You remind me very much of someone I used to know. Are you by chance related to Rachel Randall?"

Millie was shocked. This woman knew her mother!

"Yes, I am," she said. "She was my mother. Did you know her?"

"I did. I worked with her in Beirut many years ago before she disappeared."

"She was found dead, you know," said Millie. "Did you hear that?"

"Yes, I did hear although I had left Beirut by the time she was found. One of the other dancers wrote and told me that Rachel's body had finally been found and that her little girl had disappeared. I was upset to hear that. Rachel was a good friend to me.

I would like very much to talk to you about your mother and to hear about what happened to you. I would love to know the story of how you became a dancer too. Please come and visit me in my house, and we'll have a lovely long chat."

The woman reached in her bag and gave Millie a card with her address and telephone number on.

"I know you will probably be busy with the show for a few days but, when things settle down, do come and see me."

Millie slipped the card in her bag and said she would go and visit Dinah as soon as she could.

They had several days of intense rehearsals to smooth out the few rough edges of the show and as soon as she had some hours free, Millie rang Dinah who invited her over. Millie didn't tell Valentina where she was going and slipped away while her friend was still in bed. She left a note to say she had gone shopping.

She drove to the street where Dinah lived. It was a wide road in the oldest part of the town. The trees were taller here than in the rest of Las Vegas and the vegetation well-watered and manicured. Huge palm trees were planted in island borders down the middle of the road. The houses in the road had been built in the 1920s and 30s, mostly in a rambling mountain cabin style with big stone chimneys and wooden tile sidings. Millie walked up to the front door, made of wide, rough-hewn timbers studded with big black nails and rang the doorbell.

Dinah opened the door, a big smile on her face. She was wearing a pale blue velour leisure suit and her face was clean of make-up.

"Come in, come in. I am so glad you came." Dinah led the way into her completely circular stone-walled living room. It had a high conical wooden ceiling and in the middle of room was a round stone fireplace with a big cone-shaped beaten copper cowl leading to a chimney suspended from the center of the ceiling. They sat down on big squashy sofas facing the fireplace.

"What a lovely room," said Millie.

"I like it," said Dinah. "Can I get you a cold drink or a coffee or tea?"

"I'd love a fruit juice of some sort, if you have any," said Millie.

Dinah went and fetched two glasses and a jug of orange juice, ice cubes clinking on the glass. She passed Millie a glass of juice and then sat down.

"Why don't you tell me what happened to you after Rachel disappeared."

Millie told Dinah how her nanny Sofia had had to move out of Rachel's apartment because she couldn't pay the rent and how they had moved to the big house and how Nabila and Ali had come to live with them. She told her how Sofia had died and then she started to tell Dinah about how Hassim had taken her to a man's house. Dinah leaned forward and stopped Millie.

"Hassim? You did say Hassim, didn't you?"

"Yes," said Millie, puzzled. "Hassim was Sofia's son."

"Your mother was frightened of someone called Hassim. She didn't say he was her nanny's son. She only said that she was being hassled by someone called Hassim. He was always trying to get her to sleep with him and she told me that he had followed her home several times. This was just before she disappeared. I always wondered if he had anything to do with her disappearance. I told the police about him, but they were worse than useless, really."

Millie was stunned. Was Hassim responsible for her mother's death? She put her head in her hands. All those years he had been there because he was Sofia's son. Millie had not known that he had harassed her mother. She remembered how he had beaten her when he had brought her back to the big house after the man had abused her. He had been vicious and uncontrolled. She imagined him beating her mother and leaving her dead in the forest. What could she do? Too many years had gone by.

Dinah said, as she laid a sympathetic hand on Millie's knee, "I am so sorry, Millie. This has obviously been a terrible shock for you."

"It's okay. I already loathed Hassim for what he did to me. If he killed my mother, it gives me more reason to hate him."

"I know you must want justice for your mother, my dear, but there is probably nothing you can do. The police would not be interested after all these years."

"I know," said Millie. "There has been a war there too, hasn't there? Hassim might not even be still alive."

"Well, I sincerely hope he isn't," said Dinah emphatically. "Tell me what happened to you after Beirut."

Millie told her about how Marie and Jim had found her and helped to find her grandmother. She described how she had found her father, too, and that they had made a home together first in Canada and then in Paris. She told Dinah about meeting Valentina and getting the job in the *Lido* together.

"And now, here you are, dancing in Las Vegas. If she hadn't disappeared, I think your mother would have liked to come to Las Vegas. She thought she would be able to make a better life for you here, and I know that Hassim following her around made her feel anxious and insecure. I was so upset about Rachel's disappearance that I left Beirut myself soon afterwards. If Rachel had been found dead before I left, I would have tried to find out what had happened to you. I suppose we all thought her family would know about you and that you had gone to live with them. I am sorry, Millie… We all let you down."

Millie reassured Dinah, "There was nothing you could have done. Sofia and I had moved on and no-one knew where we had gone. The police couldn't find me, so you wouldn't have been able to either. What did you do after you left?"

"I took a job here in Las Vegas. I danced here for years and then I met my husband and stopped dancing. Sadly, he died last year. He left me this house and a decent income. I was born in England but have lived here for so many years, I am happy to stay here forever now."

"It is a lovely house. I can see why you would be happy here. Have you any children?"

"No, I never wanted children and neither did my husband. Some people make good mothers, but I was not one of them. Your mother, on the other hand, simply adored you. I hope you will always remember that she absolutely lived for you. She never went out partying like the rest of us. She came to work and went straight home after work. It was a terrible tragedy."

"I know she loved me," said Millie, "but after a few years I found it hard to remember her face. Nabila gave me a little case containing her papers and there were some photographs of her in it. I still have them, and some others given to me by my English grandmother and my father, so I try to keep her memory alive."

"I glad you have happy memories of her. She was a lovely person."

Millie had to leave then to go to work. Dinah kissed her cheek and told Millie that she could come and see her anytime and, if she thought of any questions she wanted to ask, all she had to do was telephone. Millie thanked her and ran off to her car. She would have to hurry as she had to pick up Valentina before she went to work.

Valentina was hopping up and down anxiously when Millie arrived at the apartment.

"Where have you been? We'll be late for work."

"Well, come on then, let's go," said Millie.

Chapter Twenty-Four – Break a Leg

During the show that night, Millie's thoughts kept returning to her mother and the possibility that Hassim was responsible for her disappearance. During one of the dance numbers, she had to climb up on a piece of scenery that rose high in the air. Her thoughts were on her mother and what Hassim might have done to her, so she was not concentrating as she should have been and went too near the edge. Panicked and horrified, she felt herself falling from the platform. Millie landed hard on the stage out of view of the audience, so two stagehands ran on immediately and carried her off stage into the wings.

Sandro had been in the audience and hurried backstage. He could see that Millie had badly damaged her leg and would not let her get up. He sent a stagehand to call an ambulance. She was taken to hospital and Sandro went with her in the ambulance. Valentina was still dancing on stage and had not realised that Millie was not there until the end of the number.

"It was a good thing we had done our solo," said Millie wincing with pain as the doctor examined her leg.

"Well, someone else will have to learn it quickly because you are not going to be dancing for a while," said Sandro irritably.

Millie had to stay in hospital for a while as she had broken her leg in three places. The doctors told her that she might not be able to dance again, at least not in such a physically demanding show. Millie was devastated but she did not cry. She had accepted that she would have to convalesce for a while but was very upset to hear that she might not be able to go back to working in the show.

While Millie remained in hospital, Sandro visited her and brought Valentina. They were both distraught to hear that Millie's dancing career was in jeopardy. Valentina cried copiously and would not be consoled.

Sandro drove Millie home from the hospital. He settled her on the sofa, her leg stretched out in front of her, plastered up to the thigh. He put her crutches within reach and went to make them all some coffee. Valentina sat in the chair near Millie and took her friend's hand.

"It is not the same without you. We have danced together for so long. I really miss you being there. It's awful, I will never get used to it."

"I know. I miss dancing with you too. Our lovely mirror dance, I enjoyed doing that so much. Who is doing it with you?"

"That French girl called Bernice. She does it okay, but nowhere as well as you. We don't get as much applause as you and I used to do. She doesn't understand the humour of it, and just does it straight. I think they might cut the number out if they can't find someone to do it better than her."

Sandro came back in with the coffee. He sat down and they talked about the show and how long Millie would be recuperating. Millie said the doctors had told her that the plaster would be on for at least eight weeks as she had more than one break. After that, she would need some physiotherapy. Only then would they be able to judge whether she could dance again. Millie said the doctors had warned her not to expect to dance such demanding roles as she had done before.

She smiled at the two gloomy faces looking at her as she spoke. "It's not so bad. There is always the chance that they are wrong, and I will be able to dance again. If not, well, I am lucky that I can always go back to Paris and live with my father again."

Sandro reassured Millie that she would not have to pay the hospital bills. He said he had persuaded the hotel management that having her dance on such a high platform without an adequate safety guard might give Millie reason to sue the hotel. He had suggested to the management that if they paid her hospital bills, he would make sure that she would not sue. He asked her to accept this as taking the hotel to court was not a good idea. They could afford the best attorneys and it would cost a lot of money to hire lawyers to fight for compensation.

"I have no intention of taking them to court, and I would be very grateful for the hospital bills to be paid. Please thank the management for me and reassure them," said Millie.

Valentina had to leave to go to work. She was anxious about leaving her friend alone on her first night out of hospital, but Sandro reassured her that he would stay with Millie for the evening.

When Valentina had gone, Millie looked at Sandro, a sad little smile on her face.

"I have often wondered what you would have said if

I had got pregnant that night in Los Angeles."

"Well," said Sandro with a grin, "I would have declared it a miracle. I had a vasectomy years ago. If I hadn't, my wife would have gone on having babies *ad infinitum.*"

Millie pouted a little. No wonder he had not been worried about making her pregnant. He had not been concerned about protecting her from infection either. She had heard many stories since their trip to Los Angeles about Sandro and his many conquests; it was well known that he simply liked the chase and lost interest when he had what he wanted. In spite of that, she still had a soft spot for him. He had, after all, showed her that making love could be pleasurable, even if she had been a bit drunk at the time.

Sandro stayed with her and when they got hungry, he went out and came back with a takeaway and a bottle of wine. They had a relaxed conversation while they ate and Millie enjoyed a glass of wine. Sandro took a sip of his wine and smiled at her, "You know, Millie, if ever I would have left my wife for anyone, it would have been you. I could leave my wife, but I could not leave my children. They are everything to me. But, of all the girls I have known, you would be the one I would choose, if I were free to choose."

"Well, Sandro, that's a very sweet thing to say, but I would not want you to leave your wife. I don't regret our night together, for my own reasons, but I would not want to live with you, even if you were free."

Sandro was taken aback by her bluntness. He was not accustomed to being treated so coolly by a girl he had slept with. Normally he had quite a bit of difficulty convincing them that he was no longer interested in them. It challenged his ego that Millie was not apparently bothered in any way by his neglect.

"What are 'your own reasons'?" he asked, his curiosity piqued.

"Ahh," said Millie smiling, tapping her nose, "Wouldn't you like to know?"

"I can see you are not going to tell me, so I refuse to be interested." Sandro grinned at her.

It was refreshing to be with a beautiful girl in such a relaxed way, especially as she was badly hurt and had reason to be weeping and wailing. Instead, she was cheerful and calm. "*She really was a very unusual and intriguing girl,"* Sandro thought to himself.

Sandro stayed with Millie until Valentina came home. It was quite a struggle at first to move about with the awkward plaster cast, but over the weeks Millie got used to it and hobbled about the apartment with her crutch. Sometimes, Valentina took her out for a drive just to get a change of scene and some fresh air. She occasionally sat on their balcony sunbathing and joked that she would have one brown leg and one white one when the plaster came off.

Eventually the plaster was removed, and she started physiotherapy. After two months, the doctor examined her again. He said that she should take a few dance classes, starting gently, and see how she coped. Millie arranged for a dance teacher to give her lessons on her own to start with, as she felt awkward with able-bodied dancers around her, and she soon realised there was no way she could keep up with them. After a few days of classes, she realised that it would be a long time, if ever, that she would be able to dance well enough to go back to dancing at the level she had before. Her damaged leg was just not strong enough.

Sandro kept in touch and sometimes visited her in

the evening when Valentina was at work. He had once made overtures to Millie to see if she were willing to make love with him again, but she laughed and said that he couldn't make her drunk enough to repeat her first mistake. Sandro was taken aback at this cheeky remark, but he was genuinely fond of her and didn't hold a grudge.

Chapter Twenty-Five – Magical Interlude

When it was clear that Millie could not take her place back in the show with Valentina, they had serious talks about what Millie should do. She thought seriously about going back to Paris and her father. She had not told him about her accident yet. She did not want to worry him.

One evening Sandro telephoned her with a suggestion for a temporary job she could do while she continued having physiotherapy. Sandro had a contact in another hotel who had told him about a magician in his show who had lost one of his girl assistants. It was not a dancing role but required enough flexibility to fit inside secret compartments in the illusions featured in the act.

Sandro asked Millie if she thought she could manage such a job. She thought about it and said, "Could I go and meet this magician and see what I would have to do? I have no experience of magic acts and have no idea what's involved."

Sandro said he would find out and call her back. The next day he called back and said he would pick her up the following morning to go and meet the magician whose stage name was "The Great Frederico," who was just plain Freddie Brown from Yorkshire, England.

Sandro drove Millie to the Desert Sun Hotel where The Great Frederico was headlining. They went backstage where the illusionist was rehearsing. He had some sort of big illusion on the stage and was shouting rather irritably at a harassed-looking woman with long, blonde hair and a small dark girl with glossy black hair tied up in an untidy bunch. All three turned to look at Millie as she walked toward them. Freddie came over to shake Sandro's hand and he in turn introduced Millie to all three of them. The blonde woman was Freddie's wife Vanessa, and the small dark girl was no relation. Her name was Anita.

Freddie explained to Millie what his assistant was required to do. She had a go at squeezing into the secret compartment of the illusion they were rehearsing and found it relatively easy. Freddie said it was rarely necessary to be in the secret places for long. After some discussion and Freddie showing Millie all the illusions that she would be involved in, she said she thought she could cope with the demands of the job quite well.

Freddie told her what her salary would be and Millie accepted it, though she was a little apprehensive of the man. He seemed to be irritable and impatient, so when she accepted the job, she would only agree to a three-month contract just to make sure she could cope with the demands of the position. Freddie accepted her terms.

In truth, he was desperate for another assistant and Millie had the right colouring and size. Many of his illusions required his wife to disappear and reappear again. In fact, she would disappear, and another assistant would reappear dressed identically. It was not physically possible for the same woman to reappear instantly in all his illusions. While he was short of an assistant to be his wife's double, he had been forced to leave his best illusions out of the act and the management had been complaining.

Millie agreed to spend the rest of the day rehearsing in the hope that she could appear in at least some of them that very evening. They rehearsed all the rest of the morning and all afternoon. Freddie was a hard taskmaster; although he spoke harshly to his wife and Anita, he stopped short of being unpleasant to Millie. Millie also tried on all the costumes and wigs she was required to wear for the act. Most of them fitted quite well or were a little too big. Freddie was pleased that he would not have to get new costumes made for Millie.

Even with the extensive rehearsal, Millie was extremely nervous about appearing in the act that very night. Freddie pleaded with her to do it. He could not risk the management complaining about the missing illusions much longer.

Being in a magic show was a very different experience for Millie. She felt under pressure that first night, but it was much less physically demanding than being a dancer. She managed competently and the show went very well. Freddie was pleased with her performance and hoped the hotel management would now be happy that the act was back to normal. Over the next few days, Millie became more proficient at her various appearances and disappearances.

All four of them in the act had to share a dressing room, although it was quite a spacious one. Millie was unhappy at having to change costume in the same room as Freddie, who ogled and leered at her and Anita the discomfort of his rather nice but rather downtrodden wife. Millie and Anita both went to extreme lengths to change their clothes when Freddie was not looking. Anita had winked at Millie the first night and shown her how to avoid letting Freddie see them in their underwear.

Anita whispered to Millie during the evening while they were waiting backstage, "Don't take any notice of old Fred," she said. "He's a dirty old man but he's all mouth and no trousers, if you get my meaning."

Millie didn't really, but assumed that Anita meant that Freddie would look but not touch.

Anita did most of the difficult illusions. She was tiny and very light, so she did the tricks which involved floating or being elevated in the air. She also did the illusions involving very tiny hiding places as she was extremely limber.

Anita told Millie that her previous act had been as a contortionist in rather seedy clubs in Europe which was where she had met Freddie and his wife. She had grown up in the circus and learned to be a contortionist in her parent's circus act after first training as an acrobat as a tiny child. Her parents both died in a car accident and she was still a teenager when she started work for Freddie and his wife. She had been with them for years and was very fond of Vanessa, Freddie's wife. She disliked Freddie, who was prone to rages and indulged in too much drink at times, although never before a show.

Millie avoided Freddie as much as she could. She found his overbearing and boastful character very irritating. When she had been in the show for a few days, he had started shouting at her as much as he did his wife and Anita. Millie said nothing but doubted that she would stay beyond the three months she had agreed to. She was grateful to be earning some money and not having to dip too much into her savings, but she became more depressed as the weeks went by. Millie liked Vanessa very much and hated to see her husband verbally abusing her. He shouted at her and blamed her for everything that went wrong, and Millie could not understand why she put up with it. Anita explained that it was because, no matter what Vanessa said, Freddie would just keep arguing until his wife was exhausted. Anita explained that Vanessa has just got used to ignoring him while he shouted and let it go over her head as much as she could.

Millie found his bad-tempered bullying quite stressful as it reminded her of Hassim. She wanted to answer Freddie back on Vanessa's behalf. Once she had defended Vanessa and Freddie had just stared at her, his eyes blazing. His wife no longer faced up to him and Anita didn't bother; he was not used to being challenged. He glared at her but said nothing. Millie had seen him then pinch his wife's arm cruelly when he thought she wasn't looking. It seemed better after that not to argue with him.

Millie told Valentina how much she disliked Freddie and how unhappy she was in the act. Valentina insisted she must leave at the end of her three months.

Millie looked at her friend, "How would you feel if I went back to France? I have no future here now and I might as well go back to live with my father. I suppose I had better think of another way to make a living. Why don't you ask about at work and see if you can find someone else to share this apartment with you if I go to France?"

Vanessa looked sad. "I shall miss you dreadfully if you leave."

"I will miss you too, but it is awful not being able to dance as I did before. I hate being in Freddie's act and can't bear to see how he mistreats his wife."

Valentina agreed to find someone to share the apartment with when Millie left, and Millie told Freddie the next day that she was not staying in the act after her three months was up. When he asked her why, she hesitated for a moment and then told him that she didn't want to work for a man who was so horrible to a wife who worked so hard for him and didn't deserve to be treated like that. Freddie frowned and said it was none of her business and what happened between him and his wife. She agreed with him but said that Vanessa might be willing to put up with him but that she, Millie, was not.

Freddie hardly spoke to her after that until her last night. He had finally found another girl to take her place and they had been rehearsing during the day. Millie finished the last trick for the last time and found her heart soaring with relief. She said goodbye to Vanessa and Anita and, without a word to Freddie, she drove back to the apartment.

Valentina had found another dancer to share the apartment; she was ready to move in whenever Millie left. Millie also had telephoned Guy to ask if he was okay with her coming home. He said he was thrilled that she was coming back, but he was very anxious when she told him about her accident. She reassured him that she was recovering well but not well enough to dance in a strenuous Las Vegas show. He said he was impatient to see her, that he had a nice surprise for her. Millie wondered what the surprise was. Perhaps he had met a woman, someone who would love him despite his disability. She hoped that was the surprise. She wanted her father to be happy.

Millie gave Valentina the car and Valentina cried at the kindness of her friend. She was dreading Millie going away but realised that it was not good for her to stay in Las Vegas when she could no longer dance as she loved to do. Sandro took them both out for lunch the day before Millie left and, although she was sad to be leaving Valentina, Millie was surprised at how unconcerned she was to be leaving Sandro. She had also expected to be more upset at the abrupt finish to her career but, strangely, she had come to terms with it quite quickly.

Millie was more concerned with the fact that Hassim might have killed her mother. It was in the back of her mind all the time. She intended to discuss it with Guy when she got back to France and to ask him what he thought they should do. Millie could not accept that doing nothing was an option.

Valentina drove Millie to the airport as Millie didn't want Sandro to take her. After parking the car, Valentina helped Millie into the airport terminal with all her bags. She was taking everything with her as she did not intend to come back. Valentina was crying, sniffing into her already sodden handkerchief.

Millie hugged and kissed her friend. "When you come back to visit your parents then we shall see each other again. We will always be friends even when we are apart."

"I know," sniffed Valentina, "But it will not be the same without you. I think I will write to Madame Bluebell to see if she will have me back when my contract here is ended."

"That would be fantastic," said Millie. "Your mum and dad would be thrilled too."

Millie checked in her luggage, and soon it was time for her to go through to the Departure Lounge. The two girls hugged again and then Millie went through, waving goodbye to her friend.

Chapter Twenty-Six – Tripoli

Still in Kamel Khoury's employ, Hassim was now working full-time in clandestine activities for his boss. Sometimes he was sent to the airport to watch who amongst Mr. Khoury's business acquaintances arrived or departed and who among Mr. Khoury's enemies and business rivals met them. None of his business deals were done with people who trusted one another farther than they could spit. It was a 'dog eat dog' world and Hassim fitted in perfectly.

He had no scruples in doing anything his boss required him to do, and if he was expected to make someone disappear permanently then he would happily oblige. He had not been asked to do this often but often enough, and unobtrusively for Mr. Khoury to pay Hassim a decent salary.

Hassim had a nice car and could afford to rent an apartment in a smart block as near Mr. Khoury's house as he could find. His apartment was filthy inside as he did not trust anyone in to do the cleaning and he thought that to do it himself was beneath him. He occasionally considered getting a woman in to keep house and clean for him, but his distrustful nature always decided against it.

He was often asked to shadow people and, over the years, he had picked up tips from some of Mr. Khoury's more experienced cohorts. He had become very skilled at following people without their knowledge. Occasionally he had to go to Tripoli on business for his boss, and never failed to keep a look out for Millie, Nabila, and Ali. He had never forgotten or forgiven them for getting the best of him. Over the years his grudge against them had not abated at all. He still harboured murderous feelings of revenge for all three of them.

Once, while he was in Tripoli shadowing a sight-seeing American business associate of Mr. Khoury, Hassim thought he had caught sight of Nabila, or at least a woman who looked a lot like her but plumper and more prosperous looking. The woman was holding the arm of an upright, scholarly-looking man. They were wandering around the fish market, looking at the fish on the market stalls. Unfortunately, the American chose that moment to veer off towards the mosques up the hill and Hassim had to follow him. He did not dare to lose his mark. Mr. Khoury did not believe in forgiving carelessness and Hassim wanted to keep his job.

He glanced behind him as he followed the American and the woman looked up and saw him. She started then bowed her head and moved behind the man so he couldn't see her anymore. Hassim was not sure if it was Nabila and she had recognized him, or she was just a modest woman lowering her eyes when a man looked at her. He was fuming that he had to leave before he could be sure. He followed his mark up the hill and then glanced behind again. The couple had gone.

The woman in the market was indeed Nabila. She was there with Mr. Massoud, now her husband. It was rare for them to come to Tripoli, but Mr. Massoud had business in the bank, and it had entailed a trip to the city. It was just the most awful co-incidence that the very first time they had gone to the city in over a year they had to encounter Hassim.

As soon as he had turned his back, Nabila had whispered urgently in her husband's ear that she had seen Hassim. They turned quickly round and sought refuge in a back-street shop. They stayed there for a while and Nabila peeped out and saw that no one had followed them. They hurried back to where they had left their little car and drove home. Nabila looked anxiously behind them all the way, but the road was quiet and empty of cars. No one was following.

"I wonder if I shall ever be free of worrying about that man," said Nabila to her husband, Khalil.

"I know, my love, it is a worry, but we shall just have to continue to be very careful when we go to the city. Perhaps you should wear a scarf over your head? I don't like women having to wear those things, and we are not Muslims, but it might give you more feeling of safety in the city."

"You are right. Next time we go to Tripoli I will wear one." Nabila kissed her husband tenderly.

They had been incredibly happy since their marriage. Before their marriage, Nabila had a terrible life and had suffered dreadful poverty since she was a child, but her character was basically good and kind. She was always brave and positive despite all the hardships she had endured. Khalil recognized and loved her sweetness and gentleness and her natural intelligence. His love had given her confidence and complete happiness, and in return she lavished love on Khalil. When they had first married it had been more of a practical arrangement between two practical people who valued each other. Over time, it had become a deeper relationship and now they loved each other deeply.

Khalil was an invalid when Nabila had come to work for him. He had been very ill, but his recovery was held back by loneliness. When Nabila came into his life, he had steadily grown stronger and was now almost completely well. He still had to take tablets for his heart, but his doctor told him to go and live a normal life. When they had been married for two years, Nabila found she was pregnant. When she told Khalil, he was over the moon.

Strangely, neither of them had expected her to get pregnant. Nabila had not expected it as she had never become pregnant after she had Ali, although she had been forced to have sex with many men by her first husband. Mr. Khalil had not expected it as he was not a young man anymore. They worried if Ali would react with jealousy when Nabila was holding a little brother or sister, as he had always been very possessive of his mother. But Ali had learned to share his mother with her husband and, when a baby girl was born, he surprised them both by seeming to love the baby as much as he loved Nabila.

Ali was now an adult in size and strength, but still a small child in his mental development. The relaxed and contented atmosphere that the little family lived in suited Ali well and he was now always calm and placid. He pottered happily around in their large garden and helped the kind and patient old man who tended it. He did not need to cling to Nabila anymore as he felt secure, and the huge man-child was content to follow the gardener around all day if necessary. Nabila was so happy that she and Ali had found such a wonderful refuge. She often felt she was in paradise and she would plant a kiss on her husband's cheek in gratefulness.

They called the little girl Sofia after Nabila's old friend. When she called her daughter's name as she toddled around the house, Nabila would think of Millie and wonder where she was. She had never expected to receive an answer to her letter. It just seemed too unlikely that Millie, once reunited with her family, would want to contact anyone who would remind her of the horror of what had happened to the little girl she had once been.

Khalil was sad for his wife that they received no reply from Millie and asked her if she wanted to write again.

Nabila shook her head. If Millie did not want to remember her past, she could understand and accept that. When she thought of her own past and the shock of seeing Hassim, Nabila would shiver with fear and shame. She could understand it if Millie just wanted to put the past behind her, as she had done thanks to her beloved Khalil.

Nabila's letter to Millie had indeed reached England and was delivered to the house where she had lived with her grandmother. The new owner of the house put the letter on a heavy old chest in the hall and planned to take it to the estate agent to pass on to Millie's family. However, one of her children accidentally pushed the letter down the back of the chest where it lay, forgotten and hidden until, many years later, the family moved on and the chest was picked by the removal men. One of the men picked up the letter and passed it to the lady of the house. She tutted irritably and scribbled the estate agent's name on the letter. She dropped it in the agency post box on the way to her new home.

Chapter Twenty-Seven – Paris

Millie landed in Paris very tired and her leg was aching badly from so many hours in a cramped airplane seat. She only had two big suitcases as she had given Valentina all the Las Vegas-style clothes which she knew would not be appropriate in France. She found a taxi and the driver loaded her bags in the trunk. As the taxi drove off, Millie looked out of the window and was lost in her own thoughts. She was coming home but it did not feel as if she were. She had moved so many times that she did not feel truly at home anywhere. Millie was startled back to reality when the taxi drew up outside the apartment and her things were unloaded. She paid the driver and he was on his way.

Millie had not told her father that that she was coming back to Paris that day, and she hoped it would be a good surprise. She still had her key and let herself into the downstairs apartment feeling a little nervous. Guy was sitting on the sofa, not his wheelchair and, to Millie's astonishment, as soon as he saw her, he hauled himself upright using a walking stick for balance and a huge grin of happiness spread across his face.

"Oh, what's happened?" Millie was puzzled by Guy's

change in circumstance. "Can you walk now? Oh, that's wonderful, why didn't you tell me?" Millie ran over to her father and hugged him.

"Whoa, whoa," he said. "I can only just stand up as yet. I still can't walk without crutches but the doctors say it might be possible now."

"Tell me, when did this happen?" said Millie eagerly.

"Well, when I was shot, the bullet lodged close to my spine and it was too near to my spinal cord for the doctors to remove it. A few months ago, I felt a terrible pain in my back and went to see the specialist here. He said the bullet had shifted a little away from my spinal cord and he thought he could safely remove it. I went into hospital to have it removed and within a few weeks I started to get feeling back in my legs. This is as far as I have got, but the prognosis is hopeful that I might be able to walk again, but perhaps only with crutches or a stick."

"That's so wonderful," said Millie. "I am so happy to see you again."

She kissed her father tenderly. She was surprised at how glad she was to see him again. A strange feeling had woken in her to see him standing there with a big smile on his face. She felt a rush of love for him wash over her. She put her arms around him and laid her head on his chest. He dropped his cheek on her head, and they stood together, father and daughter.

Guy and Millie talked and talked. She remonstrated with him for not telling her he had gone into hospital for an operation. He reminded her that she had not told him about her accident nor that she was was coming home.

"You are right. I should have told you. I have been a bit distracted by something I found out about my mother recently."

Millie told him about meeting Dinah and what she had revealed about Hassim stalking and harassing her mother, and how Rachel had talked about leaving Beirut to get away from him just before she disappeared.

"I am wondering if I should go to Beirut to see if I can find him and to get the police to arrest him. What do you think, Dad?"

Guy thought for a while. "I don't think the police in Beirut will be interested in pursuing such an old case after all these years. How would you find Hassim? You have no idea where he is living now, and you have no proof it was him."

Millie sighed. "That's just what Dinah said. I just feel that my mum didn't get justice. She didn't deserve to get killed. She was a good person, always loving and gentle. It is not as if she had anything to do with men. Dinah told me that she never socialized, not even with other dancers. She always came straight home to me. It is not fair that he should get off scot-free and not pay for her murder."

"You don't know for sure it was him," said Guy.

"No, I don't, but Dinah said that he was the only person who my mother said bothered her and she was very afraid of him. He was Sofia's son, and she and I were very afraid of him too. My mother might not have wanted to hurt Sofia by saying bad things about him."

"That's quite possible. Listen, darling, I don't think you should go there yourself. It is an appallingly dangerous place these days. I will contact some of my reporter friends to see if anyone knows of someone with knowledge about Beirut in those days. It is possible we might be able to find something out that way. Do you want me to try?"

"Yes please, Dad," said Millie gratefully. She couldn't think of anything else they could do.

Millie and Guy settled down to living together more contentedly than Millie could have imagined. They went together to see Guy's physiotherapist, he to try to learn to walk again and Millie to exercise her weakened leg. Guy managed to walk with crutches within a few weeks of Millie's return and it made him immensely happy to walk the short distance down the road in the evening to have dinner at a restaurant, instead of being tied to his wheelchair.

He had telephoned and written to all the contacts he knew who might have knowledge about Beirut in the time that Rachel was there. Several friends replied with contacts but none of the people could help when Guy actually talked to them.

Everyone said that it was very unlikely that they would find Hassim without knowing his other name. There had been unrest going on for years. Many people had died, and Beirut was definitely not a safe place to visit. There was little chance of finding Hassim by just turning up in Beirut and asking around. Even if Millie could find any of his old haunts, the buildings might not now still be standing. It was an impossible fool's errand, they were advised. Millie was disappointed but tried to put it out of her mind.

One day she received a letter from Irene. She opened it and another fat envelope fell out. First, she read the letter from Irene. She was getting old, she said, and her arthritis was playing her up. She wondered how Millie was and invited her to come and visit whenever she liked. She enclosed a letter that had come from the estate agents who had sold their house. Apparently, it had been lost behind a piece of furniture for years and only found when the people moved again.

Millie looked at the writing on the envelope. It was from a Professor at the University of Beirut. She read the letter and gave a cry of surprise. It was a letter from Nabila. She showed it to Guy:

Dearest Millie

I am so happy to discover that a kind rescuer helped you to find your family. I have been very worried about you ever since we lost each other in the marketplace.

I am living here at the address above with a very kind employer whose friend discovered that you were safe. My employer is writing this letter for me. I am glad you are not here as I saw Hassim recently and he seemed to be looking for someone. Maybe he is still looking for us. I will not go to Tripoli again as I am frightened of him.

Mr. Massoud, my employer, is a very kind man and Ali and I are very happy living here in his beautiful home. I was very sad to hear about your mother's murder.

If you would like to write to me, you can write to me at the address on this letter. I hope one day we shall see each other again.

With love from your friend,

Nabila

"Don't you think that this is fate, Dad? I shall write to Nabila and ask if I can come and visit her. Maybe she will know how to find Hassim."

"Remember Millie, this letter was sent to you twelve years ago. Nabila may not still be living in the same place. Even if you could get a visa, it would not be safe for you to go back there. Why don't you write to Nabila and see if you get a reply? You can decide what to do then." Guy was quite desperate to stop Millie trying to go back to Lebanon.

"Okay, Dad," said Millie. "That is the sensible thing to do. I agree."

"In the meantime," said Guy, "while your leg is still healing, and you don't know for sure whether you can dance again, why don't you go over to England to visit with Irene and Jim and Marie. They haven't seen you for years and still telephone regularly to see how you are. If I hear any news, or a letter comes for you, I will call you right away."

"I think I will go to England," said Millie thoughtfully. A plan was beginning to form in her mind.

Chapter Twenty-Eight – England

Millie telephoned Irene who was thrilled that Millie was coming to visit. Then she telephoned Marie and Jim. They were very happy, too, and said they would come over to Irene's to see her.

She flew to England and took a train from London to the town where Irene lived. She then took a taxi to the bungalow that Irene shared with her sister. Millie rang the doorbell, and the two old ladies came bustling to the door, both trying to be the first to hug and kiss her. She was hugged tightly to two soft bosoms smelling sweetly of old-fashioned talcum powder. She kissed them both gently, trying to hide her shock at how old and frail they had both become since she had last seen them. They bustled about bringing tea and delicious home-made cake into the lounge.

Irene had very bad arthritis and her hands, having been constantly immersed in hot water in her former housekeeper's job, were twisted and gnarled. However, she ignored this and managed, as she always had, to continue cooking and cleaning. Her sister, Janet was less robust than her sister, but between them they managed to look after the house themselves. The sisters also told Millie that they had a "gorgeous young man" to do their gardening for them.

Millie told them all about Canada, about the house in Paris and her father and his family. She told them about Las Vegas and described the fantastic show she had danced in.

"Such a pity that you had your accident," said Irene. "Are you very sad not to be able to dance?"

"Not as sad as I expected to be," said Millie. "At first, I was upset, of course, but even before I left hospital, I had accepted it. I suppose I have often had to get used to big changes and disruptions in my life. My friend, Valentina, was much more upset than I was. We had done everything together since we were teenagers and she had to get used to doing things without me. But I had got used to being alone a long time ago, so it was easier for me. I really loved being a dancer, but the accident was my own fault. My mind was not on what I was doing that night and I knew I had to take great care on that platform. I was thinking about my mother."

Millie told them about meeting Dinah and how she had described that Hassim had been harassing her mother just before she disappeared.

"You can't be sure it was him though, Millie," said Irene.

"I know," said Millie, "but my mind keeps going back to that and I feel I have to find out."

Irene begged Millie not to go back to Lebanon. "You can't bring your mother back, Millie. She would want you to get on with your life, not to risk it going back there."

"You could be right, Irene. I have decided that it depends if I get a reply from Nabila. If I hear from her then one day maybe I will go back to see her. If I can find Hassim and report him to the police for them to investigate again then that's what I'll do. If I don't hear from Nabila, then I will try to forget about it and get on with my life. If I can't dance again, I will have to find something else to do. Perhaps I will train to be a dance teacher, I don't know. I think something will turn up to make my decision for me. I have this strong feeling that it will happen despite any plans I make."

Later that evening Marie and Jim phoned. It was wonderful to talk to them. They were obviously thrilled to be able to see her again and Millie felt very guilty that she had been so taken up with her own life that she had not kept in closer touch with them. They arranged that they would drive over to Irene's in a week's time and pick her up. She would go and stay with them at their house for the remainder of her holiday.

The week with Irene and Janet passed quickly. They went into the nearby market town to shop in the market. Irene and Janet liked to buy as much as they could afford from local traders. The two old ladies were full of spirit and engaged in much teasing and banter with the people in the shops they visited. This amused Millie very much and she was glad to see that Irene was enjoying her life with her sister. The two old ladies spoiled Millie and would hardly let her do anything to help. She insisted on helping round the house even though Irene was adamant that she was a guest. Millie had to threaten to leave if they wouldn't let her help and, in the end, they gave in gracefully.

Jim and Marie arrived, and Irene stuffed them all full of food before they set off. Millie hugged Irene and Janet and thanked them for a wonderful holiday even though her trousers were now much too snug thanks to all the good food they had given her. The two old ladies stood at the door, waving goodbye, mopping at their tears with lacy handkerchiefs.

Millie waved goodbye until they were out of sight and then leaned forward to put her arms round her friend Marie's neck.

"I am so sorry I haven't kept in touch more. Please forgive me. I was a stroppy teenager there for a while. I can tell you that my father has not had an easy time of coping with me. It has only struck me since my accident how ungrateful I have been to all the people who have been so kind to me. I think I have been secretly feeling sorry for myself for what happened to my mother. Now I see that I have a lot to be thankful for."

Marie twisted round in her seat and smiled at Millie.

"No one could blame you for being a stroppy teenager for a while. Actually, it was a quite normal thing to be; you were a teenager after all. You had a dreadfully bad start and Jim and I have always said that the way you overcame that was fantastic. You had a right to be angry and bitter and you never seemed to be."

Millie reached forward to touch Marie's shoulder. "I was always angry though, I just kept it hidden. I had always kept my real self hidden. I thought I was protecting myself from disappointment, but I missed out on so much. If I had been more open at boarding school, I could have made friends, but I shut everyone out. It wasn't until I met Natalie and Valentina that I really started to trust other girls. Valentina is such an extrovert that when she decided to be my friend, she just swept me along with her. She taught me to grab life with both hands and live it. It wasn't until I was in hospital that I realised how much I had changed, and it was all due to her. I still haven't told her how much I love her for being my friend. I have had something on my mind."

When they got to Marie and Jim's house, Millie had a chance to really look at her friends. They were much the same but getting older, of course. Marie was plumper, but still as sleek as a little bird. Jim was thinner than ever and more grizzled looking. His frizzy hair was almost completely grey and he now wore glasses, but his grin was a wide as ever. They had bought a Chinese takeaway on the way home and Jim opened a bottle of wine.

"Now, tell us all your news," said Jim as Marie sipped her wine, smiling encouragingly.

Millie told them about how she and her dad had now become closer, and how wonderful it was that he seemed to be getting the feeling back in his legs and might even walk unaided in time. Marie and Jim thought that was marvellous news.

She described her time in Las Vegas and about meeting Dinah, and about recently getting the twelve-year-old letter from Nabila.

"I think getting that letter was a sign. I think fate kept that letter hidden until it was the right time for me to get it. I think I may have to go back to Lebanon and find my mother's killer."

Marie and Jim looked at each other with concern. Marie put her hand on Millie's arm.

"Millie, darling. There has been a war for years there. It is an incredibly dangerous place now. It was quite a dangerous place in some ways even when we were there. Please. Promise me that you won't go back there again."

Millie looked calmly at her friends. "Everyone says the same thing. Don't worry. If it is meant to be, I will go there. If it is not meant to be, I won't. Dad suggested that I write to Nabila. I know he is hoping I will not hear from her and that will be that. I think I will hear from her and that maybe I will go back. Something in me is quite sure about it."

Marie and Jim were unable to shake Millie's resolve, and, in the end, they gave up.

"Well, never mind that," said Marie. "Jim has a half-term holiday starting on Monday and I have taken some annual leave. Why don't we go off on the boat for a few days?"

They all agreed and sat up until the small hours talking and laughing. The next day Jim had to go to work while Marie and Millie had a lay in. They got up late and sat about in their pyjamas, talking while they ate breakfast.

Marie wanted to know all about Guy and Millie's French family. She told Marie how she had not really felt any love for Guy until she had come back from America and that she thought her lack of trust in men had made her hold back from him. Guy had always been consistently there for her but had never tried to force her to show affection. He had waited for her to come to him on her own terms. She had only recently appreciated how understanding of her feelings he had been. Now she felt love for him as her father and trusted him as a girl should be able to trust her father.

"Sometimes I do wish I had grown up with a mother and a father, as I would have done if Dad's mother had not interfered. But you can't change the past, and I am sure his mother was just trying to protect her son in the best way she knew how. See how much I have grown up," Millie said to Marie with a cheeky grin, "I can even forgive my battle-axe of a grandmother."

Marie laughed, "Wow, how grown-up is that. How about Aunt Vicky? Can you forgive her?"

Millie giggled. "That's asking too much. In truth, I don't hold much against her. Whatever her reasons for being a cold-blooded cow were, I don't really care anymore. When I look back, Granny was always kind to me, and Irene was wonderful. She was more of an auntie to me than ever Vicky was. I had no idea about families then. I had nothing to base them on. I suppose Sofia and Nabila were my family until then... When you think how much was against them, those two dear women tried their best to keep me safe. They fed me and looked after me. Many children all over the world don't get even that."

Marie sipped her coffee, "What about the French family, apart from your dad, that is."

"Well, Cousin Natalie is great, very much like a big sister. She is getting married soon so she will be moving out of the family home. Benoit is quiet and doesn't say much. He is a bit under his mother and father's thumb really, but a nice man at heart. Uncle Henri and Aunt Denise are quite kind but in an off-hand way, but that's just how they are. They are the same with their own children. They are sort of old-fashioned. Natalie is a bit of a thorn in their side really." Millie giggled. "They try so hard to get her to do what they want. She smiles sweetly, agrees with everything they say and does her own thing anyway. It is marvellous to watch really. She should be a politician!"

"Natalie sounds quite a character. Who is she marrying?"

"Dad says François is a complete innocent, and that Natalie will lead him round by the nose, but that he will enjoy every moment of it." Millie and Marie laughed at the visual image Millie described.

"Natalie sounds like quite a girl."

"Oh, she is. I wish I was more like her. I think she is

more like Grandmother than she knows, but much more loving of course. She has our grandmother's strength of character and an incurable habit of trying to manage people's lives. This was a fault in Grandmother, as she tried to force people where they did not want to go. Natalie is wiser and tries to coax people to go where they would be happiest. But the urge to manage everything definitely comes from Grandmother."

They then got onto the subject of America. Marie wanted to know all about the show. Millie described their dance numbers and had brought some photographs of her and Valentina posing in their mirror duet costumes. They were the only photographs she had of her time in Las Vegas. Marie was very impressed and thought they both looked gorgeous.

Millie had also brought the letter from Nabila to show Marie. "I didn't think she could read or write," said Marie, "And who is this Professor chap whose name is on the envelope?"

"Nabila couldn't read or write, at least not then. Perhaps her boss wrote it for her. She says in the letter that he is kind. I don't know how the Professor comes into it."

"I really hope you don't go back to Beirut, Millie. Even if Hassim is the man who might have killed your mother, the police there may not be able to prove he did it after all this time. If you did find him, he was a very dangerous man then. He may be more dangerous now, especially if he is a murderer. They have had years of civil unrest there; things have changed a lot in that time. There are unlikely to be many Europeans there now. It is much too dangerous. Please don't go."

Millie looked at her friend and then hugged her. "I will only go back if Nabila writes back and tells me it is safe to go. I may not even be able to get a visa to go back even if she says it is safe. Maybe my father will be able to go back with me. It could be years before we can go, Dad says. Please don't worry, it will probably never happen."

Marie was appeased, at least for the moment and they discussed Marie and Jim's future plans.

"We have not had a long trip on the boat for a few years now. It takes longer and longer to save up enough money to go away for a few months or a year. Everything costs more these days. Maintenance, storage costs, everything is so expensive. I think that next time we go, we will go for a whole year and rent our house out this time to cover some of the costs. It will probably be the last time we go away on the boat for a long trip. We will have to start being sensible one day."

"Perhaps you could stop by Tripoli during your next trip," said Millie grinning. "If you timed it for when I am there visiting Nabila, you could be on hand in case I need rescuing again."

"Oh, Millie, don't joke. It is not right to joke about it. I have often wondered what would have happened to you if we hadn't found you asleep on our boat."

They all went down to the boat on the Saturday and sailed around the coast for a week. The weather was sunny and the sky blue, but it was windy and cool, and the sea was quite choppy. Millie found it very exhilarating and had a wonderful time. They sailed back to the berth where Marie and Jim kept the boat when they were not using it. They drove back to the house and found the answer phone flashing.

Chapter Twenty-Nine – Letter from Lebanon

It was a message from Guy, asking Millie to call him back. Millie asked if she could call him on their telephone and Marie said, "Yes of course." Guy answered the telephone and Millie asked him if anything was the matter.

"Millie, a letter has come from Tripoli. I think it is from Nabila. I haven't opened it. I also had a bit of luck tracing the professor. He is in America now, in Chicago. I wrote to him, and, by coincidence, I received his reply this morning. He is a friend of the man who wrote the letter for Nabila. He says his friend was Nabila's employer, but they have been married for years, have a little girl called Sofia, and are very happy, it seems. We will read the letter together when you come home, darling."

"I'll fly home tomorrow, Dad. I am so excited to think Nabila is married and has a baby. She named it after Sofia too. That's so wonderful. I'll see you tomorrow night, probably."

Millie turned to Marie. "I hope you don't mind if I go

home tomorrow. I just can't wait to read Nabila's letter."

Marie smiled, "Of course, I understand, but Millie, please don't think of going to Beirut at least until it is peaceful again."

"Don't worry, Marie. Dad feels just the same as you. I will probably not be allowed to go there without a squad of soldiers to protect me."

Marie flew home to Paris the next day. Her flight was a late one and she got home at midnight. She kissed her father affectionately when she arrived.

"I think I am too tired to read the letter tonight, Dad. Can we do it tomorrow?"

Guy sent her off to bed and she fell asleep immediately. Next morning, Millie woke to the delicious smell of fresh coffee. She brushed her teeth, combed her hair, and put on her dressing-gown. She went into the dining room and found the table laid ready with coffee and croissants.

"Oh, lovely! You are spoiling me, Dad."

"Nonsense. Your break has done you good. You look rested and you seem to have caught the sun… You even have a bit of a tan on your cheeks!"

"Marie and Jim took me sailing. It was lovely weather, just a bit cold and windy. I am not tanned, I'm weather-beaten."

They both laughed. After breakfast, Guy gave Millie the letter from Nabila. Millie opened it and read it carefully then handed it to Guy to read.

Dearest Millie

My husband Khalil is writing this for me. He can read and write English. As you can tell I am married to Khalil. He has been so kind to me and Ali. Ali is well. Although he still like a small child, he is very tall.

Khalil and I have been blessed with our little girl who we named for my dear friend, Sofia. She is six years old now and is a joy to us both. We are lucky that Ali is not jealous of her at all.

We would love you to come and visit us one day. It is not safe yet, although it is getting better. You must not come until we write and tell you it is safe.

We have seen Hassim in Tripoli three times over the years, the most recent time was about three

years ago. We don't often go to Tripoli now as he
seemed, when we saw him to still be looking for
us. He was obviously looking for someone. Who
else could it be? The last time we noticed him, I
hid in a shop and Khalil followed him. He drove
off in a new Mercedes car. Hassim was very well-
dressed and looked prosperous.

Until it is safe, we beg you to not to come. We will
write whenever we have any news.

I enclose a photograph of us all in front of our
home.

With love and blessings from your friend

Nabila Massoud

Millie handed the letter to Guy to read. After he read
it through several times, they both studied the
photograph. Nabila looked plump and was smiling
widely. Her handsome husband looked like a gentle
and kindly man. The little girl, Sofia, stood solemnly in
front of them. She had huge dark eyes and was sucking
her finger. She had a kitten tucked under her arm.
Beside them loomed Ali but with a peaceful expression
on his face.

"It appears your friend Nabila has managed to find happiness with Khalil. I think that is wonderful."

"So do I," said Millie enthusiastically. "Nabila deserved to find happiness. Ali's father was terribly cruel to her, and it cannot have been easy to cope with a child as disabled as Ali. I am so glad she found a kind husband and has had a little girl. It is wonderful to hear of someone as good as her being rewarded for her goodness." Millie smiled at her father. "I think I am lucky, too. I am so glad that I have found my kind and loving father."

Guy put his arms around and kissed her gently on her forehead.

"I am proud to have such a lovely daughter. I love you very much."

Millie wrote back to Nabila and enclosed some photographs of herself, her French family, her father and Natalie. She told Nabila about her life now, reassuring Nabila that she would not come to Lebanon unless it was safe to come. Millie closed by asking her friend to be careful not to let Hassim catch up with her.

Millie talked to Guy and Natalie about her future. She needed to think of another career. She could, of course, train to be a dance teacher but thought it might be too upsetting to be teaching people to do what she could not do. Natalie agreed and suggested that Millie might like to work in her interior design business with her. Millie laughed.

"I have no idea of colour or design. That's your talent, Natalie, I just have not got it."

Millie spent a lot of time in the next few weeks wondering what new career she should choose, in the meantime, she went along with Natalie on some of her jobs to help in any way she could. She was surprised at how enjoyable it was to revamp someone's home, and it was lovely to see how delighted people were with the work Natalie was doing. She had a natural ability to match the décor of a person's home to harmonize with their personalities and their way of life in a subtle but exciting way. She was a genius with colour, and never sacrificed comfort for style, so that people found their new look rooms easy to live with. Millie enjoyed it, but she knew she did not have Natalie's gifts and doubted that it was a skill that could be learned.

Chapter Thirty– Nabila

Nabila was very contented with her life in Lebanon. Now she knew Millie was safe and back with her family, her mind was at peace. When she tended her roses, it always reminded Nabila of how Millie as a little child would bury her small nose in the soft petals of the roses and blissfully breathe in their scent. She wondered if the tragic events of the girl's life had caused any lasting damage to Millie's wellbeing. She knew it was far too dangerous for Millie to visit them in their home. It was even hazardous for them at times, although living out in the countryside was some protection.

Ali was not a problem anymore. He had developed such a strong bond with their gardener and his wife that Khalil suggested they could now take a holiday, so he set about procuring passports for Nabila and Sofia. When these arrived, he sat down with Nabila and they discussed where to go to. Nabila was extremely nervous at the thought of flying, so Khalil wrote to his friend, Mahmoud, who had a sailing boat, to ask if they could hire him to take them to Cyprus. He wrote back and said he would be happy to do it. Mahmoud also recommended a hotel where he knew they would be well taken care of, near the town of Famagusta where his boat would dock.

Nabila and Kahlil were discussing their holiday when Nabila said, "Oh, Kahlil, why don't we suggest that Millie come to Cyprus to meet up with us? She will be able to come to Cyprus safely and we may never get a better chance to meet up with her."

"That is a wonderful idea, my darling. I will write to her and her father immediately and suggest it," replied her husband, dropping an affectionate kiss on her forehead. Nabila's beautiful dark eyes glowed and, wrapping her arms around her husband's waist, she laid her head on his chest. *"How blessed I am to have this wonderful husband,"* she thought. The letter was duly sent, and Khalil added their telephone number so that Millie could call them.

When Millie received the letter, she was pleased. She had the chance to meet Nabila again and also Kahlil and their little daughter, Sofia. She also would not have to make the risky journey to Lebanon to do so. She showed the letter to her father and Guy read it with interest.

"I think this is a great idea and, if you don't mind, I

would like to come with you. I would like to meet Nabila to thank her for taking care of you as well as she could, in view of her own problems."

Millie smiled at her father. "I would love you to come with me. It will be our first proper holiday together."

Guy telephoned Khalil's number and they discussed how they could meet and what dates would suit them both. Millie asked to speak to Nabila but as she had forgotten much of her Arabic, the conversation was a little stilted. She hoped that meeting in person would make communication easier.

Now both parties had agreed a date, Khalil contacted his friend, Mahmoud, to arrange to sail to Cyprus. His friend also made the reservations at the Golden Palm Hotel, his cousins's hotel. Once Khalil had confirmation of their booking, he texted the address to Guy.

Guy and Millie decided to make their own hotel reservations at a different hotel. For one thing, they did not know how the meeting would go and on the other hand, they knew that Nabila and her family were on holiday, so they did not want to intrude too much.

As the time approached for their meeting in Cyprus,

Millie found her feelings were seesawing between huge excitement at meeting Nabila and her family and a strange feeling of dread. She often forgot about her childhood for long periods of time, but the prospect of seeing Nabila again raised a maelstrom of mixed emotions and memories.

Millie happily remembered the peaceful times she had spent with Sofia and Nabila, and her cat Peter. However, the awful experiences she had suffered at the hands of Hassim were also resurrected. She could not seem to enjoy the good memories without the bad ones intruding.

Looking back at Hassim's actions with the eyes of the child she had once been, she re-lived the fear and feelings of helplessness – but thinking as a grown woman, her feelings towards Hassim were simply of utter hatred and revulsion. She had met a few imperfect and unpleasant people in her short life, such as her grandmother, but she had not come across anyone as inherently wicked as Hassim. The thought that he might have murdered and abandoned her mother's body in such a callous way made her so angry that she believed that only bringing Hassim to justice would ever give her real peace.

For the most part, she had repressed the memories of the terrible night she had been abused but they had suddenly surged back to life. Tears filled her eyes at the memory of the horror she had experienced and how helpless she had been. She reminded herself that it was in the past, but Hassim had been responsible for her being in that man's house and he was the focus of her hatred and longing for justice, for herself and for her mother.

Chapter Thirty-One – Reunion

Nabila, Khalil, and Sofia sailed to Famagusta on their friend's boat. Mahmoud took them to their hotel and introduced them to the owner, a cousin of Mahmoud's wife. They were pleased with their comfortable room and the wonderful sea view from their balcony. After unpacking, they went down and sat outside in the pavement café to have some lunch. While they had coffee, the hotel owner came and sat with them, telling them about all the local sights he thought worth visiting. The men smoked while Nabila and Sofia nibbled olives and pistachio nuts.

Khalil left a message at Millie's hotel to let her know they had arrived. Eventually, Millie rang to say they had also arrived at their hotel, the Grecian Bay Hotel. They arranged to join Khalil and Nabila for dinner that evening.

Millie and Guy got settled in their rooms and, after unpacking and showering, they dressed ready to travel by taxi to the Golden Palm. They had decided that it was better for them to travel to meet Khalil and Nabila as they had Sofia with them. As the taxi drove them across the city to the Golden Palm, Guy looked at his daughter. She was looking more subdued than he expected. He reached for her hand.

"Are you okay, Millie? You're very quiet. Aren't you looking forward to seeing Nabila?"

Millie smiled at her father, "Yes. Of course, I am really looking forward to seeing her and also meeting her husband and daughter, but I must admit, it is also reminding me of some really bad memories."

Guy put his arm round his daughter. "I am sure when you see Nabila and how good her life is now, you will just be happy to see her."

"I am sure you are right, Dad. I hope we can talk to each other without language being a problem."

They arrived at the hotel and were glad to see that Nabila and Khalil were waiting in the outside café and as soon as Millie spotted Nabila, a feeling of love flooded through her as she saw that Nabila was looking so well and so happy in the company of her handsome, silver-haired husband. A dear little dark-eyed child was peeping shyly round her father's legs. Nabila threw her arms around Millie and kissed her on both cheeks, chattering away in Arabic. To Millie's surprise she found she could still understand some of what Nabila was saying.

"I was so unhappy to have lost you near the port. I dragged Ali around for hours, trying to find you and it broke my heart to think of you alone and frightened!" Nabila put her hands on Millie's cheeks and was so happy to see Millie grown up and with her father.

Guy and Khalil shook hands and immediately liked each other. Millie could not remember enough Arabic to explain things to Nabila, so she told Khalil how she had found an English couple and how she had hidden on their boat. Then she told them how she had been taken to her grandmother and then eventually had found her father. Khalil translated the story for his wife.

Millie and Nabila sat together with clasped hands. Nabila called her daughter to her, and Millie hugged the little girl. "Nabila, she is so beautiful."

"How is Ali?" Millie asked. Khalil explained that Ali was safe at home and how he was much improved, and that he was very attached to their gardener and his wife who were caring for him in their absence.

"He saved me, really, Nabila, didn't he? If Ali hadn't hit Hassim, I think he would have killed us both. He was completely out of control."

Nabila nodded, it was true that Ali had inadvertently prevented Hassim killing or seriously injuring both Nabila and Millie. The women gazed at each other, remembering how frightened they had been and how they had fled, constantly terrified that Hassim would catch them.

Khalil told them how they had seen Hassim several times and how Nabila had resorted to wearing a scarf round her face when they went into town. They told Guy and Millie that they felt that Hassim had been looking for them when he was in their town. Nabila was sure that he had not forgotten about them.

Millie told them that she suspected, from information from her mother's friend, that Hassim had been the person who had murdered Rachel. Nabila and Khalil were shocked to hear this. Nabila knew that Hassim was wicked, but she had not really imagined he could be a cold-blooded murderer.

For a moment all four sat quietly, then Guy said, "This is not the time to be gloomy. We are also celebrating too. We are so happy that you found each other and are happy, of course, that you have this dear little girl." Guy smiled at Sofia. She gazed at him shyly for a moment and then smiled at him.

"You are right, Dad," said Millie, turning to her friend. "I am so thrilled to know that you found happiness, Nabila, and I am so grateful to you, Khalil, for your kindness to Nabila."

Khalil explained that Nabila had brought him great happiness too. He had never expected to have a child and that Sofia was the light of his life. Khalil and Nabila looked at each other fondly.

They all had dinner together in the hotel restaurant, and Millie and Guy together told the story of how Millie had contacted him and all about her dancing career and her accident.

Nabila was very content to see Millie grown up and safe with her father. How different all their lives would have been in Ali had not come to their rescue, even if he did not know exactly what he had done. She thought fondly of her poor son, and hoped he was content at home without her there.

After their dinner, Guy and Millie bid the couple goodnight as Sofia had fallen asleep on her father's lap. They arranged to meet at the Grecian Bay the following day for lunch. Guy and Millie sat quietly in the taxi back to their hotel.

Each was thinking about their meeting with Nabila and Khalil in different ways. Guy was thinking how much he had liked Khalil and how obvious it was that he and Nabila had a wonderfully united marriage. His thoughts drifted back to his lovely Rachel and wished that he had taken better care of her. They could have had such a wonderful marriage if his mother had not chased Rachel away from him.

Millie's thoughts were careening around in her head. She had loved seeing Nabila and Khalil's happy marriage but seeing her again had opened a Pandora's box of memories and emotions. Long-suppressed images whirled around her mind in a kaleidoscope.

She remembered Sofia's careworn face and how she had done her best to care for Rachel's abandoned child. She remembered Hassim's surly face and felt again the terror he had made them all feel. She grieved anew for Sofia and her little cat Peter, and for the terror she had felt when in the clutches of the horrible man in the white house in Beirut. The memories of the fear she had felt rose in her chest and made it hard to breathe.

Guy took Millie's hand and gradually the fear

receded. In its place rose an implacable anger at Hassim and at what he had done to her, and probably her mother too. Somehow, some day, she would make sure Hassim paid for what he had done.

Chapter Thirty-Two – Retribution

By awful co-incidence, Mr. Khoury and his bodyguards, including Hassim, had flown to Cyprus the same day as Guy and Millie and, with several hired cars to carry his entourage, checked into a luxury resort hotel. Khoury was meeting with several of his cronies for one of their week-long business and party meetings. High-class prostitutes were flown in from London and Paris to provide their services to Mr. Khoury and his guests.

Once Mr. Khoury was ensconced in his suite, he dismissed all but his two most trusted bodyguards. He had no intention of paying for all of them to stay in the same hotel as him at a nightly rate of more than £1,000 per person. They would be staying in a much cheaper establishment nearby, handy to answer a call from their boss.

Hassim, who was allocated the job of driving one of the hire cars, was rather peeved at being housed in a far less luxurious hotel. He also envied his employer taking his pleasure with the long-legged lovelies he had seen gathering in the hotel lobby. When he was off duty, he decided to go out for a drive to see if he could find a woman for himself, but he had no intention of paying for his pleasure. He drove about the streets but failed to find a woman on her own that would suit his tastes.

Frustrated, Hassim drove around near the beach and spotted a group sitting on the terrace outside a hotel. He did a double-take when he saw a woman from behind with long curly, honey-coloured hair just like Rachel's had been and opposite her was a woman who looked like Nabila. Two men sat with them and between them, a small child.

He quickly parked his car and moved closer to the group, keeping well out of their sight. The group stood up and started to hug. With a better view, Hassim was now certain that one of the women was Nabila and his anger surged. One of the men and the girl with the hair like Rachel moved away and stood waiting for a taxi.

Hassim saw that the young woman with the long hair was very much like Rachel. It must be the child, Millie, now grownup. Hassim watched with black vengeance in his heart as Nabila, the other man and the child went inside the hotel. He ran back to his car and followed the taxi with Millie and her father back to their hotel. He swore to return when he was free and make Millie and Nabila pay for outwitting him.

The next morning, Hassim had a call from one of his boss's main bodyguards who instructed Hassim to attend Mr. Khoury during breakfast. Hassim was surprised, having rarely been alone with Mr. Khoury, so he hurried to the hotel and found Mr. Khoury outside in the garden, sitting alone. Mr. Khoury told Hassim to sit down at his table and to pour himself a coffee. Mr. Khoury looked curiously at Hassim. He was well aware of all the various illegal and sometimes lethal activities that Hassim had carried out for him, and he was curious about the man.

He asked Hassim questions about his life and Hassim assumed his boss was as venal as he was himself and he did not hold back in bragging about his many crimes. He found himself bragging about raping and killing the English woman, Rachel, because she would not willingly have sex with him. He also told his boss about his efforts to make money from the murdered woman's child, not noticing the frown that flitted over My Khoury's face like a shadow.

"Go on," encouraged Mr. Khoury, tenting his fingers

under his chin. He was inwardly disgusted at his employee's dreadful bragging.

Hassim had seriously misjudged his boss. Believing that Mr. Khoury was in tune with his own lack of moral code, Hassim told his boss about taking Millie to the man who had abused her. He related how angry he had been as Millie's behaviour towards his customer had cost him money. He never noticed the disgust on Mr. Khoury's face and, full of his own importance, went on to describe how Millie, Nabila and Ali had evaded his retribution until now.

Mr. Khoury had no compunction about ordering his men to inflict revenge on the criminal people he did business with if they thwarted or betrayed him, but he would *never* cause harm to women or innocent children. He imagined how he would react if any man did to his own daughter what Hassim had done to Rachel's child. He was infuriated that this employee of his had murdered a woman just for not wanting to sleep with him. Intense anger rose in his heart, but Mr. Khoury kept his face blank.

With unbridled excitement, Hassim told his boss how he had spotted Millie and Nabila in a restaurant right there in town that very night.

"What are you going to do about it?" said Mr. Khoury, feigning indifference.

"Well, when I am off duty, I am going to follow that girl and that damn woman around and find a way to teach them a lesson for getting away from me." Hassim grimaced with anticipation of his revenge.

Pretending to approve of Hassim's plans, Mr. Khoury decided to make a few enquiries of his own. He asked Hassim which hotels Millie and Nabila were staying in. Hassim told him.

"I need you here tomorrow," said Mr. Khoury, but after that you can have as much time off as you need."

"Thanks, Boss," said Hassim. Mr. Khoury sat quiet, deep in thought, and Hassim drank his coffee and stayed silent until Mr. Khoury dismissed him.

Millie and her father met Nabila and her family for lunch the next day. They were perfectly content to be together. Guy and Khalil were both similar characters and enjoyed their conversations about books they had read and world events. Millie and Nabila managed to communicate, despite Millie having forgotten much of the Arabic she had spoken as a child. Mostly the two women were content to sit and feel close to each other. Sofia gradually lost her shyness towards Guy and Millie and even became brave enough to climb onto Millie's knee. She would play with Millie's long curls, fascinated by the colour of her hair.

Millie was quite enchanted by the pretty little child and loved to cuddle her. Looking at the sweet little girl who had never been afraid or lacked care, she could not help remembering her own less fortunate childhood. She looked at Nabila, smiling fondly at her daughter; Millie knew that Nabila had done her best to protect her in those far off and dangerous days, and she put her arm around Nabila's shoulders and kissed her tenderly on the cheek. Nabila smiled happily at Millie, revealing the unevenness of her teeth.

Millie wondered if she would ever have a child herself. Such thoughts had never entered her head before, but the feeling of the child on her lap and her soft and sweet-smelling little body created a sudden longing in her heart to have a child of her own one day.

They arranged to meet the next day and to have a lunchtime picnic on the beach. Khalil said that he would arrange to have the picnic made by his hotel and they arranged to meet on the beach nearby. Khalil pointed out that, behind the beach was a grassy area with some trees, where they could sit in the shade if the sun became too strong.

The following morning, after taking breakfast outside their hotel, Millie and Guy took a taxi to the Golden Palm. They did not notice Hassim driving behind them, an angry scowl on his face. Khalil, Sofia, and Nabila were waiting outside their hotel with a large cooler. Their hotel had also provided some rugs for them to sit on and a couple of folding chairs.

Khalil led the way towards the beach. They set up the chairs and blankets on the grass edging the sand. They all took off their shoes and prepared to enjoy their day together on the beach. Sofia immediately wanted to paddle in the sea. Millie took her hand, and they paddled in the little waves frilling the edge of the water. Millie helped the little girl build a sandcastle and decorate it with pebbles and tiny shells.

They ate their picnic later in the morning and then, leaving the two men sitting in the chairs watching Sofia play in the sand, Millie and Nabila wandered off, arm in arm, into the cool of the trees. They could hear the voices of the men talking and Sofia's chattering. As they wandered along the edge of the beach among the trees, the sounds of their family's voices faded away and all they could hear was the whispering of the trees and the waves on the beach.

Out on the sea they could see a speedboat moving slowly along in the same direction as they were walking. There were two men in the boat and Millie vaguely wondered if they were fishing but could not see any fishing rods.

Suddenly, Nabila fell to the ground. Turning to see what had happened to her friend, Millie was shocked to see Hassim behind them, a gun in his hand. He had hit Nabila on the head with the gun. Her first thought was for her friend and she started to go to her, but Hassim raised his arm.

"Don't move, bitch," Hassim smiled nastily. "Did you think you were safe from me? Well… you were wrong. I am going to give you what I gave your mother."

Millie gasped. It *was* Hassim who had killed her mother! She looked down at Nabila who had blood running from a wound on her temple. She started to move towards Nabila again, but Hassim moved to stand between them. Millie backed away as she stared at the gun pointing at her. Her thoughts raced wildly in her mind. She couldn't call her father or Khalil. They didn't have any way to defend against a gun. She looked around frantically: there was nowhere to run. The sunlight on the sea flickered through the trees and she thought she glimpsed the motorboat getting closer to the shore.

Millie kept backing away from Hassim until she was on the sand again. She saw that some rocks were between her and her father and Khalil. Nabila moaned as she stirred, so Millie kept backing away, hoping to draw Hassim away from her friend. Hassim followed her, the gun still pointing at her.

"Did you think I had forgotten you and Nabila? I have been looking for you both for years. I even caught sight of her once or twice, but she evaded me. I never forget anyone who gets the better of me. I am going to make sure you suffer before you die… as I made your bitch mother suffer!"

Hassim walked menacingly toward her; the gun dipped a little. Millie looked round frantically. Should she run? Should she call her father? She tripped and fell to her knees.

Hassim started forward her holding the gun out straight in front of him. Suddenly, a shot rang out and Hassim dropped to the ground, the gun falling from his hand. The shot seemed to have come from the speedboat, which had suddenly put on a burst of speed. It wheeled around and out to sea, before vanishing round a curve on the land, the sound of its engine diminishing until it was all quiet.

The sound of the shot brought Guy and Khalil running. Millie stood, shocked by Hassim's sudden fall. Khalil ran to his wife who was now sitting up and gazing at her own hand covered in blood from where she had touched the painful place on her temple.

Guy looked down in horror at the dead man lying on the ground, his gun fallen from his hand.

"Millie, what happened? Who is that man?" Guy's tone was frantic.

Millie got to her feet, shivering with shock and Guy took her protectively in his arms.

"That's Hassim. He told me he had killed my

mother." Her face white with shock, she pointed out to sea. "Someone on that boat shot him."

"I wonder who was on that boat and why they shot him," said Guy, holding Millie tight. "He must have had other enemies. We should be grateful to them, but this is all so awful. I think we should get the police."

They went over to Khalil and Nabila. "Are you okay, Nabila?" asked Millie.

"I think she is alright; it is just a deep cut." Kahlil looked at Millie. "Who was that?" he said pointing at Hassim.

Nabila, hanging on her husband's arm, spoke in a quivery voice, "That is… was… Hassim. He was going to kill us both."

The two men talked about what to do. They had to involve the police but decided that to tell the police about all the history of Hassim's involvement in their lives in the past would complicate things unnecessarily. They decided to just say that the man was a stranger, and they did not know why he had attacked them. They had no idea who the people in the boat were, but they were very grateful to them.

Guy waited by the body while Khalil went back to the hotel with Sofia, Nabila and Millie to call the police and to tend to Nabila's injury. Their hotel owner said that he would call the police and explain things. Khalil took Sofia and Nabila up to their room and bathed her forehead tenderly.

"I don't think you will need stitches, but you will have a painful bruise for a while."

The hotel owner sat Millie in a chair in the coffee shop and sent one of his staff to fetch the picnic things back to the hotel.

The police arrived and they were shown up to the woodland and Hassim's body, the gun still laying by his hand. They questioned Guy closely, their skepticism that he did not know the man apparent in their faces. When Guy told them how people in the boat had shot Hassim before he could shoot Millie, their faces registered utter disbelief. They could see that Hassim's gun had not been fired.

The police accompanied Guy back to the hotel, and they questioned Millie closely. She repeated the story Guy had told and was adamant that someone from a boat had shot the man who was threatening her. She insisted that she did not know the man or why he was intent on killing her.

The police questioned other residents of the hotel, and several had witnessed the boat slowly moving up the coast, the sound of a shot and then seeing the boat speeding off and out of sight. Eventually they accepted Millie's story and decided that they should go and investigate this speedboat and its occupants. They discovered that the dead man was an employee of Mr. Khoury, and he and his men were questioned. Mr. Khoury, shrugging indifferently, maintained that Hassim was only a chauffeur, and he had no idea what he did on his day off. Soon realising that they would never get any useful information from such a powerful man as Mr. Khoury, the police gave up and went away to investigate the speedboat and where it might have been hired.

Later that evening, two of Mr. Khoury's most trusted bodyguards were shown into his suite. Money changed hands and, shaking their hands, Mr. Khoury said, "Have you cleaned up behind you?"

The two men, who had been professional snipers in their past military careers, assured him that neither the boat nor the rifle they had used would ever be found. Like Mr. Khoury, the two men had their professional standards and a man like Hassim who targeted women and children was less than vermin in their eyes.

Chapter Thirty-Three – Aftermath

After the police had gone, Nabila put Sofia to bed and the two couples sat together in the garden of the hotel, too shocked to eat. They talked over the events of the day in hushed voices.

"One good thing," said Khalil, his arm round his wife, "we no longer have to worry about meeting up with that man again. He has gone from our lives for good."

Millie looked fondly at Nabila who was slumped in her chair, leaning against her husband. At last, she knew for sure who had killed her mother. How different the day would have unfolded if the people on the boat had not killed Hassim before he could kill her and probably Nabila too. She wondered who those people were, but she could not help being glad Hassim was dead. He had cast a long shadow on her life and on Nabila's life, too. Now Rachel had been avenged at last. Perhaps they now could all live a normal life.

Guy and Millie got up and said goodbye to Khalil and Nabila. They arranged to come back to the hotel in the morning.

When Guy and Millie were leaving the hotel in the

morning, they were shocked to find a crowd of reporters and TV cameras pointing at them. They pushed through the crowd and got into the waiting taxi. When they reached the Golden Palm, they were dismayed to see that the reporters had followed them. Because of Guy being an author, the story of the gunman being killed before he could kill Millie was big news.

Millie and Guy dashed into their friend's hotel, refusing to make any comment to the reporters. Khalil was waiting in the foyer, and he took them up to their room.

"We do not like these people chasing us pestering us for comments," said Khalil. Nabila was sitting on one of the beds cuddling Sofia. She looked apologetically at Millie.

Khalil spoke for his wife, "I hope you will forgive us, Millie, but we just want to go back home. Mahmoud is taking us back this afternoon on his boat. Nabila cannot bear all this fuss. We could not even sit outside to have our coffee this morning. Those people kept shouting at us and poking microphones and cameras in our faces. I think it is best if we just leave."

Guy patted Khalil on his shoulder and Millie went over to sit by her friend. She said, "Of course, we understand completely. We have decided to leave today ourselves if the police say we can."

They all felt sad that their meeting up after so many years had been spoiled by Hassim's actions. None of them wanted to stay there; after such a close encounter with death, getting back into their former holiday mood was impossible.

Millie hugged her friend and Sofia and wished her peace and happiness now that Hassim was not going to spoil her peace of mind ever again. Guy and Khalil shook hands, and they all said their farewells.

Millie and Guy ran the gauntlet of the media, jumped into a taxi, and returned to their hotel. Guy rang the police and received the good news that they could leave if they left their contact details. They booked a flight back to Paris and the hotel helped them leave quietly by calling a taxi to the rear employee exit.

When they got back to Paris, they discovered that the events in Cyprus were well covered in all the main international newspapers. Their French family were very happy to have them both back safe and sound.

Guy asked them not to say anything to the press who hung round the door, shouting questions at everyone who went in or out. Millie and Guy stayed at home and refused to comment. There was, of course, wild speculation about who Hassim had been and Mr. Khoury was also being mentioned as Hassim had been his employee. Mr. Khoury maintained his indifferent attitude and refused to comment.

The newspapers scented that there was a deeper part to this story and Guy was well known but no one had known that he had a daughter. They wanted to know why someone from Lebanon would try to kill her. In the absence of any information from Millie or her family, the clamour gradually died away.

Over a few days the press, with nothing new to report, lost interest and life went back to normal for Millie and Guy. They had a telephone call from Khalil to say that Nabila had recovered from her injury; she was very happy to be home and back to her normal life.

When all was quiet again, Millie and Guy decided to go to England to visit Irene and for Guy to meet Marie and Jim for the first time. Guy wanted to thank the couple for rescuing his daughter from what could have been a much more tragic life. Natalie came with them to drive as Millie had not yet got a European license, and Guy was still not strong enough to drive long distances.

First, they went to visit Irene. She and her sister were getting older and quite a bit frailer, but they were still happy with their lives and still making amazing cakes. They had read the papers, of course, and were so glad that Millie and Nabila had escaped safely. Millie told them the whole story and how she had discovered that Hassim, the man who had attacked them, had confessed to murdering Rachel. The two old ladies listened with eyes like saucers and promised, when Millie asked them, not to talk about it to anyone.

Then the three of them drove to visit Marie and Jim. Millie was surprised and a little saddened to see that they, too, were getting older. They were both still working part-time and had sold their boat.

Jim explained that he was too old for it now and it was too expensive to maintain. They had bought themselves a little campervan and it was obviously Marie's pride and joy. They also had got a rescue dog, a delightfully shaggy mongrel with saucy eyes peeping out of his fringes. Marie had wanted a dog for many years and Millie was so happy to see what comfort the little dog brought to her friend. It made her think of Peter, her long-dead cat, and how she had loved him.

Guy thanked Marie and Jim for the care they had given his daughter.

"It was our pleasure. We often say, don't we Jim?" said Marie, leaning on her husband's arm, "what an amazing coincidence it was that bad weather made us stop in Tripoli that time. We hadn't intended to stop there at all. I don't like to think what might have happened to Millie if we hadn't had that storm."

After their visit, when they got off the ferry, they drove back to Paris slowly, making stops on the way to visit different towns in Normandy, enjoying the beautiful but quiet countryside. When they got back to Paris, Guy went back to work on his writing and Millie wandered about the city aimlessly, wondering what to do with herself. She knew she should decide on a career and study for some qualifications but, now that dancing was not possible, she could not think of anything she wanted to do for the rest of her life.

She shopped for things she did not really need and

spent too much time sitting in pavement cafes watching the world go by, just to fill up the hours of the day.

Millie knew she needed a purpose in life but, although she spent hours thinking about what she could do, nothing captured her imagination. She worried about her future, which now loomed empty before her. It began to seem impossible that she would find something she really wanted to do.

A few weeks later, Guy's publisher wrote from Canada. Guy opened it and discovered another letter inside, addressed to Millie. He called to her and, when she came into the room, he gave her the letter.

Millie sat down and slit open the envelope. She looked up at her father, her eyes big with surprise.

"It's from Antoine, one of my friends from school in Canada." Guy raised his eyebrows. Millie had never mentioned a friend called Antoine.

"We were very close," said Millie hesitantly. "But we stopped being friends. We had... had a sort of disagreement"

"Well, read the letter and see what he has to say."

Guy left the room to give her privacy and Millie read

the letter. She noticed Antoine had included his address and telephone number in Canada.

Dearest Millie,

I read in the newspapers about your terrible experience in Cyprus. It made me feel that I must write to you to ask you what caused our breakup. I have never stopped caring about you. When you went to Paris with your father, I had to accept that you didn't feel the same about me as I felt for you. I had been so sure till then that we had something wonderful together.

When I read about you in the paper, I decided that I had to try and find you and to ask if there was any chance for us. I realised that if that gunman had succeeded in killing you, I would never have seen you again and that idea broke my heart.

I would be prepared to visit you wherever you are, if you tell me that there is any hope for me.

With love always
Antoine

Millie smoothed the letter on her knee. Antoine still had feelings for her! Hope flowered in her heart. Through all the places she had been and all the adventures she had experienced, Antoine had always been in the back of her mind and in her heart as a precious memory. Could they possibly build a relationship, she wondered? She was sitting smiling happily to herself when Guy came back into the room.

"What is making you smile?" said Guy, smiling himself.

Millie told her father all about Antoine and why she had suddenly been willing to leave Canada and move to Paris. Guy read the letter again and looked fondly at his daughter.

"I think you should telephone this young fellow and invite him to visit us. After all you have been through, I think you deserve to have a brand-new start and Antoine sounds like a nice lad."

Millie hugged her father gratefully, happy tears in her eyes. She went to the telephone and dialed Antoine's number, a huge smile on her face. When she heard Antoine's voice, she said. "Hello Antoine, it's Millie. I got your letter. How do you fancy a trip to Paris?"

Acknowledgements

Grateful thanks to the little beggar girl I saw in Hamra Street, Beirut in the Lebanon in 1969. She touched my heart and stayed in the recesses of my mind through the years of my busy life, until I was just compelled to imagine what her life might have been.

Thanks to Lisa Talbott, fellow writer, for leading me to Michael Hurd.

Lastly, my grateful thanks to Michael Paul Hurd, Author/Publisher, Lineage Independent Publishing, for treating my baby with thought, kindness and for being so understanding.

Printed in Great Britain
by Amazon